Jingle All the Way Home

Mistletoe Falls Series, Book #6

Tara Baisden

Sterling Ridge Press LLC

Copyright

Jingle All the Way Home © 2025 by Tara Baisden

All rights reserved. No part of this book may be reproduced, distributed, or transmitted in any form or by any means, including photocopying, recording, or other electronic or mechanical methods, without the prior written permission of the author, except in the case of brief quotations embodied in critical reviews and certain other noncommercial uses permitted by copyright law.

This is a work of fiction. Names, characters, places, and incidents either are the product of the author's imagination or are used fictiously. Any resemblance to actual persons, living or dead, events, or locales is entirely coincidental.

Cover designed by Sterling Ridge Press LLC

Published by: Sterling Ridge Press, LLC www.sterlingridgepress.com

ISBN: 978-1-966093-41-1 Printed in the United States of America

First Edition: November 2025

For permissions, contact: tara@tarabaisden.com or visit www.tarabaisden.com

Dedication

For every woman who ever walked away from what looked perfect on paper to build something real.

For the skilled tradesmen who create beauty with calloused hands and teach us that true strength is measured in character, not credentials.

And for my own small town, where coming home never requires an explanation, only an open door and a warm welcome.

This one's for the brave ones who choose authenticity over applause, who understand that sometimes the best foundation is built on honesty and hard work, and who believe that it's never too late to renovate your entire life.

May you always have the courage to strip away what doesn't serve you and rebuild something beautiful.

With love and warm holiday wishes,

Tara

Contents

Prologue

Renee Bentley stood at the floor-to-ceiling windows of her Manhattan condo, watching pedestrians sixteen stories below rush past each other like water around stones. The view had cost her dearly—polished hardwood floors, exposed brick accent walls, a kitchen with marble countertops she rarely used for anything beyond reheating takeout. Every piece of furniture had been selected by an interior designer who understood the language of success: clean lines, neutral tones, and nothing that suggested a life actually lived here.

She pressed her forehead against the cool glass. Two weeks ago, on a Monday, her boss had called her into his office with that particular expression people wore when delivering bad news they'd rehearsed. The company was restructuring. Downsizing. They valued her contributions, of course, but the board had decided to consolidate departments. A generous buyout package awaited her signature—enough to soften the blow, he'd said, as if money could cushion the sudden free fall of losing the identity she'd spent years constructing.

She'd signed the papers the following Friday afternoon.

Now she had nowhere to be.

Her phone sat on the kitchen island beside an untouched bagel, its screen dark and silent. No morning emails. No calendar notifications. No time-sensitive requests that only she could handle. The absence felt louder than any alarm.

Renee picked up the phone and scrolled through her contacts, past colleagues and clients and the handful of acquaintances who passed for friends in a city where everyone was too busy networking to actually connect. Her thumb hovered over her mother's name.

She pressed call before she could reconsider.

"Renee?" Her mother's voice carried the warm Tennessee drawl that Renee had spent years softening in her own speech. "Honey, is everything all right? Shouldn't you be at work right now?"

The concern in those last four words nearly undid her.

"Hi, Mom." Renee turned away from the window and sank onto the leather sofa that had cost more than her first car. "I'm fine. I just... I needed to hear your voice."

"Well, that's never a bad thing." Michelle Bentley's tone shifted, that maternal radar picking up on what wasn't being said. "But you don't usually call on a Monday morning. Shouldn't you be in meetings or presentations or whatever it is you marketing executives do?"

Renee let out a breath that felt like it had been trapped in her chest for days. "That's actually why I'm calling. The company I work for—worked for—is downsizing. They offered me a buyout package, and I took it."

Silence stretched across the line, the kind that preceded either sympathy or a lecture. Renee braced for both.

"Oh, sweetheart." Her mother's voice gentled. "How are you feeling about all this?"

"Honestly?" Renee stood and began pacing the length of her living room, counting steps between furniture pieces. "Relieved. Terrified. Maybe both at once. I've been thinking about starting my own marketing consultancy—something smaller and more personal. Mom, I'm just so tired. The rat race, the city, the constant pressure to be on all the time. I don't have a life—I had a career that swallowed everything."

"You've been running pretty hard for a long time," Michelle said. "Maybe this is a chance to catch your breath and figure out what you really want."

"I've been thinking about that." Renee stopped at the window again, watching a delivery truck maneuver through the traffic below. "What if I sold the condo? Moved back to Mistletoe Falls?"

The squeal of delight that erupted from the phone made Renee pull it away from her ear.

"Are you serious? Oh, Renee, that would be wonderful! Your father and I have missed you so much, and your sister would be over the moon. You could help local businesses, build something meaningful right here at home."

The enthusiasm was infectious, and Renee smiled for the first time in days. "I'm not saying it's definite, but I'm considering it. Really considering it."

"Well, you know what's funny? I was just thinking the other day about your Aunt Holly's place. The Jingle Bell Inn. It's been sitting empty for four years now, can you believe it? Nathan still hasn't sold it."

The name hit Renee like a bell chiming in the distance, clear and resonant.

The Jingle Bell Inn.

She hadn't thought about Aunt Holly's Victorian home in years, but suddenly, she could see it perfectly: the wraparound porch strung with white lights, the carved wooden sign swaying in the mountain breeze, the smell of cinnamon and pine that seemed to live in every room. She'd spent countless afternoons there as a child, helping Aunt Holly arrange guest rooms and fold linens that smelled like lavender.

"Nathan's still trying to sell it?" Renee's mind was already moving, pieces clicking into place with the satisfying precision of a well-executed campaign strategy.

"Last I heard. I think he's just keeping the utilities on and having someone check on it monthly. You know how Nathan is about Mistletoe Falls—couldn't wait to shake the mountain dust off his shoes and never look back."

Renee knew. Her cousin had always been more interested in New York's skyscrapers than Tennessee's mountain peaks. They'd crossed paths occasionally at industry events, exchanging polite conversation before returning to their separate ambitious lives.

"The Jingle Bell Inn," Renee repeated softly, testing the words. "I haven't thought about that place in years."

"Oh, it was such a gem when Holly was running it. Every room was decorated for Christmas, with fresh pine garland on the banisters, and the kitchen always smelled like something wonderful was baking. Do you remember helping her make gingerbread cookies for the guests when you were younger?"

Renee did remember. She could almost taste the cinnamon and molasses, feel the weight of the rolling pin in her small hands while Aunt Holly hummed carols and told stories about the families who stayed there each season. "I remember the sitting room with the fireplace. And the way the entire house seemed to glow when the Christmas lights were on."

"It could be that way again," Michelle said, and Renee could hear the careful hope threading through her mother's voice. "If someone cared enough to bring it back."

Renee walked to her kitchen and stared at the marble countertops she'd chosen for their elegance, not their warmth. How many meals had she actually cooked here? The space was beautiful and utterly unused, like a stage set waiting for a play that never started.

"What kind of shape is it in?" she asked.

"Well, it's been sitting empty, so I imagine it needs some love. But the bones still look good—Holly took care of that place like it was her child."

"Mom, do you think..." She hesitated, feeling foolish for even voicing the thought taking shape in her mind. "Do you think it would be crazy? To buy it? To actually move home and try to run it... or even turn it into a different business?"

"Crazy?" Michelle laughed, warm and bright. "Honey, I think that sounds wonderful. You've always had a gift for making things beautiful and bringing people together—isn't that what marketing really is? Telling stories that connect with people? Well, what if instead of selling someone else's story, you created your own?"

Renee's throat tightened. When had she stopped thinking of her work that way? When had creativity become strategy, and connection become metrics?

"I don't know the first thing about running an inn," she said.

"You didn't know the first thing about New York either, and you figured that out just fine. Besides, you wouldn't be starting from scratch. You'd have us, and Heather, and the whole town rallying around you. That's what we do here—we show up for each other."

Renee closed her eyes and let herself imagine it. Not the endless meetings and performance reviews and the constant pressure to prove her value. Instead, she saw morning coffee on a wraparound porch, guests arriving with anticipation lighting their faces, the satisfaction of creating a space where people felt welcomed and cherished. She could build something with her own hands, something that mattered in ways a quarterly report never would.

"I'd need to talk to Nathan," she said. "Find out what he's asking for it."

"Of course you would. But it's something to really consider. Like you said, you could buy it and run it as an inn or change it into whatever you envision this new business idea of yours to be."

"Mom, I need to go. I have to sit down with this idea for a little while and figure out if I could make this work."

"Call Nathan."

"I will. And Mom? Thank you. For listening."

"Of course, sweetheart. Call me anytime. And Renee? I really do hope you consider moving back home. I miss you."

After they disconnected, Renee stood in the center of her expensive condo and let the silence settle around her. The conversation with her mother had cracked something open inside her and created space for light to filter through.

The Jingle Bell Inn.

She walked to her home office, a spare bedroom she'd converted into command central to her career. Her laptop sat closed on the desk, surrounded by stacks of industry magazines and motivational books. She opened the computer and pulled up a search engine, typing in the inn's name.

A real estate listing appeared, and she clicked through the photos. The exterior looked much as she remembered—the Victorian architecture with its gabled roof and wraparound porch. The interior shots revealed rooms frozen in time, waiting for someone to remember them.

She could see the charm the inn still had. The original hardwood floors, the carved banisters, the oversized windows that would flood each room with light. The sitting room fireplace with its stone hearth. The dining room was large enough for communal breakfasts, where strangers might become friends over coffee and conversation.

Her marketing mind automatically began cataloging possibilities. Location: prime, in a town that drew tourists year round for its Christmas charm. Unique selling proposition: authentic Victorian inn with small-town hospitality and modern comfort. Target market: families seeking genuine holiday experiences, couples wanting romantic getaways, anyone tired of cookie-cutter hotels and craving something real.

She opened a new document and began typing, letting her thoughts flow without editing. At the top, she wrote: Marketing Consultancy or Inn? Pro/Con Analysis.

Under marketing consultancy, the pros came easily. Low overhead—she could work from anywhere. Flexible schedule. Drawing on fifteen years of expertise. Building a client base in Mistletoe Falls and surrounding areas, helping local businesses tell their stories and grow. It was safe, sensible, leveraging everything she already knew how to do.

But the cons nagged at her. Would she just be recreating her Manhattan life with a Tennessee ZIP code? Trading one set of demanding clients for another? She'd still be selling other people's visions instead of building something of her own.

Under the Inn option, she hesitated before typing. The pros felt more emotional than practical. Creating a gathering place for families and friends and, of course, guests. Restoring something beautiful that held family history. Living in a space that felt like home rather than a showroom. Using her marketing skills not to convince people they needed something, but to welcome them into an experience they'd remember.

The cons were harder to ignore. She had zero hospitality experience. Running an inn meant being available all the time—cooking breakfasts, managing reservations, handling maintenance issues. Or she could hire someone to help her. The property clearly needed updating, and the kitchen and the bathrooms she'd seen on the website needed complete overhauls. And what if she failed? What if she poured a ton of money into this idea and discovered she'd romanticized something that was actually exhausting?

Yet as she stared at the two columns, one truth became clear: only one option made her heart beat faster.

She could start small, she reasoned. Get the inn operational, handle the guest side herself while slowly building a small marketing consultancy on the side. Help a few local businesses with their branding and online presence. The two ideas didn't have to be separate—they could support each other. The inn would give her credibility in the community. And the marketing work would provide additional income while the inn found its rhythm.

Renee pulled out a calculator and began running numbers. The buyout package, plus what she'd get from selling the condo, minus Nathan's asking price and possible renovation costs. It was doable. More than doable—she'd have breathing room, time to figure things out without the pressure of a mortgage she couldn't afford.

She opened another browser tab and searched for information about running an inn. Articles appeared about licensing requirements, health inspections, insurance considerations, and marketing strategies for small hospitality businesses. The learning curve would be steep, but nothing on that list looked impossible. Just different.

Her phone lay on the desk beside her laptop. She picked it up, then set it down again. Picked it up.

What was she afraid of? That he'd say no? That he'd say yes? That making this call would set in motion something she couldn't take back?

Maybe that was exactly what she needed—something she couldn't take back. A choice that felt like jumping instead of carefully calculated risk management.

Renee stood and walked back to the living room windows. Sixteen stories below, people rushed through their Monday, heads down against the October wind, each person absorbed in their own urgency. How many of them were happy? How many were just going through the motions they'd learned to mistake for living?

She'd been one of them for years.

She pulled up Nathan's contact information and pressed call before doubt could creep back in.

He answered on the third ring, his voice sharp with the efficiency of someone who billed by the hour. "Renee. This is unexpected."

"Hi, Nathan. I hope I'm not catching you at a bad time."

"I'm between depositions. What do you need?"

Straight to business. Some things never change.

"I heard the inn is still on the market."

A pause. "The inn. You mean my mother's place in Mistletoe Falls."

"The Jingle Bell Inn, yes."

"It's listed." His tone flattened. "Why?"

Renee took a breath. "I'm interested in buying it."

Another pause, longer this time. "You want to buy an old Victorian inn in a town that thinks a traffic light is progress?"

"I want to go home," Renee said simply.

She heard him exhale. "That house needs updating. There's nothing structurally wrong with it. I've kept the utilities on and pay someone to check on it, but it's been sitting empty for four years."

"What's your asking price?"

He named a figure that made her heart skip—not because it was too high, but because it was a little less than what was listed on the realtors' website.

"If you're serious," Nathan continued, "I'll sell it to you for half that. Sell it directly and avoid realtor costs. Consider it a family discount. Honestly, Renee, the place drains me. Every month I write checks to keep it maintained, and every time I think about going back there to deal with it properly, I just... don't want anything to do with it. If you want it, it's yours. I'll have my assistant draw up the paperwork."

"Half the asking price?" Renee pressed her palm against the window, feeling the vibration of the city through the glass. "Nathan, that's incredibly generous."

"It's practical. Your family, you actually have fond memories of the place, and frankly, I want it off my books and out of my mind. My mother loved that inn. I don't."

They talked logistics for another ten minutes—inspections, timelines, the legal steps that would transfer a piece of family history from one Bentley to another. When they hung up, Renee's hand trembled slightly as she set the phone down.

She walked through her condo slowly, taking inventory. The designer furniture, the artwork chosen to impress rather than inspire, the closet full of tailored suits in shades of gray and black and navy. How much of this actually mattered? How much of it was armor she'd worn to prove she belonged in rooms where people measured worth in titles and square footage?

Outside, the city hummed with its usual chaos—sirens and car horns and the constant drone of ambition pushing against ambition. She'd loved it once, or thought she had. Maybe she'd just loved the idea of being someone who belonged here, someone important enough to deserve a view like this.

But standing here now, she couldn't remember the last time she'd felt peace.

Renee picked up her phone one more time and opened her notes app. At the top of a blank page, she typed: Things to do before moving home.

The cursor blinked, waiting.

For the first time in years, she had no idea what came next—and somehow, that felt less like falling and more like the first breath after finally breaking the surface.

Chapter 1

The mountain road curved sharply ahead, and Renee eased her foot off the accelerator, letting the new SUV hug the bend as autumn trees blazed gold and crimson on either side. Three weeks. That's how long it had taken to sell the condo, pack up ten years of carefully curated Manhattan life, and ship what she could live without for a week or so. The rest fit in the back of a vehicle she'd purchased specifically for mountain winters.

The GPS announced that she was twenty minutes from her destination. Twenty minutes from the choice she still couldn't quite believe she'd made.

The road climbed higher, and with each curve, the air grew crisper, cleaner, carrying the scent of pine and mountain streams instead of exhaust and street vendor pretzels. She'd forgotten how the landscape here seemed to breathe—rising and falling with the rhythm of ridges older than any skyscraper, peaks that wore their age like wisdom instead of decay.

A sign appeared ahead: **Welcome to Mistletoe Falls—Where Christmas Magic Lives Year-Round**. Someone had hung a fresh evergreen wreath beneath the lettering, and Renee smiled despite the butterflies doing aerobics in her stomach.

The road narrowed as she approached the Snowbell Covered Bridge, its weathered timber frame spanning Mistletoe Creek in the same spot it had for over a hundred years. Garland wrapped around the entrance posts, and she could see strands of white lights woven through the greenery, ready to transform the bridge into something magical once evening fell.

She slowed to a crawl as she entered the covered tunnel, sunlight striping through the gaps between boards. The sound of her tires on wooden planks echoed in the enclosed space, familiar and foreign all at once. How many times had she crossed this bridge as a child, counting the seconds it took to pass through, making wishes in the darkness before emerging into light on the other side?

The bridge released her, and she could see downtown Mistletoe Falls ahead.

After driving a few more moments, Mistletoe Lane curved around the town square, exactly as she remembered, yet somehow more vivid. The century-old brick buildings stood shoulder to shoulder, their facades painted in complementary shades of cream and burgundy and hunter green. Gas lamp-style streetlights marched down both sides of the wide brick sidewalks, each one already wrapped in evergreen garland.

She drove slowly, drinking in details her mind had filed away but never quite forgotten. The Fireside Diner, her parent's place, with its vintage neon sign promising "Home Cooking & Warm Welcomes." The Sugarplum Bakery, one of her favorite spots for a sweet treat and a great cup of coffee. The Once Upon a Time Bookshop, which she visited every time she was back in town, to stock up on books from her favorite authors.

The sidewalks weren't crowded at this hour on a Monday, but she spotted a few people moving between shops—a woman carrying a bakery box, an older man sweeping the entrance to his store, two women chatting outside her sister's floral shop. Everyone moved without a rush, pausing mid-conversation to wave at a passing car, clearly in no hurry to get anywhere.

When had she stopped moving like that? When had every step become calculated for maximum efficiency?

The town square was on her left as she continued along Mistletoe Lane, its Victorian gazebo standing white and proud at the center of a space that would soon be transformed for Christmas. She could already imagine it—the massive tree that would anchor the square, the lights that would turn every branch into starlight, and the way families would gather on cold evenings to sing carols and drink cocoa.

She'd grown up with these traditions. Even after moving to Manhattan, she'd come home for Christmas every year, and usually managed a summer visit when work allowed. But driving through now, preparing to stay instead of just visit, she felt the difference in her bones. This wasn't just a brief visit. This was coming home.

Mistletoe Lane curved gently around the town square, and she signaled her turn onto Icicle Lane. Her pulse quickened. Three more blocks.

She passed a boutique clothing store, a photography studio, and several other businesses, and then she saw it.

The Jingle Bell Inn, a three-story white Victorian with burgundy trim that caught the morning light beautifully. The wraparound porch extended across the front and curved around both sides, exactly as she remembered. Gingerbread trim decorated the eaves and porch posts, intricate patterns that some long-ago craftsman had carved by hand.

The carved wooden sign still swung from its wrought-iron post near the walkway, the lettering—The Jingle Bell Inn—faded but readable. The small brass bells attached to the bottom no longer gleamed, but they'd be easy enough to polish. Wreaths hung in every window, remnants from the last Christmas Aunt Holly had celebrated here.

Renee pulled into the paved parking area on the side of the building and shifted into park, but her hands stayed on the wheel. This was hers. She owned this. The deed sat in a folder on her passenger seat, signed and notarized and completely legal. Nathan had been almost laughably eager to finalize the sale, his assistant handling most of the details while he focused on cases that actually interested him.

She'd gotten it for a steal—half of what it was worth. Family discount, Nathan had called it, though they both knew it was more about him washing his hands of a place that meant nothing to him.

For Renee, though, this inn meant everything to her. A fresh new start, possibilities, and cherished memories. Aunt Holly had made this inn into a haven, a place where guests became friends and every meal felt like Thanksgiving dinner. She'd taught Renee that creating beauty and welcome wasn't frivolous—it was one of the most important things a person could do.

But Aunt Holly had also been here every day, pouring her whole self into this place. Could she do the same? Did she even know how?

She grabbed her purse and got out of the vehicle. The temperature had dropped during the drive, probably somewhere in the mid-fifties now, and she was grateful for the cardigan she'd pulled on at the hotel this morning.

The front porch steps creaked under her feet, the sound both welcoming and warning. She'd need to check those. Add it to the list.

The key Nathan's assistant had given her slid into the lock smoothly, and the front door swung open with only a slight protest from hinges that needed oil. The smell hit her first—not terrible, but definitely the scent of a house that had been closed up too long.

The foyer opened before her, its hardwood floors scuffed but solid. The staircase rose to her right, its banister carved with the same attention to detail as the exterior trim.

She moved through the first floor slowly, her footsteps loud in the silence. The sitting room to her left still held Aunt Holly's furniture—two sofas facing each other before a stone fireplace that was gorgeous. The wingback chairs needed reupholstering; their fabric faded in spots where sunlight had touched them year after year. But the bones of the room were beautiful. High ceilings with original crown molding, built-in shelves flanking the fireplace, and windows that would flood the space with light once the heavy curtains were replaced.

The dining room held a long farmhouse table that needed refinishing, but the wrought-iron chandelier overhead was a treasure worth keeping.

But the kitchen made her stop short.

Aunt Holly had loved this room, had spent hours here creating the breakfasts that made guests ask for recipes. However, time and neglect had not been kind. The appliances were decades old, their avocado green proclaiming their vintage loud and clear. The laminate countertops were chipped and stained beyond saving. Cabinet doors hung slightly crooked on hinges that had loosened over time. The hardwood floors needed refinishing.

This wasn't going to be a simple update. This was going to be a complete gut job, just like she had guessed when she had viewed the images online on the realtor's website.

Renee leaned against the wall and let herself feel the weight of that reality. Standing here, seeing it in person, the scope of work seemed enormous. The kitchen alone would probably take weeks.

She walked to the window above the sink and looked out at the backyard. The lawn needed mowing one last time before winter. The flower beds had gone wild. But beyond that, she could see the edge of the forest that bordered the property, mountains rising in the distance, morning light painting everything in shades of gold and amber.

This view alone was worth every challenge waiting inside these walls.

Renee continued her exploration. The main floor bathroom made her wince—floral wallpaper peeling at the seams, fixtures that had probably been installed in the 1990s and not updated since. The office was decent and functional.

She climbed the stairs to the second floor, testing each step carefully. They seemed solid enough, though they'd need refinishing as well. The second floor held the six guest rooms, each one themed for Christmas exactly as she remembered. The Candy Cane Suite with its red and white color scheme. The Silver Bells Room in soft blues and silvers. The Mistletoe Room with its pine green accents.

They all needed work, but mostly cosmetic work. Remove the wallpaper, paint, updated light fixtures, new bedding and curtains. The private bathrooms were dated, but not disasters like the kitchen or downstairs bathroom.

On the third floor, which would become her home. The bedroom suite was large, and the walk-in closet would easily hold her wardrobe once it all arrived. The second bedroom would work as an office. The bathroom, though? That was getting gutted. No question.

She stood in the living room and looked out the dormer windows at the town spreading below her. From here, she could see the town square in the distance, and the mountains cradling the entire town.

Renee descended the stairs and returned to the first floor, standing in the foyer where she'd started. She looked at her reflection in the mirror on the wall—a woman in jeans and a cardigan, hair pulled back in a ponytail, face bare of the makeup she'd worn like armor in Manhattan. She looked younger somehow. Or maybe just more real.

The inn waited around her, patient and willing. It had welcomed strangers and made them family. It had held laughter and Christmas carols and the smell of gingerbread baking.

It could be all those things again.

But first, she needed to figure out where to even start.

Chapter 2

Renee stepped into The Fireside Diner, and the familiar scents of coffee, bacon grease, and fresh-baked bread hit her like a wave of homecoming. Red vinyl booths lined the front windows and down both sides of the restaurant. Black-and-white checkered floors gleamed under vintage light fixtures, and the lunch counter stretched along the back of the diner, chrome stools anchored at regular intervals like sentries.

Her mother burst through the kitchen door, apron strings flying, her eyes bright with tears. Michelle Bentley might have grayed at the temples and added a few laugh lines around her eyes, but she moved with the same energy—quick and purposeful, as if standing still meant missing something important.

"Renee!" Michelle said as she wrapped her in a hug. "Oh, sweetheart, you're really here. You're really home."

"I'm really here."

Carter Bentley emerged from the kitchen more slowly, wiping his hands on a towel tucked into his apron. Where Michelle was all motion and expression, Carter moved with deliberate calm, his solid presence filling space without demanding it. When he reached Renee, he pulled her into a hug that spoke volumes.

"Welcome home, honey," he said, and Renee had to blink hard against the sting in her eyes.

"You look tired. Are you eating enough? You didn't drive straight through from Manhattan, did you?" her mom asked.

"I stopped in Virginia last night. Got a hotel room and had a decent night's sleep." Renee smiled at her mother's immediate shift into nurturing mode. "I'm fine, Mom. Just a little road-weary."

"Well, come sit down. Have you eaten lunch?" Michelle was already steering her toward a corner booth, the one with the best view of Main Street.

The diner held maybe a dozen other customers scattered throughout—an older couple sharing a piece of pie, a man reading the newspaper while nursing coffee, and three women in the center booth who kept glancing over with obvious curiosity.

Carter slid into the booth across from her, while Michelle flagged down a young waitress with a blonde ponytail. "Kayla, would you mind bringing us three iced teas? And we'll order in just a minute."

"Sure thing, Mrs. Bentley." Kayla smiled at Renee. "Welcome back. I heard you bought the old Jingle Bell Inn."

"News travels fast," Renee said, returning the smile.

"Always does." Kayla headed toward the drink station, and Renee watched her go, marveling at how young she looked. Had everyone in town gotten younger, or had Renee just gotten older?

Michelle reached across the table to pat Renee's hand. "We're so glad you're here. I know we talked on the phone, but seeing you in person, having you home for good, I'm so happy."

"Your mother's been cooking extra batches of everything all week," Carter added, his eyes warm with affection as he glanced at his wife. "Freezer's full of casseroles and soups, all labeled with your name on them."

"Mom. You didn't have to do that."

"Of course I did," Michelle said, as if the alternative had never occurred to her. "You're going to be busy getting that inn up and running. The last thing you need to worry about is cooking."

Kayla returned with three glasses of sweet tea, condensation already beading on the outside. She pulled out her order pad. "What can I get you, folks?"

"Meatloaf platter for me," Renee said without even looking at the menu. "With mashed potatoes and green beans. And a dinner roll."

"Make that two," Carter said.

"A chicken salad sandwich, please. With fruit instead of fries." Michelle waited until Kayla left before leaning forward. "So. Tell us everything. How does the inn look? Did the cleaning service you hired do a good job? Are you pleased with the condition?"

Renee wrapped both hands around her tea glass, organizing her thoughts. "The cleaning service did well—everything's dust-free, at least. And honestly, it's both better and worse than I expected."

Carter's eyebrows rose. "How so?"

"The building itself looks good. The original craftsmanship is beautiful—crown molding, built-in shelves, those gorgeous banisters. The wraparound porch seems sturdy, and the windows look like they're in good shape." Renee paused, taking a sip of tea. "But the interior? That's where the work is."

"Walk us through it," Michelle said.

Renee began describing her tour of the inn, starting with the foyer and working her way through each room. When she got to the kitchen, Carter winced.

"Complete gut job?" he asked.

"Complete gut job," Renee confirmed. "Dad, the avocado green appliances belong in a museum, the laminate counters are chipped beyond repair, and the cabinets are dated and need more than just new hinges. The whole room needs to be stripped down."

"That's going to be expensive," Carter said, his practical nature showing through.

"I budgeted for it. I have enough from the buyout and the condo sale to cover renovations with plenty of room to spare." Renee appreciated her father's directness. No tiptoeing around money—just honest assessment. "But seeing it in person, the scope of work feels... bigger somehow."

Michelle reached across the table and squeezed her hand. "That's normal, honey. Looking at a project on paper is different from standing in the middle of it. But you're not going to tackle everything at once, right?"

"I'd rather just take care of it all before opening. The kitchen will be the first priority," Renee said. "And the third floor—my living quarters—needs work too. The bathroom up there is getting completely redone. I refuse to live with pink and burgundy tile from the eighties."

Carter chuckled. "Fair enough. What about the guest rooms?"

"They're not terrible. Mostly cosmetic things—remove the wallpaper, paint, new fixtures and minor updates to the bathrooms. Nothing structural as far as I could tell." Renee pulled out her phone and opened the notes app, where she'd listed everything. "The hardwood floors on the first and second floors need refinishing. The main floor powder room on the first floor is stuck in the nineties. All the wallpaper is coming down, then the whole house needs to be painted."

"You're going to need a good contractor," Carter said.

"I know," Renee said. "I've been trying to figure out who to call. I looked online before I left Manhattan, but it's hard to tell who's actually reliable versus who just has a good website."

"Morrison's Construction," Carter said without hesitation. "Tom Morrison's been our hardware supplier for years. Good man, runs a solid business. His sons, Jake and Dawson, started the construction company several years ago and built it into something impressive. They do quality work—no cutting corners, no rushing jobs. Half the renovations in town have Morrison's fingerprints on them."

"Tom and Betty are wonderful people," Michelle added warmly. "Their boys are hardworking and trustworthy. You won't find better."

Renee pulled out her phone to make a note. "Morrison's Construction. I'll give them a call."

Kayla arrived with their food, and the conversation paused while plates were distributed and napkins arranged. The meatloaf looked exactly as Renee remembered—thick slices glazed with ketchup and brown sugar, surrounded by creamy mashed potatoes and green beans that had been cooked with bacon and onions. The dinner roll still steamed when she broke it open.

"This is so good," Renee said after the first bite. "I didn't realize how much I missed real food until right now."

"Manhattan doesn't have food?" Carter asked with a slight smile.

"Expensive food, trendy food, food that looks like art on a plate. But it doesn't have this." Renee gestured at her plate. "Comfort. Home. The taste of every Sunday dinner I grew up eating."

Michelle's eyes softened. "I'm glad you're home, sweetheart. I know it's a big change, leaving everything you built in New York. But you look... I don't know. Happy. Calmer, maybe. This past summer, when you came for a visit, you looked like you were carrying something heavy, and now you look less stressed."

Had she? Renee considered while cutting another bite of meatloaf. In Manhattan, she'd measured her days in meetings and deadlines, her worth in completed campaigns and client satisfaction scores. Success had been quantifiable, provable, something she could point to and say: See, I matter.

But she'd also been exhausted. Lonely. Running on a treadmill set to a speed that never allowed her to catch her breath.

"I was heavily stressed," Renee said slowly. "The constant pressure to prove myself was overwhelming. I was really struggling... this whole past year, if I'm being honest." She looked at her parents, these two people who'd built a life on serving others good food and warm welcomes. "You guys never seem to struggle."

"Oh, honey, we have struggled plenty," Michelle said with a laugh. "There were years when the diner barely broke even, when we wondered if we'd made a terrible mistake sinking our savings into a restaurant. But we had each other, and that was enough."

"It's still enough," Carter added. "Different challenges now—keeping up with food costs, adapting to changing tastes, and managing staff. But the foundation hasn't changed. We feed people; they leave fuller and happier than when they came in, and that matters. Simple as that."

"That's what I want with the inn. Not just a place to sleep, but a place where people feel welcome. Where families make memories and couples reconnect and everyone leaves feeling like they matter."

"You're going to do just fine," Michelle said firmly. "You've got the heart for it, and you've got the skills. Marketing, management, organization—you've been training for this your whole career, you just didn't know it."

"I don't know anything about hospitality," Renee pointed out.

"But you know about creating experiences. Isn't that what marketing is? And hospitality is just creating experiences in person instead of on paper." Michelle smiled. "You'll learn the rest. We'll help. The whole town will help if you let them."

That was the key, wasn't it? Letting people help. Renee had spent years being the one with the answers, the one others relied on. Admitting she needed help felt uncomfortable.

But maybe that's exactly what she needed to learn.

They ate for a few minutes; the diner sounds providing a soothing backdrop—clinking silverware, low conversation from other booths, the hiss and sizzle from the kitchen grill. Through the window, Renee watched people pass by on the sidewalk. A mother with a stroller. An older man walking a small dog. Two teenagers sharing earbuds and laughing at something on a phone.

Life at a different pace. A pace she could learn again if she gave herself permission.

"So, what's your timeline?" Carter asked, pushing his empty plate aside. "When are you hoping to open?"

"I don't have a firm date yet," Renee admitted. "I need to meet with a contractor first, get a realistic schedule for the renovations. I was really hoping to open before Christmas, but after walking through the house today... I'm thinking that probably won't happen."

"Well, give Morrison's a call. They'll be honest with you about timelines," Carter said.

Kayla returned to clear their plates. "Can I get you any dessert? We've got fresh apple pie."

Michelle glanced at Renee. "Apple pie?"

"Always apple pie," Renee said.

While they waited for dessert, the conversation drifted to lighter topics—updates on Renee's sister Heather's flower shop, changes in the town since Renee's last visit, and who'd gotten married or had babies or retired. The rhythm of small-town gossip felt foreign after Manhattan's anonymity, but also comforting.

The pie arrived warm, with vanilla ice cream melting into cinnamon-spiced apples. Renee took a bite and closed her eyes. "How does this taste the same as when I was twelve?"

"Same recipe," Carter said simply. "Why mess with what works?"

They lingered over pie and coffee, in no rush. Other customers came and went, several stopping by the booth to welcome Renee home and express excitement about the inn reopening. She fielded questions about her plans and accepted well-wishes with growing warmth. This was what she'd missed without realizing it—belonging to a place where people cared about your success because it contributed to the whole community's wellbeing.

She checked the time. "I should get going. I need to stop at the grocery store. And I should probably start unloading my SUV before it gets dark."

"You're staying at the inn tonight?" Michelle asked, concern flickering across her face.

"Of course. I own a house full of bedrooms that are just fine to sleep in, and the bathrooms work even if they are outdated or ugly. I'll be fine."

They slid out of the booth and hugged each other goodbye. Michelle held on longest, patting Renee's back in that universal motherly gesture that somehow communicated everything important without words.

"We're so proud of you. Welcome home, honey," Michelle whispered.

"Thanks, Mom. I'm glad to be home."

"You need anything—and I mean anything—you call us. Day or night. Doesn't matter." Carter said.

"I will," Renee promised, and meant it.

Chapter 3

Jake Morrison's work boots hit the front porch steps of The Jingle Bell Inn, and the old wood creaked under his weight—not worrisome, just the sound of a house that had been standing here long before he was born and would likely stand here long after. He'd driven past this place countless times over the years, watched it sit empty after Holly Bentley passed, and felt that particular sadness that comes from seeing something beautiful go neglected.

"Renee Bentley," Dawson Morrison said from beside him, clipboard in hand. "You remember her from high school?"

Jake had recognized the name the moment their secretary, Linda, had mentioned it yesterday when she'd scheduled this consultation. Renee Bentley. Cheerleader, smart, popular, always surrounded by friends. He'd been too busy being the arrogant quarterback to pay much attention to anyone who wasn't on the football team or dating someone on it, but he remembered her.

"I remember her," Jake said, reaching for the doorbell. "Haven't seen her in years."

The door opened, and Jake's prepared greeting died somewhere between his brain and his mouth.

Renee Bentley stood in the doorway, and she was—

Different. Completely different from the teenage girl he vaguely remembered. She'd grown into her features, her face showing the kind of confidence that came from years of knowing exactly who she was and what she was capable of. Her chestnut hair fell just past her shoulders in natural waves, and her blue eyes held intelligence that made him suddenly conscious of himself.

She wore jeans and a simple sweater, nothing fancy, but she wore them like someone accustomed to boardrooms and corner offices. Poised and put-together. Completely out of his league in every way that mattered.

"Jake Morrison?" she said, and her smile was warm and genuine. "And you must be Dawson. Thank you so much for coming out on such short notice."

"No problem at all," Dawson said smoothly, stepping forward to shake her hand while Jake remembered how to make his body move. "The Jingle Bell Inn is a local treasure. I always hated seeing it sit empty."

Jake finally managed to extend his hand, and when Renee's palm met his, he felt the contact register somewhere deeper than a professional handshake should. Her grip was firm and confident.

"Good to see you again. It's been a while," he said, finding his voice.

"Thirteen years," she said. "You've changed. Both of you have."

"You've changed too," Jake said, then worried that sounded wrong. "I mean—you look good. Different. Grown up."

Smooth, Morrison. Real smooth.

Renee just laughed, a sound that reminded him of why people had liked her in high school. "We all had to grow up eventually. Though I hear you've done more than that—my parents spoke highly of Morrison's Construction. Said you've built quite a reputation."

"We have," Dawson said, shooting Jake a glance that clearly said, Get it together. "Why don't you walk us through the inn and tell us what you're hoping to accomplish? Linda mentioned you're planning to reopen it as an inn; is that correct?"

"That's the goal." Renee stepped back, gesturing for them to come inside. "Though I'll be honest—standing here yesterday, looking at everything that needs updating, the scope of work felt a bit overwhelming. I know what needs to happen; I'm just not sure where to start."

Jake crossed the threshold and looked at the space with professional eyes instead of whatever that had been when she'd opened the door. The foyer was solid—good bones, as his father would say. The hardwood floors needed refinishing but weren't damaged beyond repair. Crown molding original to the house, detailed and beautiful. The staircase banister was hand-carved, the kind of craftsmanship you couldn't buy anymore at any price.

"Let's start with what's not wrong," Jake said, pulling his notebook from his back pocket. "This place was built to last, and Holly Bentley took care of it. We looked at the foundation before we knocked, and it looked good. The roof looks solid from the outside. You're not looking at outdoor structural repairs, which is half the battle."

"That's good to hear."

"So, from what Linda told us this morning, you're looking at cosmetic updates and modernization," Dawson said. "Bring the systems up to current code, update the bathrooms and kitchen, refinish what can be saved, and replace what can't. It's work, but it's the good kind of work—making something beautiful again instead of trying to save something that's rotting from the inside."

"That's exactly what I want," Renee said. "My Aunt Holly loved this place. Every room was decorated with such care that every guest felt like family. I don't want to just update it—I want to honor what she built while making it functional for today."

Jake looked at her more carefully. Most clients talked about ROI and resale value and getting the most bang for their buck. But Renee was talking about legacy and love, and that changed everything about how he'd approach this job.

"Why don't you walk us through what you're thinking?" Jake suggested. "Room by room. Show us what you like and what needs to change."

They started in the sitting room. Renee spoke about her aunt with obvious affection, describing mornings when guests would gather by the fireplace, how Holly always kept a puzzle going on the side table for anyone who wanted to add a piece, and the way the room felt like the heart of the house even though the kitchen was where the cooking happened.

"The fireplace needs a thorough cleaning," Renee said, gesturing to the stone hearth. "And I'd like the chimney checked to make sure it's safe to use. These light fixtures in here are probably original to the 1980s renovation, which is not the era I want."

"The fixtures we can update easily," Jake said. "There are companies that make historically appropriate lighting that's wired for modern electrical standards. We can keep the period feel without the fire hazard."

"Fire hazard?" Renee's eyebrows rose.

"Probably not," Jake said. "But wiring from the eighties is pushing forty years old. It's worth updating while we've got the walls open, anyway. Safer, and it'll give you more capacity for modern appliances and electronics."

"That makes sense." Renee pulled out her phone and made a note. "What about the hardwood floors?"

"Refinish," Dawson said immediately. "They're original to the house and in good shape under all this wear. Sand them down, stain or seal them, and they'll look brand new."

They moved to the kitchen, where her enthusiasm dimmed slightly.

"This is the big one," she said. "Complete gut, right?"

Jake nodded, already mentally cataloging what needed to happen. "Complete gut. But that gives you the freedom to design it exactly how you want it. What are you thinking—modern functionality with period-appropriate aesthetics? Or do you want to go full modern?"

"Modern functionality, classic feel," Renee said without hesitation. "I want guests to feel like they've stepped into a beautiful historic home, but I need to be able to work efficiently. Commercial-grade appliances that don't look commercial. Storage that makes sense. Enough counter space to prep breakfast for a full house."

"How many guest rooms are you planning to keep operational?" Dawson asked.

"All six on the second floor," Renee said. "The third floor will be my private residence. But I'd like to be able to serve breakfast for twelve people comfortably, assuming some rooms have couples."

Jake did the mental math. "You'll want a six-burner range, double oven. Commercial fridge that's paneled to match the cabinetry, so it doesn't look industrial. Deep farmhouse sinks—those are back in style anyway, so you'll be period-appropriate and functional. And lots of counter space, which means we'll need to reconfigure the layout."

"Can I add an island?" Renee asked. "I've always loved kitchen islands for prep work and serving. And I want more electrical outlets in here."

"We can add whatever you want," Jake said. "It's a gut job, so we're basically building a new kitchen in an old space."

They spent twenty minutes in the kitchen alone, Renee asking questions that showed she'd done her homework. She knew what she wanted, but she also knew what she didn't know, and she wasn't afraid to ask. Jake appreciated that. Too many clients pretended to understand construction and then got angry when reality didn't match their Pinterest boards.

Renee visibly winced when she showed them the downstairs bathroom. "This is getting gutted too. The wallpaper alone is a crime."

"Agreed," Dawson said with a grin. "The nineties were not kind to bathrooms."

"Can we expand it at all?" Renee asked. "It feels cramped."

Jake studied the layout, checking the walls with his knuckles. "This wall here isn't load-bearing. We could push into the office nook and borrow a couple of feet. Give you space for a larger vanity, maybe a linen closet."

"Would that compromise the office space too much?"

"You're not planning to use the first-floor office for business operations, are you?"

"No, I'll keep my business stuff upstairs in my personal space. The office down here will be for guests. I'll add a small desk and computer where they can check email or look up local attractions."

"Then borrowing two feet won't hurt," Jake said. "You'll still have room for a desk and some shelving if you like."

They climbed to the second floor, and Renee showed them each of the six guest rooms. Jake had to admit that even neglected and outdated, the Christmas theming was charming. Each room had its own personality. Renee clearly intended to preserve that.

"The bathrooms all need updating," she said as they moved from room to room. "New fixtures, new tile, replacing the outdated vanities, and better lighting. But I don't need them gutted like downstairs. Just modernized."

"We can do that," Dawson said.

"What about the bedrooms themselves?" Renee asked. "The wallpaper has got to go; I want each room painted."

"Remove all the wallpaper, repair any damage to the plaster underneath, and prime and paint everything fresh," Jake said. "New light fixtures throughout. Update the electrical outlets—code requires more outlets than these rooms currently have, and guests will want places to charge phones and plug in laptops."

"Will that require opening walls?"

"Some fishing of wires, but not a major demo. It's not fun work, but it's not catastrophic work."

They reached the third floor, and Jake could see this space meant something different for Renee. This was going to be her home, not just a business project. She showed them the bedrooms, the reading nook, the small kitchenette, and the living area. Everything was functional but outdated, clearly decorated in the style of twenty years ago.

"All the wallpaper up here has to go. I want all the light fixtures replaced and more electrical outlets up here as well," Renee said. "But the bathroom?" She opened the door to reveal pink and burgundy tile, a clawfoot tub with rust stains, and fixtures that had seen better decades. "This is getting completely redone. I refuse to live with this."

Jake couldn't help but smile. "Can't say I blame you. That color combination is... bold."

"That's a generous word for it," Renee said with a laugh. "I want this gutted and rebuilt as a modern bathroom. Nothing historic about it—I want good water pressure, a shower that actually drains properly, storage that makes sense, and colors that don't make me feel like I'm living in a museum of bad choices."

"We can do that," Jake said. "Complete gut, modern rebuild. You want a tub or shower only?"

"Tub-shower combo."

Jake made notes while Dawson measured the space. The bathroom was a decent size—plenty of room to work with for a full modern redesign.

"What about the kitchen up here?" Dawson asked.

"I need to think about this space a little more, but for now, new appliances—the ones here are ancient—better lighting, and new countertops. Possibly new cabinets. But it's just me, so I don't need anything fancy. Functional is fine."

They discussed finishes and fixtures, timelines, and sequences. Jake explained how they'd approach the work—start with the major demolition on the first-floor kitchen and bathrooms, then work through the second-floor updates while the main floor was being rebuilt, and work on Renee's third-floor bathroom and kitchen in between as time allowed.

"How long?" Renee asked. "Realistically?"

Jake exchanged glances with Dawson, doing the mental math. "With our entire crew? Eight to ten weeks for everything, assuming we don't run into surprises. Could be less if the demo goes smoothly and we don't hit any issues."

"That would put us at early January," Renee said, her brow furrowing slightly. "I was thinking maybe a soft opening around Christmas, but that's probably too ambitious, isn't it?"

"It would be pushing it," Jake said honestly. "And even if we could get a couple of rooms technically finished by Christmas, you'd still have active construction happening. Guests don't typically appreciate staying somewhere with saws running and workers traipsing through. The noise alone would be a problem, and there's dust to consider even with our best containment efforts."

Renee nodded slowly, and Jake appreciated that she didn't argue or try to pressure him into an unrealistic timeline. "You're right. I was probably being too optimistic anyway. Early January makes more sense—gives me time to do this properly instead of rushing and cutting corners."

"Plus, it gives you time to get your systems in place," Dawson added. "Reservations, marketing, and the business side of things. Better to open when you're truly ready than to open half-ready just to hit a date."

"That's true," Renee agreed. "And January is still a good time for bookings here—ski season in the mountains, people wanting winter getaways. I can work with that timeline."

Jake found himself impressed. Most clients wanted perfection immediately and got frustrated when reality interfered with timelines.

"What about costs?" she asked.

Dawson pulled out his tablet and opened their estimating software. "Based on what we've seen and discussed, I'd estimate between seventy-five and ninety thousand for everything. That includes materials, labor, permits, and a contingency budget for surprises. We can get you an itemized quote by tomorrow afternoon."

"That's within my budget. Send me the detailed quote, and if the numbers work, I'd like to get started as soon as possible."

"We could start Thursday," Jake said. "Demo work on the first floor, which will be loud and dusty but relatively quick. Get the kitchen gutted and start the bathroom renovation. Meanwhile, we'll order materials for the second floor."

"One thing," Renee said, and something in her tone made Jake look up from his notes. "I want to be involved. Not just making decisions and writing checks—I want to actually help with the work. Learn as we go. I know I don't have construction experience, but I'm a fast learner, and I would like to be part of remodeling this place."

Jake blinked, not sure if he'd heard correctly. "You want to help? Like, actual physical labor?"

"Is that a problem?"

"No, it's just—" Jake tried to figure out how to phrase this diplomatically. "Most clients want to stay out of the way. Especially clients with your background. Corporate executives usually prefer to let the professionals handle the messy work."

"I'm not a corporate executive anymore. I'm an inn owner who intends to understand every inch of this place. If I'm going to run this business, I need to know how it works. If something breaks in the middle of the night when I have guests, I need to at least have a basic idea of how to handle it until I can call for help."

Jake glanced at Dawson, who was grinning as if he found this entire conversation hilarious.

"She's got a point," Dawson said.

"I'm not afraid of hard work," Renee continued. "I might not know which end of a hammer to hold right now, but I can learn. And I can follow directions."

Jake studied her. From the rumors he'd heard, she'd left a successful career to come home and reopen her aunt's inn. Now she apparently wanted to swing a hammer alongside his crew instead of staying safely out of the way in her clean clothes and manicured hands.

"All right," he said. "You can help. But you follow safety protocols, you do what we tell you when we tell you, and if something's beyond your skill level, you step back and let the professionals handle it. Deal?"

"Deal." Renee extended her hand, and Jake shook it, trying not to notice how her smile made something in his chest shift sideways.

"We'll need you to sign off on the quote once we send it," Dawson said. "And we'll need a deposit to order materials and get things scheduled. Linda can handle all that paperwork."

"Perfect," Renee said. "I'll watch for the quote tomorrow."

They walked back downstairs, Jake's mind already sorting through project sequences and material orders. This was going to be a good job—interesting work, a client who actually cared about quality, and enough scope to keep his crew busy through the holidays.

It wasn't until they were back in the foyer, heading toward the front door, that Jake realized he'd spent the last hour and a half genuinely enjoying himself. Not just the work talk—though that was always satisfying—but the conversation itself. Renee was smart and funny, asked good questions, and didn't treat him like hired help. She'd listened to his suggestions, offered her own ideas, and somehow made discussing bathroom fixtures feel less like a business transaction and more like a collaboration.

"Thank you both for coming out," Renee said. "This feels manageable now. Yesterday it felt overwhelming, but having a plan makes all the difference."

"That's what we do," Dawson said easily. "Turn overwhelming into achievable. You'll have that quote tomorrow, and we'll be back Thursday morning ready to work if all is agreed upon."

"I'll be ready," Renee promised.

"One question—do you have somewhere else to stay while we're doing the demo work? It's going to get loud and dusty, and you probably don't want to be living here for the worst of it."

"I'll be fine," she said. "I've got the third floor set up, and I can close the doors to keep most of the dust out. Besides, someone should be here to keep an eye on things."

"Fair enough. Just warning you—demo day is not quiet."

"I survived Manhattan. I think I can handle construction noise."

Jake grinned. "We'll see about that."

Chapter 4

The scent hit Renee the moment she opened the door to Pinecone & Ivy Florist—fresh earth, pine, and the sweet perfume of flowers. Wooden floorboards gleamed beneath soft white lights, and rustic tables near the entrance displayed hand-tied bouquets nestled in simple glass vases. Each arrangement looked effortlessly elegant, as if it had grown that way naturally.

"Renee?"

Her sister's voice came from behind a worktable near the back, and then Heather was rushing forward, her honey-blonde hair escaping in soft curls around her face. They met in the middle of the shop, and Heather pulled her into a hug.

"You're really here," Heather said, pulling back to study Renee's face. "I mean, I knew you were coming, but seeing you in person—it's different."

"I'm really here," Renee confirmed, returning her sister's smile. "And this place, Heather. It's more beautiful than I remember."

"You haven't been in here since I remodeled two years ago." Heather gestured around the shop, pride evident in her voice. "I expanded the design studio in back, added more shelving for the potted plants, and added more coolers for floral arrangements."

Renee turned slowly, taking in the details. Along one wall, reclaimed wooden shelves held potted herbs and indoor plants—succulents in hand-painted pots, miniature evergreens, and trailing ivy. A chalkboard sign above them read, in Heather's neat handwriting: Bring a bit of the mountains home. The opposite wall featured decorative containers—hand-thrown pottery, antique milk glass vases, and vintage tins.

"It's gorgeous," Renee said. "Very you. Grounded and beautiful and—" She paused, searching for the right word. "Real."

Heather's expression softened. "That's what I was going for. Nothing pretentious, nothing trying too hard. Just flowers and beauty and a little bit of mountain magic." She tilted her head, studying Renee. "You look different. Good different. Happier, maybe?"

"That's what Mom said."

"Mom's usually right." Heather gestured toward the worktable where she'd been arranging sprigs of winter greenery in a low wooden box. "Come sit. Tell me everything. How's the inn? Have you met with contractors yet? Are you still thinking about the marketing firm idea?"

Renee settled onto a stool while Heather returned to her arrangement, her hands moving with practiced ease as she listened. The workspace was organized chaos—buckets of fresh flowers grouped by color, spools of ribbon, shears, and wire cutters.

"The inn is both better and worse than I expected," Renee began. "The structure's solid, which is good. But the updates needed are extensive. The kitchen's a complete gut job, the bathrooms need work, and the floors need refinishing throughout the first and second levels.

I met with Morrison's Construction this morning—Jake and Dawson Morrison. They seemed knowledgeable and professional."

"Jake Morrison," Heather said, tucking a sprig of holly into the arrangement. "I remember him from high school. He and his brother have built quite a reputation with their construction company."

"That's what Mom and Dad said. They do excellent work, from what I've heard." Renee watched her sister work, the way she tested each piece before placing it, ensuring balance and beauty. "They gave me an eight-to-ten-week timeline for everything."

Heather added another piece of greenery, then stepped back to assess her work. "What about the marketing firm? Are you still thinking about that?"

"I am. Maybe not right away—getting the inn operational is a priority. But eventually, I'd like to help local businesses with their branding and online presence. There's so much potential here that people aren't tapping into."

"Like what?"

Renee leaned forward, warming to the topic. "Like you, for instance. Your Instagram is good, but you could be doing so much more with it. Behind-the-scenes content showing your creative process, tutorials on seasonal arrangements, and showcasing local weddings where you did the flowers. You're an artist, Heather. People would eat that up."

"I barely have time to keep up with orders, let alone create content."

"That's where a consultant comes in. Help you develop systems that don't drain your time but expand your reach. Sorry. I'm not trying to give you unsolicited advice."

"No, it's good." Heather smiled. "I like seeing you passionate about something. You always loved problem-solving, even as a kid. Finding ways to make things work better."

"Manhattan beat that out of me for a while. Everything there was about metrics and quarterly reports and proving your value with numbers that never felt meaningful. Now I want to help people build something that matters. Like you did here. This is yours. You created it, you nurture it, and you get to see people's faces when they walk in and smell the flowers. That's worth more than any high-rise corner office."

Heather set down her shears and came around the table to perch on the stool beside Renee. "I'm glad you're home. Not just because I missed you—though I did—but because you seem like you're finally where you're supposed to be. Does that sound weird?"

"No," Renee said. "It sounds true."

They sat in comfortable silence for a moment, the kind that only exists between people who know each other well enough not to need constant conversation. Through the front windows, Renee could see people passing on the sidewalk, the pace of life so different from Manhattan's constant rush.

"Oh!" Heather sat up suddenly. "Speaking of people you should reconnect with—Cindy Allen is right next door. She owns the Ginger Jar now."

"Cindy Allen?" Renee's heart lifted. "My Cindy Allen? From high school?"

"The very same. She opened the cookie shop about three years ago, and it's become one of the most popular spots in town. You have to go say hello."

"I can't believe we lost touch," Renee said, already standing. "We were inseparable in high school."

"Life gets busy. But she's right next door. Go surprise her." Heather shooed her toward the door. "And Renee? I'm going to stop by the inn soon. I haven't been inside since Aunt Holly passed. I'd like to see what you're planning."

"I'd love that. Fair warning—it's currently a construction zone in waiting."

"Even better. I want to see it at the beginning, before the transformation."

Renee hugged her sister again, holding on for an extra beat. "Thanks for being excited about this. For not thinking I'm crazy for giving up Manhattan."

"You're not crazy. You're brave. There's a difference." Heather pulled back, her green eyes serious. "Now go find Cindy before I put you to work stripping stems."

Renee laughed and headed for the door, the bell chiming softly as she stepped back onto the sidewalk. The afternoon sun had warmed the November air to something almost pleasant, and she paused for a moment, orienting herself. The Ginger Jar was next door, its hand-painted sign—a whimsical ginger jar surrounded by holly leaves—swaying gently in the mountain breeze.

She'd taken maybe three steps toward it when she spotted him.

Jake Morrison was coming down the sidewalk from the opposite direction. He moved with an easy confidence she'd noticed yesterday, comfortable in his skin.

He saw her at the same moment, and his face broke into a smile that did something unexpected to her pulse.

"Hi Renee," he said as he approached.

"Hi Jake."

"We got your signed contract earlier this morning. We appreciate your getting it back to us so fast. Linda's processing everything now. I'm glad I ran into you. Do you have time this afternoon to sit down and discuss your kitchen and downstairs bathroom in more detail? I want to get a better sense of what you're envisioning so we can order materials."

"I have time. What did you have in mind?"

"Would you be able to come by our office? I've got sample books for countertops, tile, and fixtures—it's easier to look through everything in person than trying to explain options over the phone. Plus, you can meet the rest of the team if they're around."

"That sounds perfect. When?"

"How about an hour from now? That gives you time to finish whatever you were doing." Jake pulled a business card from his pocket and handed it to her. "Address is on there. We're on Cranberry Court, behind the hardware store."

Renee took the card. "I'll be there in an hour."

"Looking forward to it." Jake took a step back, then paused. "Fair warning—our office is not fancy. It's functional, but don't expect polished corporate vibes."

"I left polished corporate vibes behind in Manhattan," Renee said. "Functional sounds perfect."

He grinned at that and continued down the sidewalk. Renee watched him go, then firmly redirected her attention toward The Ginger Jar.

The cookie shop's front window displayed cookies so beautiful they could pass for art—snowflakes dusted with fine white icing, gingerbread houses trimmed with candy pearls, and sugar cookies shaped like mittens and stars.

Renee pushed open the door, and a wave of scents greeted her—vanilla, almond, cinnamon, and the buttery warmth of cookies fresh from the oven. The space was bright and cozy, with warm light spilling across marble and glass display cases. Soft Christmas music played in the background, mixing with the faint whir of mixers from somewhere in back.

Behind the counter, a petite woman with warm brown eyes and auburn hair pulled back in a ribbon was arranging cookies in the display case. She glanced up automatically, probably preparing to greet another customer, and then froze.

"Renee Bentley?"

"Hi, Cindy."

Cindy Allen's face transformed, her expression cycling through shock to disbelief to pure joy in the space of three seconds. She rushed around the counter and hugged Renee with the same enthusiasm she'd shown in high school when they'd pulled all-nighters studying for AP exams or planning prom decorations.

"Oh my gosh, oh my gosh!" Cindy pulled back, her hands on Renee's shoulders as if to confirm she was real. "What are you doing here? When did you get into town?"

"I moved back," Renee said, laughing at her friend's rapid-fire questions. "Yesterday, actually. And I just found out you owned this place about five minutes ago when Heather mentioned it."

"You moved back? Like, permanently?" Cindy's eyes went wide. "But what about New York? You're this big, fancy marketing executive. What happened?"

"Long story. Do you have time to talk?"

"Time? Renee, I will make time." Cindy glanced at the wall clock, then toward the front of the shop, where two customers were browsing the display cases. "Give me two minutes."

Renee waited while Cindy handled the customers with cheerful efficiency, boxing up a dozen assorted cookies and chatting about the upcoming Christmas season. When they left, Cindy flipped the sign on the door to "Back in 15 Minutes," grabbed two cookies from the display case, and steered Renee to one of the small café tables near the window.

"Okay," Cindy said, sliding into the chair across from her. "Talk. Start from the beginning and don't leave anything out."

Renee explained the buyout, the exhaustion that had been building for months, and the phone call with her mother that had sparked everything. She told Cindy about Nathan's half-price offer and the three weeks of frantic preparation to leave Manhattan.

Cindy listened with the same focused attention Renee remembered from high school, occasionally gasping or reaching across the table to squeeze her hand.

"I can't believe you bought the Jingle Bell Inn," Cindy said when Renee finished. "That place was magical when your Aunt Holly ran it. Is it in bad shape?"

"It needs a lot of work. Morrison's Construction is starting renovations Thursday."

"Jake and Dawson Morrison? They're good. My brother used them when he renovated his house last year." Cindy broke off a piece of her cookie, a gingerbread that smelled like Christmas morning. "So you're really staying? Like, this isn't a temporary thing where you try small-town life for six months and then run back to the city?"

"I'm really staying. I sold my condo, Cindy. I burned the bridges."

"Good." Cindy's smile was fierce. "You always belonged here, even when you didn't realize it. I used to watch your Instagram and think, 'She looks successful, but does she look happy?' And the answer was always no."

Renee felt her throat tighten. "I wasn't, not for a long time. Now I'm terrified and excited and convinced I'm either making the best decision of my life or the worst one. But I feel alive again. Does that make sense?"

"Perfect sense." Cindy reached across the table and took both of Renee's hands. "Welcome home, Renee."

They spent the next twenty minutes catching up properly. Cindy explained how she'd gone to culinary school in Knoxville, worked in a bakery for five years, and then come home to Mistletoe Falls when the space next to Pinecone & Ivy became available. She'd poured her savings into the cookie shop, and it had taken off faster than she'd dared hope.

"I love it," Cindy said simply. "Every day is different, and I get to make people happy with sugar and butter and a little bit of artistry. What more could I want?"

"A life partner?" Renee suggested gently. "You always talked about wanting a family."

Cindy's expression turned wistful. "Someday. Right now I'm married to this place. But I'm only thirty-two. There's time." She brightened. "What about you? Any romance in your life?"

"None, and I'm not looking for any either. I just got here." Renee said with a grin as she glanced at the wall clock and realized with a start that forty-five minutes had somehow passed. "I have to go. I'm meeting Jake Morrison at his office in fifteen minutes."

"Jake Morrison," Cindy repeated, her grin turning knowing. "Interesting."

"It's business."

"Mm-hmm, business. He's single, you know," Cindy said as she stood and walked her to the door, flipping the sign back to "Open," as they went. "We need to get together for some girl time, maybe lunch or something. When are you free?"

"I don't know yet. Once the renovations start, my schedule's going to be crazy."

"Then we'll make it work around the craziness. Give me your number."

They exchanged phone numbers, hugged again at the door, and Cindy made her promise to stop by the shop anytime she needed cookies or conversation or both. Renee stepped back onto the sidewalk, feeling lighter than she had in months. Years, maybe.

Her SUV was parked half a block down, and she walked toward it with a growing sense of rightness about her choices. Heather's warm welcome, Cindy's enthusiastic acceptance—these were the connections she'd lost in Manhattan. The relationships that made a place feel like home instead of just a location.

She slid behind the wheel and pulled up the GPS, entering the address from Jake's business card. Morrison's Construction, 717 Cranberry Court. Five-minute drive.

Chapter 5

Renee opened the door to Morrison's Construction. The reception area was modest but welcoming. Photos of completed projects lined one wall. A woman in her late fifties sat at a sturdy wooden desk typing on a computer. A bulletin board covered in job schedules and thank-you cards from satisfied clients was behind her.

The woman looked up with a smile that crinkled the corners of her eyes. "You must be Renee Bentley. I'm Linda. Jake said you'd be stopping by."

"That's me," Renee said, returning the smile.

Linda reached for the phone on her desk and pressed a button. "Jake? Ms. Bentley's here." She listened for a moment, then nodded. "He'll be right out. Can I get you some coffee?"

"I'm fine, thank you."

Renee took the moment to look around; through an open doorway to the side of Linda's desk, she could see into a larger workspace—a long drafting table beneath tall windows, shelves holding paint swatches and material samples, and a meeting table covered with rolled blueprints. The faint sound of voices drifted from somewhere deeper in the building, punctuated by the occasional clank of tools being organized.

A door opened down the hall, and Jake emerged. When he spotted her, his face broke into a smile.

"Renee. Thanks for coming by. Come on back. I've got everything set up."

She followed him through the doorway and into the heart of Morrison's Construction. The space felt alive with purpose—blueprints weighted down on the drafting table, sample books stacked on shelves, and a cabinet with rows of design catalogs.

"This is our design center, for lack of a better term," Jake said, leading her to the large meeting table. "We meet with clients here, go through options, and make plans. More comfortable than trying to do everything at a job site." He pulled out one of the sturdy chairs for her before moving to the opposite side of the table. "Let me grab some materials."

He disappeared into what looked like a storage room and returned carrying several thick sample books. "Okay. Before we dive into specific choices, I want to understand your overall vision. When you picture the finished kitchen, what do you see? What do you want guests to feel when they walk into that space?"

"I want them to feel welcome. As if they've stepped into someone's home rather than a commercial space. But I also need efficiency."

Jake nodded, pulling a notebook closer and making notes. "So we're balancing warmth with functionality. That's doable. The farmhouse sink helps with that—gives you the capacity you need while maintaining that homey feel. What about cabinetry? Are you thinking painted or natural wood?"

"I'm not sure yet. What would you recommend?"

"Depends on the overall feel you want. Painted cabinets—white or cream—would give you a brighter, more cottage-style kitchen. Natural wood, especially if we go with something like cherry or maple, would feel more traditional, maybe a bit more formal." He stood and walked to the cabinet, returning with a binder full of cabinet door styles. "Let me show you some options."

He opened the binder and began pointing out different styles, explaining the pros and cons of each. Shaker-style doors for clean lines. Raised panel for more traditional elegance. Beadboard for cottage charm. His hands moved as he talked, and Renee found herself watching the way he gestured—confident but not aggressive, using his hands to emphasize points rather than dominate the conversation.

"Can I see the Shaker style in both painted and natural wood?" she asked.

Jake flipped to different pages, laying the binder open so she could compare. "The Shaker style is popular because it's classic without being fussy. Works well in historic homes because it doesn't compete with original architectural details."

Renee studied the samples, her marketing brain automatically analyzing how guests would perceive each option. The painted white felt fresh and inviting. The natural cherry felt rich and established. "What's your honest opinion? Based on the inn's character?"

Jake leaned back slightly, considering. "If it were my project? I'd go with painted. Probably a soft white or cream. The inn has beautiful original woodwork—the banisters, the built-in shelves. Painted cabinets would let those features stand out instead of competing. Plus, lighter cabinets will make the kitchen feel larger."

"That makes sense." Renee made a note on her phone. "Painted Shaker style. Soft white."

"Good choice. Now, countertops." Jake pulled forward another heavy book, this one filled with samples of stone and quartz. "You mentioned wanting durability yesterday. In a working kitchen that'll see daily use, I'd steer you toward quartz over granite. Less maintenance, no sealing required, and it's non-porous, so it won't harbor bacteria."

He opened the book to a section showing various quartz patterns. "You can get quartz that looks almost identical to natural stone—marble veining, granite speckles, whatever aesthetic you want. But you get the benefit of modern engineering."

Renee leaned forward to examine the samples more closely. The quartz options were stunning—some mimicking marble so well she wouldn't have known the difference. "What about this one?" She pointed to a soft gray with delicate white veining.

"That's a popular choice. It's called Calacatta Mist. Gives you that classic marble look without the maintenance headaches." Jake pulled the sample from its slot and handed it to her. "Feel the weight of it. That's a good indicator of quality."

The sample was cool and solid in her hands, heavier than she'd expected. She turned it over, examining the consistent pattern and smooth finish. "I like this. It feels substantial."

"It'll hold up well. And the gray tones will work nicely with white cabinets—gives you contrast without being stark." Jake made a note. "We'll need to do final measurements before ordering, but I can give you an estimate based on what we saw yesterday. You'll need counters along the perimeter, plus the island. Figure roughly forty square feet total."

"And the island—how large can we make it without overwhelming the space?"

Jake pulled out a sheet of graph paper and quickly sketched the kitchen layout from memory. Renee watched his pencil move with efficient strokes, blocking out walls, windows, and the existing doorways. "The current kitchen is roughly fourteen by sixteen feet. If we remove the old cabinets and appliances, we'll have a clear footprint to work with." He drew a rectangle in the center. "I'd recommend an island about six feet by three feet. Large enough to be useful for prep work, but it still leaves adequate walkway space on all sides."

"Could we do seating on one side? A couple of stools?"

"Absolutely. We can extend the counter on one side to create an overhang. Put two or three stools there, and you've got casual seating for guests who want to chat while you cook." He sketched in the overhang. "Some innkeepers like having that interaction—it makes the space feel more social."

"I'd like that." Renee could already picture it—early morning conversations over coffee, guests sharing stories while she prepped their breakfast. "What about storage on the island?"

"We can do cabinets on the opposite side from the seating. Drawers would be more functional—easier to access than lower cabinets where you have to get on your knees to reach the back." Jake looked up from his sketch. "You'll want to think about what you'll store there. Pots and pans? Baking sheets? Small appliances?"

"Probably pots and pans. I'll use the perimeter cabinets for food storage and dishes."

"Then we'll do deep drawers with dividers. Keep everything organized and accessible." He made another note. "Now, commercial-grade appliances. The key is getting professional performance without the industrial look."

Jake pulled out a catalog from a manufacturer Renee didn't recognize. "This company specializes in residential-commercial hybrids.

Their ranges give you six burners and double ovens with the BTU output you'd find in a restaurant kitchen, but they're designed to look at home in a residential space." He opened to a page showing a stunning stainless-steel range. "This is their most popular model. Six burners, convection double ovens, and continuous grates so you can slide pans around easily."

"That's beautiful," Renee said, genuinely impressed. The range looked professional but not institutional.

"It's also about four thousand dollars," Jake said evenly, watching her face. "I always believe in being upfront about costs. There are less expensive options, but they won't give you the same performance or longevity."

Renee appreciated his honesty. "I budgeted for quality. If this is what I need to do the job right, then that's what I'll get."

"Okay. Then we'll go with this model. For the refrigerator, I'd recommend a counter-depth unit with custom panels that match your cabinetry. You get the storage capacity of a full-size commercial fridge, but it looks built-in rather than like you installed a restaurant cooler."

He showed her examples, explaining how the panels would be crafted to match the cabinet doors exactly. The refrigerator would blend seamlessly into the design rather than dominate the space.

They worked through the remaining appliances—a dishwasher that would be similarly panel-ready, a microwave that could be mounted in a cabinet to keep the counters clear, and even a small wine fridge for guests who wanted to chill a bottle.

"Now, the sink." Jake turned to another section of samples. "You liked the farmhouse sink idea when I mentioned it yesterday. These are also called apron-front sinks. They're deeper than standard sinks, which is helpful when you're dealing with large pots or baking sheets."

He laid out several options—white porcelain, stainless steel, and even a warm cream color. "The classic look is white porcelain. It's what you'd have found in historic kitchens. But fair warning—they can chip if you're not careful. Stainless is more forgiving."

Renee ran her finger along the edge of the white porcelain sample. "I like the white. It feels right for the inn. And I'll be careful."

"White it is." Jake smiled.

They moved on to lighting, and Jake pulled out yet another catalog. "Kitchen lighting is about layers. You need good task lighting over the work areas, ambient lighting for overall illumination, and maybe some accent lighting to highlight features."

He showed her pendant lights that could hang over the island—simple glass globes that would provide focused light without blocking sightlines. Under-cabinet lighting to illuminate the countertops. A period-appropriate ceiling fixture that would tie the room together.

"What about the backsplash?" Renee asked, realizing they hadn't discussed it yet.

"Good question. That's where you can add personality without overwhelming the space." Jake pulled forward a book of tile samples. "Classic subway tile is always a safe choice—timeless, clean, and it won't date the kitchen. But you could also do something more decorative if you want visual interest."

He showed her various options—simple white subway tile, subway tile with contrasting grout, and even some hand-painted ceramic tiles with delicate patterns. Renee found herself drawn to a soft white subway tile with grey grout.

"That's a good choice," Jake said when she pointed it out. "Simple and clean. The colored grout is subtle enough that it won't compete with everything else, but it adds just enough interest to keep the space from feeling too plain."

"I like how you explain things," Renee said, not quite sure why she felt compelled to say it aloud. "You don't talk down to me, but you also don't assume I know things."

Jake's ears reddened slightly. "I work for you. My job is to help you make decisions, not to make decisions for you. Plus, you ask good questions. Makes my job easier when a client actually thinks about what they want instead of just pointing at pictures."

They finished the kitchen discussion with paint colors. Renee chose a soft grey for the walls that would keep the space bright without feeling sterile.

"Okay," Jake said, leaning back and stretching. "That's the kitchen sorted. Let's talk about the downstairs bathroom before you get too tired of looking at samples."

"I'm not tired," Renee assured him. Her brain felt pleasantly full, like after a productive work session in her Manhattan office. Except this was better—she was building something real, something she'd live with every day.

Jake pulled out a fresh sheet of graph paper and sketched the current bathroom layout from memory. "Right now it's about six by eight feet. Cramped for a public bathroom that'll get daily guest use. We talked about borrowing space from the office nook—if we push this wall out about two feet, we gain twelve square feet. That gives you room for a larger vanity, a linen closet, and generally makes the space feel less claustrophobic."

"Will that leave enough room in the office nook?"

"More than enough. You'll lose a bit of floor space, but it'll still fit a desk and chair comfortably. And since you're not planning to use it as a primary office, the smaller footprint won't matter."

"Then let's do it."

Jake sketched the new layout, his pencil moving with the same confident efficiency she'd noticed earlier. When he finished, he pulled out a catalog showing bathroom vanities. Most were modern and sleek, but a few had more traditional styling that would work in a historic inn. "What are you thinking—single sink or double?"

"Single is fine. It's not like couples will be using this bathroom together. And a single vanity leaves more counter space for guests to set down their things."

"Smart thinking." Jake pointed to a cream-colored vanity with simple lines and plenty of drawer storage. "This one would work well. It's substantial enough to feel like quality, but it's not so ornate that it looks out of place."

Renee nodded. "I like that one. What about the top?"

"You could do the same quartz as the kitchen and keep things cohesive. You could do white if you want more contrast or stick with the gray to tie it all together."

"Let's do the gray. I'm in favor of creating visual connections between the spaces."

They worked through the remaining bathroom details—subway tile for the walls, hexagon tile for the floor in keeping with historic bathroom styles, a framed mirror instead of a medicine cabinet to maximize the period feel, and sconce lighting on either side of the mirror for even illumination.

"Last thing," Jake said, flipping to a section on shower fixtures. "You'll probably want a good shower curtain rod—curved, so it doesn't feel so cramped in there—and maybe even a rainfall showerhead for that luxury hotel feeling. That is if you plan to keep the tub-shower combo in the downstairs bathroom."

"I would like to keep it. Will we need to upgrade the plumbing for a rainfall showerhead?"

"Possibly; it depends on what we find when we open the walls. If the supply lines are old, we'll replace them anyway to prevent future problems. Better to do it now while everything's torn apart than to deal with a leak two years down the road."

"That makes sense. Do whatever needs doing to make it right."

Jake made a final note, then set down his pencil and met her eyes. "I think we've got everything we need to start ordering materials. Linda will put together a detailed materials list and timeline, and we'll submit it for your approval before we order anything."

"How long before the materials arrive?"

"Most of this we can get within a week. The custom cabinets will take three to four weeks, but that's fine—we won't need them until after we've done the demo, updated the plumbing and electrical, and prepped the walls. The appliances might take two weeks. Everything else is standard stock."

Renee glanced at the samples spread across the table—tiles and countertops, cabinet samples and paint chips, all the pieces that would transform her aunt's outdated kitchen into something functional and beautiful. "This is really happening."

"It is," Jake said, and there was something warm in his voice. "You picked good materials. Quality stuff that'll last. Your aunt would be proud of what you're doing here."

"Thank you. That means a lot."

Jake began gathering the samples they'd selected, stacking them in a neat pile. "Linda will make color copies of these for your records. That way you can show them to your family or just have them for reference as work progresses."

"That's thoughtful."

"We learned the hard way that clients like being able to see what they chose, especially when decisions were made weeks before installation." He carried the samples toward the front desk. "Let me get Linda started on the paperwork, and then you'll be all set."

Renee followed him back to the reception area, where Linda looked up from her computer with a smile. Jake handed her the stack of samples and gave her a quick rundown of their decisions while Renee waited, taking in the photos on the walls once more. Each one showed a completed project—renovated kitchens, restored porches, and additions that looked like they'd always been part of the original home. The work was meticulous; the attention to detail was evident even in photographs.

"I'll have copies ready for you in just a few minutes," Linda said. "And I'll email you the materials list and timeline by tomorrow afternoon."

"Perfect. Thank you." Renee turned back to Jake, who was leaning against Linda's desk with his arms crossed, looking more relaxed than he had during the consultation. "I appreciate you taking the time to walk me through everything. It would have been overwhelming trying to make these decisions on my own."

"That's what I'm here for. It's better to spend time upfront getting it right than to rush through and end up with regrets. We'll be at the inn on Thursday morning around seven. Demo days are noisy and dusty. Are you sure you want to be around for that?"

"I'm sure. I would like to watch as everything happens, and remember, I want to help as well."

"Fair warning, it's not glamorous work. We'll be ripping out cabinets, moving appliances, and removing old drywall."

"I survived corporate board meetings. I think I can handle some construction noise and dust."

"Get yourself a good pair of work gloves. And wear clothes you don't mind getting dirty." Jake's grin was warm and genuine.

"I will."

Linda handed her a folder with the copied samples, and a business card tucked inside. "Everything you need is in here. And if you think of any questions that I can answer, just call. I'm here every day until five."

"Thank you both." Renee tucked the folder under her arm and headed for the door, Jake following to walk her out.

"Drive safe," Jake said from the doorway. "And Renee? For what it's worth, I think you made good choices in there. The inn's going to be beautiful when we're finished."

"It will be. I'm sure of it."

Chapter 6

The screech of the circular saw cutting through old cabinet bases pierced the morning air. Renee ducked under the plastic sheeting they'd hung earlier to cover the doorway, wearing the hard hat he'd given her at seven sharp.

Jake set down his pry bar and crossed to where she waited. "Billy, hold up a second," Jake called over the noise. The saw went silent, and Billy straightened, pushing his safety glasses up onto the brim of his cap.

"This is Renee Bentley," Jake said. "The owner. Renee, this is Billy Watkins. He's been with us since we started the company. Master electrician, but he can do just about anything we need."

Billy wiped his hand on his jeans before extending it. "Good to meet you, Ms. Bentley. I've heard a lot about this place from my grandmother. She used to bring me here for Christmas tea when I was a kid. Your aunt made the best gingerbread cookies I've ever tasted."

Renee's expression softened, and Jake noticed the way her shoulders relaxed. "She did love her gingerbread. I'm glad you have those memories. And please call me Renee."

"Yes, ma'am. We'll take good care of the place." Billy glanced at Jake. "Ready for me to pull the rest of these uppers?"

"Go ahead."

The saw whined back to life, and Jake led Renee toward the dining room, where Sam Rogers and Levi Adams were talking. Both men looked up as they approached.

"Sam Rogers," Jake said, raising his voice slightly over the background noise. "Lead plumber. If water flows through it, Sam knows how to make it work right."

Sam had a compact and strong build, with forearms that showed the strength of years turning wrenches. His handshake was firm. "Pleasure, Renee. Jake showed me the plans for your kitchen. That farmhouse sink is going to be a beauty once we get it installed."

"I'm excited about it," Renee said.

Levi Adams stepped forward before Jake could make the introduction. At forty-two, Levi carried himself with the quiet confidence of a man who'd spent two decades perfecting his craft. His hands were scarred from years of working with wood—small nicks and calluses that told their own stories.

"Levi Adams," he said. "Finish carpenter. I'll be handling the custom work once we get past the demo phase. Crown molding, trim work, anything that needs a precise fit."

Renee studied him with open interest. "Jake mentioned you're the one who'll make sure everything looks period-appropriate."

"That's the goal. I've worked on enough historic homes to know what details matter. The original woodwork in this place deserves to be showcased, not hidden."

"I agree completely," Renee said.

Jake watched the exchange, noting how Renee engaged with each man—not as hired help, but as craftsmen whose expertise she valued. Most clients kept their distance during the demo, treating the crew like background noise. But Renee asked questions and made eye contact.

The rest of the crew were scattered between the kitchen and the downstairs bathroom. Jake would introduce them as work allowed, but for now he needed to walk Renee through what was about to happen to her kitchen.

He turned to the dining table, where he'd spread the renovation plans earlier that morning, weighing down the corners with his tape measure and a couple of carpenter's pencils. Renee stepped beside him, close enough that he could see the faint dusting of freckles across her nose.

"All right," Jake said, pulling his focus back to the plans. "Let me show you exactly what's happening today and over the next few weeks."

He traced the kitchen outline with his finger, conscious of how she leaned in to see better. Their heads were close together over the drawings, and he could hear the quiet intake of her breath as she studied the details.

"Gutting the kitchen means we're taking everything down to the studs," he explained. "Cabinets, countertops, and appliances—all of it comes out. Then we'll assess the plumbing and electrical. Based on what I've seen so far, I'm fairly certain we'll need to upgrade both systems completely to meet current code."

"What does that involve?"

"New supply lines for the plumbing. For electrical, we're adding circuits to handle the commercial-grade appliances and the additional electrical outlets you requested. The main panel in the basement is old but serviceable—we may need to upgrade it depending on the load calculations."

Renee nodded slowly, her gaze tracking across the plans. "And you're still doing the downstairs bathroom at the same time?"

"We'll gut both spaces simultaneously. Levi and Sam will work on the bathroom while Billy and I focus on the kitchen demo. It's more efficient, and it means you get both major projects finished in the same timeline rather than stretching it out." He pointed to the bathroom layout on a second sheet. "Remember, we're pushing this wall out two feet to gain space. That's structural work, so it'll take a little extra time, but the payoff is worth it."

She was quiet for a moment, studying the drawings with the same focused intensity he'd seen during their material selection meeting. Then she straightened slightly, one hand resting on the table edge. "This is really happening. The kitchen I remember—where Aunt Holly made Christmas morning cinnamon rolls—it's about to disappear."

There was something in her voice that made Jake pause. Not quite sadness, but close. A kind of wistfulness that came from watching the past make way for the future. Renee met his eyes, and for a moment Jake forgot they were standing in a construction zone with his crew working twenty feet away. Her blue eyes held gratitude and something else he couldn't quite name.

He cleared his throat and returned his attention to the plans, tracing the proposed workflow. "We've set up dust barriers with plastic sheeting at every doorway leading from the work zones. You'll still get some dust—it's unavoidable during demo—but the barriers will contain most of it. Your third floor should stay relatively clean."

"Which doorway do you prefer me to use to go outside?"

"You can still use all of them." Jake pointed toward the back of the house. "We'll use that back entrance exclusively during work hours. Your main entrance door and stairway will remain unblocked and clear for you to use. You can come and go without navigating around tools and materials."

"And hours?"

"Seven to five, generally." He glanced at her. "If there's a morning you need quiet—sleep issues, headache, whatever—just let me know. We'll do our best to adjust."

"Well, that's thoughtful of you."

"We try." Jake rolled up the first plan and reached for the detailed drawings underneath. "These show what the finished kitchen will look like. I wanted you to see the end vision."

He spread the new drawings, and Renee leaned in again. This time she braced her hand on the table next to his, their fingers inches apart. Jake noticed the absence of rings, the neat trim of her nails, and the small scar on her thumb. He wondered about that scar—what had caused it, whether she even remembered.

Stop it, Morrison. Focus.

"The island here," he said, tapping the center of the kitchen layout. "Six by three feet, like we discussed. Seating on this side, storage on the other. The range goes against this wall with a custom hood above it. We'll tile the backsplash in that soft white subway tile you picked."

"It's going to be beautiful," Renee said.

"It will. But first, it will be a disaster zone." He met her eyes again, making sure she understood. "Demo is the hardest part emotionally. You will see bare walls, exposed framing, wires hanging out, and pipes capped off. It looks worse before it looks better. I need you to trust the process."

"I trust you."

"Good, because there'll be days you might question your decision to do this. Days when you walk through here and think, 'What have I done?' That's normal. Just remember the end goal."

"Walk me through the sequence again," Renee said. "I want to understand every step."

He walked her through the entire renovation process, from today's demo through rough framing, plumbing and electrical rough-ins, insulation, drywall, finish carpentry, cabinetry installation, countertop fabrication, appliance delivery, floor refinishing, and paint. He explained how each phase built on the previous one, how delays in one area could cascade, and why they sequenced the work the way they did.

Renee asked intelligent questions—about material lead times, about inspection requirements, and about what happened if they discovered problems behind the walls. She wanted to understand not just what they were doing, but why.

"You're thinking like a project manager," Jake observed.

"Old habits. In marketing, you learn to see how all the pieces connect. If one campaign element fails, how does it affect the rest? The same principle applies here, I suppose."

"It does. Except in construction, you can't always control the variables. We might open a wall and find water damage. Or the electrical might be worse than we thought. You have to be flexible."

"I can be flexible." She smiled. "I survived a decade in New York City. Trust me, I know how to adapt when plans change."

Jake found himself curious about that—her life in Manhattan, the career she'd left behind, and what had driven her to make such a drastic change. He'd read the basics in the initial client questionnaire Dawson had filled out, but the facts didn't tell him much about the woman.

"Can I ask you something?" He kept his tone casual, rolling up the elevation drawings. "Why did you buy the inn? It's a big leap from working in New York and having a major professional career."

Renee was quiet for a moment, her fingers tracing the edge of the table. When she spoke, her voice carried a thoughtfulness that suggested she'd examined this question more than once.

"I was burned out. Completely, thoroughly exhausted in a way that sleeping more or taking a vacation couldn't fix. I'd spent years building a career that looked impressive on paper but felt hollow in practice." She glanced at him. "I was making great money, managing important accounts, and getting promoted on schedule. And I was miserable."

Jake nodded, understanding that sentiment better than she probably realized.

"When the company I worked for offered me a buyout, I had this moment of clarity," Renee continued. "I could take the money and find another corporate job. Or I could take the money and do something different. Something mine. At first, I was thinking about coming back here and starting a marketing firm of my own. My mother mentioned the inn during a phone call, and it just clicked. This place represented everything I'd lost somewhere along the way—family, community, and purpose that went beyond profit margins."

"But you've never run an inn before, right?"

"No. And maybe that's exactly why I should try. I was a senior marketing executive, Jake. I know how to see potential, identify target markets, and create experiences that resonate with people. Running an inn is hospitality, yes, but it's also storytelling. Making guests feel like they've discovered something special. That's what I did in corporate marketing, just with different products."

Jake found himself reassessing her yet again. He'd initially categorized her as a successful professional playing at small-town life, but there was a real vision in what she'd just described. She wasn't running from something—she was running toward something.

"What about after?" he asked. "Once the inn's operational?"

"I'm still considering opening my own marketing consultancy, eventually. Help local businesses tell their stories better, build their online presence, and reach beyond Mistletoe Falls to the tourists who would love this place if they knew it existed." She smiled a little self-consciously. "That probably sounds naïve. A small-town girl thinks she can make it as an entrepreneur."

"It doesn't sound naïve. It sounds like you know exactly what you want, and you're going after it. That takes guts."

"Or foolishness." But she was still smiling. "Sometimes I'm not sure which."

"Guts," Jake said firmly. "I've seen foolish. This isn't it."

Renee held his gaze, and Jake became acutely aware of how easy it was to talk to her. And that was dangerous territory. She was a client. A sophisticated woman who'd lived in Manhattan and managed million-dollar campaigns. What would someone like her want with a contractor?

He broke eye contact first, gathering the rolled plans. "Okay, back to work. Remember to keep your hardhat on anytime you're in the work areas. And the safety glasses—don't take those off either. Flying debris doesn't care about timing." He handed her a pair of clear protective glasses from his tool belt. "Did you get those work gloves?"

She pulled them from her back pocket, and Jake examined them with a critical eye. Canvas with leather palms, decent stitching. They'd hold up.

"Those'll work. Now, ground rules." He ticked them off on his fingers. "Be careful around active demo zones. When we're using power tools, keep your distance. If you smell gas or see sparks, tell someone immediately and get outside. Don't move materials or tools; some things are staged for specific reasons. And if you're not sure about something, ask. No question is stupid when it comes to safety."

Renee nodded. "Understood. What can I actually help with today?"

Jake glanced toward the kitchen, where Billy was wrestling an upper cabinet free from its wall mounts. "Once Billy gets those uppers down, we'll start pulling the lowers. I can teach you how to remove cabinets—locate the screws, support the weight, and walk them away from the wall without damaging the floor."

"Sounds like a plan."

Jake led her back to the kitchen, where Billy had just set another cabinet on the growing stack near the back door. The walls looked naked without them, studs exposed where the cabinets had been mounted. The avocado-green appliances sat like relics from another era, waiting their turn for removal. Renee stood in the doorway, taking in the transformation that had occurred in the thirty minutes she'd spent reviewing plans.

"It already looks so different," she said.

"And we're just getting started." Jake moved to where Billy was working. "How much longer on the uppers?"

"Thirty minutes, maybe."

"Good. Once you're clear, Renee and I will start on the lower cabinets." Jake turned to Renee. "Until then, you can watch how Billy works. See how he supports the cabinet before removing the final screws? That keeps it from dropping and damaging the wall or floor."

Renee moved closer, observing Billy's methodical process.

Sam appeared from the bathroom, wiping his hands on a rag. "Water's shut off. Ready to pull fixtures whenever you give the word."

"Go for it." Jake glanced at Renee. "You want to see what's happening in the bathroom? It's less dramatic than the kitchen, but the process is similar."

"Yes, absolutely."

He led her through the plastic sheeting into the small bathroom where Sam was already loosening the bolts on the toilet. The floral wallpaper Renee had winced at during their first walkthrough seemed even more garish now under the work lights Sam had set up.

"This all has to go," Jake explained. "Toilet, vanity, tub eventually. We'll cap the plumbing, patch and prep the walls, and then build it back with the new layout we discussed—pushing into the office nook to gain that extra space."

Renee studied the room with a critical eye. "It's going to feel twice as large."

"At least. And functional in a way this never was." Jake pointed to where the wall would be removed. "Levi's measuring and marking right now on the other side. Once Sam's done in here, we'll start the demo on that wall."

Sam glanced up from where he was loosening bolts. "Give me twenty minutes and the toilet's out. Vanity will take a bit longer."

"Take your time. We've got plenty to keep us busy." Jake turned to Renee. "You want to stay and watch, or head back to the kitchen?"

"I'll watch for a few minutes."

Jake nodded and headed into the office, leaving Renee to ask Sam her questions about plumbing. Behind him, he heard her inquiring about pipe materials and replacement timelines.

"I double-checked; the wall's not load-bearing," Levi announced when Jake joined him. "We can take it out without additional support. It should only take an hour or so once we get started."

"Good. What about the plumbing in the wall?" Jake asked.

"Looks straightforward. Old supply lines, but they're copper. Should cap clean once Sam gets the fixtures out."

They worked in companionable silence for a few minutes, Levi measuring and marking while Jake double-checked the bathroom plans against what they were seeing. The layout was straightfor-ward—remove the wall and extend the bathroom into the office nook. Nothing particularly complicated, but every detail mattered when you were working in a historic home.

"She seems nice," Levi said without looking up from his tape mea-sure.

Jake kept his expression neutral. "She does."

"She seems to be the hands-on type."

"She's more involved than most," Jake agreed.

Levi straightened, meeting Jake's eyes. "You like her."

"She's a client."

"That's not an answer."

Jake exhaled slowly. "Drop it, Levi."

"Just saying. Wouldn't blame you if you did."

"She's also way out of my league," Jake said flatly. "She spent a decade in Manhattan running marketing campaigns. I spent a decade learning how to hang drywall without screwing it up. We're in differ-ent worlds."

Levi shrugged. "Sometimes different worlds collide in interesting ways."

He wandered off before Jake could formulate a response, leaving Jake alone with his thoughts. Yes, he liked Renee. Yes, he'd noticed the way she smiled when she was genuinely pleased with something. Yes, he'd caught himself watching her hands move over the material samples yesterday, the way she bit her lower lip when she was thinking through a decision.

And none of that mattered, because women like Renee Bentley didn't end up with men like him.

He pushed the thought aside and returned to the kitchen. He had work to do, and standing around analyzing his own hopeless interest in a client wasn't going to get cabinets demolished.

Billy had the last upper cabinet down and was disconnecting the range. Renee now stood near the dining room doorway, watching the process with obvious fascination. When she saw Jake, she straightened.

"Billy's explaining how to disconnect gas appliances safely," she said. "I had no idea there were so many steps involved."

"Gas isn't something to mess around with," Jake said. "One mistake and you've got a serious problem." He moved to where Billy was working. "How's it looking?"

"Clean shutoff. No leaks, no corrosion on the line. It should be straightforward." Billy glanced at Renee. "You might want to step back a bit while I finish this part. Just as a precaution."

Within minutes, Billy had the range disconnected and ready for removal. Jake helped him muscle it away from the wall, revealing decades of accumulated grease and dust. Renee made a small noise of dismay.

The refrigerator came next, and the kitchen looked even more skeletal. Just lower cabinets and bare walls, waiting for transformation.

Jake pulled on his work gloves and gestured for Renee to do the same. "Ready to learn cabinet removal?"

They worked together for the next hour—Jake showing Renee how to locate the mounting screws, how to support the cabinet weight while Billy removed the anchors, and how to walk it away from the wall without damaging the floor. She followed instructions precisely, asking questions when she didn't understand, never rushing or making assumptions.

By lunchtime, they'd removed many of the lower cabinets. Renee's face was flushed from exertion, her hair escaping from its ponytail in damp tendrils. She had a smudge of dust across her cheek, and her hands were trembling slightly from the sustained effort of holding heavy cabinets steady.

She looked absolutely delighted.

"That was incredible," she said, accepting the water bottle Jake handed her. "I've never built anything or torn anything down in my life. This is so different from sitting in meetings."

"It's definitely more physical." Jake took a long drink from his water bottle, trying not to stare at the way her cheeks were flushed or the way her eyes shone with accomplishment.

"I love it. I mean, I'm going to be sore tomorrow. But I love it."

Sam ambled over, wiping his hands on a rag. "We're breaking for lunch. There's a sub shop two blocks down. If you're interested, you can join us."

"I'll grab something from my parents' diner," Renee said. "How about if I order everyone lunch instead? My treat."

"If you're offering, we'd never turn down food from The Fireside. This crew eats anything, so whatever the special is today is fine."

"Consider it done." Renee pulled off her hard hat and safety glasses, then paused. "Thank you. All of you. For letting me be a part of this."

Billy spoke up from where he was coiling extension cords. "Most clients would've run screaming after watching their kitchen get torn apart. You stuck around and helped. I'm impressed."

"It's my inn. I want to understand every piece of it."

Jake watched her leave through the plastic sheeting, her work gloves tucked in her back pocket, her stride confident despite the morning's labor. When he turned back, he found three sets of knowing eyes on him.

"Not a word," he said.

Sam grinned.

"Your face is saying enough as it is," Billy said.

Jake ignored them both and headed for his truck, needing a few minutes alone to think. He liked her. More than liked her, if he was being honest with himself. And that was a complication he absolutely didn't need.

Chapter 7

Renee crouched in front of the last remaining lower kitchen cabinet as she looked at the pipes Jake was examining. The kitchen echoed now—every footstep, every word bouncing off the bare walls.

"See this?" Jake's voice drew her attention to where his flashlight beam illuminated a section of pipe beneath the sink. "That's galvanized steel. It's been here since the house was built, probably."

Renee leaned closer, their shoulders nearly touching in the confined space. The pipe looked dull and rough compared to the shiny copper she'd seen Sam working with in the bathroom. "And that's bad?"

"Not bad, just old. Galvanized was standard back then, but it corrodes from the inside over time. Restricts water flow, which can cause pressure problems." Jake ran his finger along the pipe, and flakes of rust came away on his work glove. "We'll replace all of this with copper. Much more reliable. Hand me that pipe cutter. The one with the red handles."

Renee reached for the tool from the collection spread on the drop cloth beside them. The pipe cutter was heavier than she'd expected, solid metal that spoke of quality and long use. She passed it to Jake, watching as he positioned it around the pipe.

"The key is making a clean cut," he said. "You tighten this gradually, rotating it around the pipe. Too much pressure at once and you'll crush the pipe instead of cutting it."

She watched his hands work—scarred knuckles, calloused palms, fingers that moved with absolute certainty. There was something mesmerizing about watching someone who knew what they were doing, who'd spent years perfecting a skill until it became second nature. She thought of her own hands, which until recently had only known keyboards and presentation clickers, and felt a strange mixture of inadequacy and determination.

"Want to try?" Jake offered the cutter.

"You trust me with that?"

"You've done well with everything else. Besides, I'm right here if you need help." He repositioned himself so she could reach the pipe more easily. "Just remember—gradual pressure, keep it steady."

Renee took the cutter. Jake guided her arms into position, his hands briefly covering hers to show the proper angle. The contact was professional and instructive, but she felt the warmth of his palms through her work gloves, anyway.

She tightened the cutter's mechanism, then began rotating it around the pipe. The metal resisted at first, then slowly began to yield. It required more arm strength than she'd anticipated, and by the third rotation her shoulders were burning.

"You're doing great," Jake said. "Just a few more passes."

She continued rotating, feeling the pipe give way bit by bit. When it finally separated with a small hiss of trapped air, she felt a surge of accomplishment entirely disproportionate to the task. But Jake was grinning at her like she'd just won an award.

"Perfect cut." He took the cutter and set it aside, then reached for a cap fitting. "Now we seal this off so we can remove the cabinet without any surprises. The last thing we need is water spraying everywhere."

"Has that happened before?"

"More times than I'd like to admit. Usually when someone forgets a shutoff valve or assumes a line is empty when it's not." He applied a kind of paste to the threads of the cap, then began screwing it onto the pipe. "Construction keeps you humble. Just when you think you know everything, a pipe bursts or a wall reveals termite damage, and you remember that you're always learning."

Renee appreciated the honesty. In her corporate world, admitting you didn't know something or had made a mistake felt like career suicide. But Jake wore his learning experiences like badges, proof that he'd put in the time to become genuinely skilled.

They worked together for the next twenty minutes, disconnecting the rest of the drain lines and preparing the cabinet for removal. Jake explained each step. The work required them to stay close, their heads bent together in the confined space beneath the sink, and Renee found herself acutely aware of his presence—the faint scent of sawdust and soap, the steady rhythm of his breathing, and his calm competence in every movement.

She'd worked alongside plenty of talented people in Manhattan. Brilliant strategists, creative directors who could sell ice to penguins, and account managers who juggled impossible demands with grace. But none of them had made her feel quite like this—respected, capable, and seen as a person rather than a title.

When her phone rang, the sound jarring in the stripped-bare kitchen, Renee nearly dropped the wrench she was holding.

Jake glanced at her. "You need to get that?"

She pulled the phone from her pocket, and her stomach dropped when she saw the name on the screen. Patricia Westbrook.

"I should probably take this," Renee said, hearing the reluctance in her own voice.

"No problem. I need to check some things in the basement anyway." Jake stood, brushing dust from his jeans. "Take your time."

He left through the plastic sheeting, and Renee watched him go before answering the call. "Patricia. Hi."

"Renee! Finally. I've been trying to reach you for two days." Patricia's voice carried that characteristic blend of warmth and urgency that had made her such an effective account director. "How's the great mountain adventure going? Please tell me you're not living in a tent."

Despite her apprehension, Renee smiled. "No tent. Just a Victorian inn that's currently undergoing major renovations."

"Ah. So you're living in a construction zone. That's almost worse." Papers rustled in the background—Patricia was probably at her desk. "Listen, I'm calling because something incredible just came up, and you're the first person I thought of."

Renee's smile faded. She knew that tone. It was Patricia's we-have-an-opportunity voice, the one that usually preceded offers that were impossible to refuse.

"Patterson & Klein is opening a new creative division," Patricia continued. "They want someone to build it from scratch—hire the team, establish the culture, and set the strategic direction. It's essentially a VP position without the official title yet, but that would come within eighteen months. They're offering two-ninety base, plus performance bonuses that could push it over three-fifty."

Two hundred ninety thousand dollars. Renee looked down at her dusty jeans, at the grime under her fingernails, and at the gutted kitchen surrounding her. Six months ago, that number would have made her heart race. Now it just felt surreal.

"That's a generous offer," she managed.

"It's more than generous—it's career-making. You'd be building something entirely new, which I know you love. Creative control, significant resources, and Patterson's reputation would open doors you can't even imagine right now." Patricia paused. "Renee, I know you needed a break. I understand burnout. But this is the kind of opportunity that doesn't come around twice. At least tell me you'll consider it."

Through the plastic sheeting, Renee could hear Billy's radio playing classic rock. She could hear Levi's power saw cutting through wood in another part of the house. The sounds of her current reality—physical work, tangible progress, and purpose that didn't require quarterly projections.

"I appreciate you thinking of me," Renee said. "But I made a choice when I left New York. I'm building something here."

"An inn. Renee, you're brilliant at marketing strategy. You have a gift for reading markets and creating compelling narratives. And you're going to use that to—what, make sure guests have fresh towels? It's not that inn keeping isn't worthwhile, but it's such a waste of your talents."

Her words stung. Not because they were cruel—Patricia didn't have a cruel bone in her body—but because they echoed the doubts that still crept.

"It's more than fresh towels," Renee said, hearing the defensiveness in her voice. "I'm creating an experience. Building something that serves the community. Using everything I learned in corporate marketing, just applied differently."

"But do you really see yourself doing this long-term? Running an inn in—where is it, Mistletoe Falls? Renee, you're thirty-two. This is the time to be building your career, not retreating to a small town that probably doesn't even have decent coffee."

"We have excellent coffee, actually." Renee stood, needing to move. She walked to the window overlooking the street, watching a young mother push a stroller past the inn. "And I'm not retreating. I'm choosing a different path."

"A path that pays significantly less, offers zero advancement opportunities, and frankly, sounds lonely. I'm not trying to be harsh. I'm worried about you. You left so suddenly, and now you're renovating an old inn in the middle of nowhere. It feels impulsive. Not like you at all."

Renee caught her reflection in the window—dusty hard hat, flannel shirt she'd bought at the general store, and her face was bare of makeup. Patricia was right. This wasn't like her. The old Renee would have never made such a drastic change without extensive planning, risk assessment, and backup strategies.

But maybe that was exactly the problem.

"I was exhausted, Patricia. Completely burned out. Every morning I woke up dreading the day. Every meeting felt meaningless. Every campaign success felt empty because I knew the next one was already waiting." Renee pressed her palm against the cold glass. "I was successful and miserable, and I couldn't keep living that way."

"So take some time. Travel. Decompress. But don't throw away everything you've built. Come back to New York. Take the Patterson position. I guarantee that within six months you'll remember why you loved this work."

Would she? Renee tried to imagine it—the morning commute, the tailored suits, and the conference rooms with their impressive views.

The adrenaline of landing a major client, the satisfaction of executing a flawless campaign. She'd loved it all at one time.

"I'll think about it, but I'm pretty sure my mind is made up."

"Of course. Take a few days. But they want an answer by next week—the position is too important to leave open long. And Renee? It really is good to hear your voice. I've missed having you around. The office isn't the same without you."

They said their goodbyes, and Renee lowered the phone, staring at the blank screen. The kitchen felt very quiet suddenly, despite the construction noise filtering through from other parts of the house. She looked at her hands, nails broken despite the work gloves, skin dry from cleaning products.

These weren't the hands of a senior marketing executive.

But they weren't useless hands either. They'd helped demolish cabinets, had just successfully cut a pipe, and had contributed to transforming this space. There was satisfaction in that work—immediate, tangible, and real.

So why did Patricia's call feel like it had opened a door Renee thought she'd firmly closed?

She walked back to where they'd been working, looking at the disconnected pipes and the lone cabinet waiting to be removed. This morning she'd felt capable and purposeful. Now she felt unmoored, caught between two versions of herself that couldn't seem to coexist.

The plastic sheeting rustled, and Jake emerged from the basement. He took one look at her and stopped.

"Everything okay?" he asked.

Renee wanted to say yes, to brush it off as nothing important. But standing in this gutted kitchen with wavering confidence and wearing a flannel shirt, she found she didn't have the energy for pretense.

"I don't know," she admitted.

Jake crossed to the cooler in the corner of the room and pulled out two water bottles. He handed her one, then leaned against the wall.

"Wanna talk about it?"

"A former colleague from New York called." Renee twisted the cap off the water bottle but didn't drink. "She called about a job opportunity. Vice president position, significant salary, building a new creative division from scratch."

"That's a serious offer."

"It is." Renee finally took a drink, buying herself time to organize her thoughts. "She thinks I'm wasting my potential here. Running an inn instead of using my marketing expertise for something more significant."

"Do you think that?"

"I don't know what I think right now. Just moments ago I was helping you disconnect pipes and feeling proud of myself for making a clean cut. Now I'm standing here wondering if I've made a massive mistake. If I threw away a career I spent years building for some romantic notion of small-town life, that's going to lose its appeal the first time I have a slow season or a major repair bill."

Jake was quiet for a moment, rolling his water bottle between his palms. When he spoke, his voice was measured. "Can I tell you something? And you can tell me if it's overstepping."

"Please."

"When I was eighteen, I had a full ride to play football at UT. I was convinced that was my path—professional sports, fame, and success. Then I screwed up badly enough that I lost the scholarship. Lost everything I thought defined me." He met her eyes. "For a long time, I was angry about it. It felt like my life was over before it had really started. But looking back now, that wasn't a failure. It was redirection. Losing football led me to construction, which led me to work I genuinely love. Work that matters in ways throwing a football never would have."

Renee heard what he wasn't saying—that his past held painful lessons learned the hard way. That he understood what it felt like to question every choice.

"I'm not saying your situation is the same," Jake continued. "But maybe the question isn't whether you made a mistake leaving New York. Maybe it's whether that life was actually serving you or if you were just serving it."

The words settled into Renee's chest, heavy and true. She'd been successful in Manhattan. Undeniably successful. But she hadn't been happy lately. She hadn't been fulfilled in any way that mattered beyond her bank account and professional reputation?

"It's like day and night," she said. "Manhattan compared to here. There, I was always on—always performing, always proving myself, and always chasing the next promotion or account. Here, I can just... be. I can learn to cut pipes and not feel stupid for not knowing how. I can talk to people without wondering what they want from me. Not only that, but I can breathe."

"That sounds like you already know your answer."

"But what if Patricia's right? What if I'm running away instead of building something real? What if six months from now I'm drowning in inn management and wishing I'd taken the safe option?" Renee pressed her fingers against her temples. "I took one phone call, and now I'm second-guessing everything. That's pathetic."

"It's not pathetic. It's human." Jake pushed off the wall and moved closer. "Big life changes are scary. And people from your old life are going to question your new one. That doesn't mean they're right. It means they care about you."

Renee looked up at him, this man who'd somehow become a steady presence in her chaotic transition. He wasn't trying to fix her doubt or dismiss her feelings. He was just standing there, offering water and perspective and the quiet assurance that questioning didn't equal failing.

"Do you regret it?" she asked. "Losing football and ending up staying here in Mistletoe Falls?"

Jake considered the question seriously. "Sometimes I wonder what my life would have looked like if things had gone differently. But regret? No. This life—building things with my hands, working with my brother, and being part of this community—it fits me in a way football never really did. I just didn't know it until the other option was taken away."

"I'm not sure running an inn fits me yet," Renee admitted. "So far, I feel like I'm playing dress-up. Marketing executive pretending to be an innkeeper. Like everyone can see that I don't really belong here."

"Everyone feels that way when they're learning something new. You think I felt like a real contractor on my first job? I was terrified I'd screw something up." Jake's mouth quirked in a half-smile. "But you... you show up every day. You ask questions, and you're willing to get dusty and make mistakes. That's not pretending—that's becoming."

Becoming. The word resonated with her. Maybe she wasn't supposed to have all the answers right now. Maybe doubt was part of the process, not evidence of failure.

"Patricia suggested I come back to New York," Renee said. "Take the position, return to the life I know."

"Are you going to?"

Renee looked around the gutted kitchen, at the exposed studs that would soon be pristine walls, at the space that was currently a mess but held the promise of transformation.

"No. I made a choice when I bought this inn. Maybe it wasn't the logical choice or the safe choice, but it was mine. And I'm not ready to give up on it just because someone else thinks I should."

Jake's expression warmed, and something in his eyes made her heartbeat stutter. Pride, maybe. Or respect.

"Good," he said simply. "Because I think you're going to be really good at this. The inn, I mean. You have vision and determination."

Renee felt her throat tighten with unexpected emotion. When had someone's belief in her felt more valuable than their approval? When had validation from a contractor in work boots meant more than praise from corporate executives?

"Thanks," she managed. "For listening. And for not telling me what to do."

"That's not my job. You're plenty capable of making your own decisions." Jake gestured toward the remaining cabinet. "But for what it's worth, I hope you stick around. This renovation would be a lot less interesting without you."

The comment was casual, friendly, exactly what a contractor might say to a client he'd come to like. But the way his gaze held hers for an extra beat suggested more.

She cleared her throat and forced herself back to practical matters. "So. Should we finish disconnecting this cabinet? Or do I need a minute to have a complete existential crisis first?"

Jake's laugh was warm and genuine. "Let's tackle the cabinet. Existential crises are better handled after the physical work is done. Trust me on that."

Chapter 8

The backup alarm on the delivery truck cut through the late morning air, and Jake looked up from the junction box he'd been rewiring in the sitting room. Through the front window, he watched a massive moving truck maneuver into position at the curb, its brake lights flashing as the driver shifted into park.

Renee walked to the front door and opened it. Even from here, he could see her smile—warm and genuine.

"Need any help?" he asked as he walked toward her. Through the doorway he could see the driver rolling up the truck's rear door. Inside, boxes were stacked floor to ceiling, each one labeled in large handwriting. Kitchen. Bedroom. Office. Personal. Books.

Renee glanced at him, her expression caught between excitement and mild embarrassment. "No, it's okay. My entire Manhattan life just arrived."

"That's a lot of boxes."

"Fifty-two. I sold all the furniture with my condo, but everything else—" She gestured at the truck. "Here it is."

The driver, a barrel-chested man in his fifties with a Yankees cap, walked toward them and handed Renee a receipt. "Where do you want them, ma'am?"

"Here on the porch is fine."

Jake pictured her hauling fifty-two boxes up two flights of stairs, one at a time over the course of days. His back ached just thinking about it. "My crew and I can take your boxes upstairs now."

Renee turned to him, surprise evident in the slight widening of her eyes. "Jake, you don't have to—"

"I know. But there are ten of us, and we can move all your boxes pretty quickly." He pulled out his phone and fired off a quick text to the crew group chat. "Besides, I'd rather spend half an hour carrying boxes than watch you struggle with this for the next week."

The delivery driver and his assistant made quick work of unloading, stacking boxes on the wide front porch in neat rows. Jake's crew appeared in ones and twos—Levi from the bathroom, Sam and Billy from the kitchen, and the others from various corners of the renovation. Dawson came last, wiping his hands on a rag as he surveyed the collection.

"Moving day?" Dawson asked.

"Apparently." Jake gestured to the boxes. "Renee's stuff from New York. We're helping get it upstairs."

"Third floor?" Levi asked, and when Renee nodded, he grinned. "Good thing we've been doing cardio."

The crew organized themselves with the efficiency of men accustomed to physical labor. Billy grabbed the first box, tested its weight, and headed inside. Sam followed with a second. Within minutes, they'd established a rhythm—two or three guys heading up at a time while others grabbed the next load.

"I'll head up and direct traffic," Renee said. "Otherwise you'll end up playing Tetris trying to figure out where everything goes."

Jake hoisted a box labeled Kitchen and followed her inside. The main staircase curved gracefully up to the second floor. Another flight beyond that led to Renee's private quarters.

By the time Jake reached the third floor, his shoulders were burning pleasantly from the weight of the box he carried.

"Kitchen boxes can go over there," Renee directed, pointing to the small but functional kitchen. "I'll sort through everything later."

Jake set the box down where she'd indicated, taking a moment to glance around. The space had good bones—high ceilings, plenty of natural light, and original architectural details that spoke to the home's history. It felt like Renee somehow, though he couldn't quite articulate why.

He headed back down for another load.

The crew settled into an easy rhythm, boxes moving steadily from the porch to the third floor. On his third trip up, Jake grabbed a box labeled Kitchen (Coffee). The weight suggested it was packed to capacity. When he set it down in Renee's kitchen, he noticed the flaps had come loose during transport. Inside, he could see bags of coffee beans.

"You have a coffee addiction?" he asked as Renee directed Levi toward the bedroom with another box.

She turned, following his gaze to the partially open box, and laughed. "That's not even half of it. There are two more coffee boxes somewhere in all this mess."

"Two more?"

"I know... it sounds completely ridiculous, right?" Renee walked over and pulled out a bag with an almost reverent expression. "But good coffee was one of my few personal indulgences in New York.

Everything else was suits and client dinners and keeping up appearances. But coffee—that was just for me."

"So you're a complete addict."

"Absolutely unrepentant." She set the bag down with a smile that transformed her face from pretty to genuinely beautiful. "I have a problem, and I'm not interested in solving it. Life's too short for bad coffee."

Jake found himself grinning back. "Fair enough. Though I should warn you, the local general store carries exactly two types of coffee—regular and decaf. The grocery store has a larger variety. But if you want specialty coffee and a large selection, try the Hearth & Coffee Mercantile down the street."

"Oh trust me, I already spotted that store, and I'll be visiting soon. I've been making do with what I brought in my car, but I was starting to get desperate." She patted the box affectionately. "Now I'm fully stocked. I could probably survive a month-long blizzard on coffee beans alone. Want to try some? I make a mean pour-over."

The offer was casual and friendly, the kind of thing neighbors might say to each other. But it felt like more. Like she was sharing something personal.

"Maybe after we finish. I'm curious what seventy-dollar coffee tastes like."

"It's life-changing," Renee assured him.

Sam appeared at the top of the stairs with another box. "Where do you want Office?"

"Second bedroom," Renee called back, then added to Jake, "I'm thinking of using it as a home office eventually. Once the inn is operational."

Jake filed that information away and headed back down for another box. The pile on the porch was shrinking steadily. He grabbed two boxes labeled Bedroom (Shoes).

Dawson fell into step beside him on the stairs, carrying a box marked Books. "She's an interesting woman," his brother said.

"She is."

"And you like her."

Jake shot him a look. "She's a client."

"Yep. A client you're making googly eyes at every time she's not looking." Dawson's grin was knowing. "Not that I blame you. If I weren't married, I'd—"

"Don't finish that sentence if you want to keep all your teeth."

Dawson laughed but mercifully dropped the subject as they reached the third floor. Jake set the shoe boxes in the bedroom where Renee was organizing space, trying not to notice the box she'd already opened. But he couldn't help seeing it—designer heels spilling out, each pair more elegant and expensive-looking than the last. Sleek black pumps. Strappy sandals with delicate gold buckles. Knee-high boots in supple leather that probably cost more than his truck payment.

These were the shoes of a woman who'd navigated Manhattan boardrooms and upscale restaurants. A woman who belonged in a world of polished conference tables and five-star hotels. Not in a construction zone in small-town Tennessee.

Jake turned away before Renee could catch him staring and headed back downstairs.

Two more trips, and the boxes were all inside. The crew dispersed back to their respective projects, but Jake lingered, ostensibly to make sure Renee didn't need anything else, but really because he wasn't quite ready to return to the electrical work waiting below.

"Thanks," Renee said, surveying the clutter of boxes filling her living space. "That would have taken me days to move by myself."

"No problem. We're used to heavy lifting." Jake noticed another open box near the sofa—this one with Office (Professional) written on the side. Papers spilled out, along with what looked like a leather portfolio, a framed certificate, and what looked like awards.

Renee followed his gaze, and her expression shifted, a faint flush creeping up her neck. "That's just—it's nothing. Old work stuff. My portfolios from the firm."

"Can I look? I'm curious about what you did before."

"I guess. But it's just corporate creativity. Marketing campaigns and brand strategies. Nothing like what you do—actual building, actual craftsmanship. This is just playing with words and images to convince people to buy things they probably don't need."

He crossed to the box and pulled out the portfolio, a heavy leather-bound book embossed with her name. Inside, each page showcased a different campaign—glossy photos, strategic breakdowns, and results metrics.

The first campaign spread showed a luxury boutique hotel in SoHo. The "before" showed a dated building with unremarkable branding. The "after" was transformed—sophisticated logo, elegant website design, social media presence that made the hotel look like the only place anyone would want to stay. The copy was clever, the visuals striking, and the results impressive: a forty-three percent increase in bookings within six months.

"You did this?" Jake asked.

"I led the team, yeah." Renee stood at a distance, arms crossed.

Jake turned the page. The next campaign was for an organic skincare line—packaging design that managed to be both minimalist and luxurious with brand messaging that positioned the products as self-care rather than vanity. Sales had increased eighty-seven percent in the first quarter after launch.

"These are pretty cool."

"They're just marketing—"

"No." He looked up at her, holding her gaze. "This is real work. Look at this hotel campaign. You didn't just make an ad. You saw what this place could be and figured out how to show everyone else that vision. That's not playing with words—that's strategy. Problem-solving."

"It's different from what you do."

"Sure. But not less valuable." Jake turned another page, this one showing a restaurant rebrand—a farm-to-table concept that Renee had helped transform from neighborhood spot to destination dining. The before-and-after photos showed the evolution, but it was the brand story that caught Jake's attention. She'd woven the restaurant's connection to local farms into every aspect of the marketing, making it feel authentic rather than trendy.

"This restaurant campaign," Jake said, tapping the page. "You connected them to local suppliers, made that part of the brand identity. That's not just marketing. That's understanding community. Understanding how businesses can support each other."

"I guess."

Jake studied another spread—this one for a startup tech company, brand identity built from scratch. The logo was clean and modern, and the messaging positioned the company as innovative but trustworthy. "How did you come up with this?"

"Research. Market analysis. Understanding what their target audience valued and how to communicate that the company delivered it." She moved closer. "That one was tricky because they wanted to seem cutting-edge without seeming unstable. Many startups fail, so I had to balance innovation with reliability."

"And you figured that out." Jake glanced at her. "Built them an entire brand identity that solved that problem. That takes serious creative thinking."

Jake closed the portfolio and set it aside, then pulled out a framed certificate from the box. Marketing Excellence Award, it read. Presented to Renee Bentley for Outstanding Achievement in Brand Strategy. The date was two years ago.

"You won awards," he said.

"A few. They hand those out pretty freely in the industry."

"Renee." Jake set down the certificate and turned to face her fully. "Stop minimizing this. You were good at what you did. Really good, apparently. And that doesn't become less true just because you chose to do something different."

She met his eyes. "It feels frivolous now. Like I spent years helping rich people sell luxury products when I could have been doing something that mattered."

"But you made people successful. Helped businesses grow. That hotel campaign—how many jobs do you think that created when bookings increased by forty-three percent? How many local suppliers benefited from that farm-to-table restaurant connection?" Jake picked up the portfolio again. "This is real work. Different from swinging a hammer, sure. But just as valuable."

Renee was quiet for a moment, studying him with an expression he couldn't quite read.

Jake flipped open the portfolio again, landing on the hotel campaign. "You should use these skills for the inn. This kind of strategic thinking, this ability to tell a story that makes people want to be part of something—that's undoubtedly what this place needs."

"I plan on creating a brand identity for the inn. Not just a logo and a website, but a whole experience. What makes staying here different from any other mountain inn?"

Jake could see her mind working, the wheels turning as she considered possibilities.

"I've also been thinking more about something else," Renee said slowly. "Once the inn is operational and I have a rhythm established and hired a couple of staff members, I'm going to open that small marketing consultancy I mentioned before."

"The second bedroom up here—the one where Sam just put those office boxes. That would make a great office space. Plenty of room for a desk and client meetings if you need them."

"That's exactly what I was thinking." Renee's smile returned, brighter than before. "I could help businesses like The Ginger Jar expand their online sales or help my sisters' place, Pinecone & Ivy, reach customers beyond Mistletoe Falls. There are so many talented people here doing beautiful work, but they don't know how to market themselves effectively."

Jake pictured it—Renee using her corporate expertise to help his neighbors, his community. Not for Fortune 500 profit margins, but for real people trying to build sustainable livelihoods. "You are going to make a big impact on people's lives here."

"Maybe. I hope so." She gestured to the portfolio. "It would feel good to use these skills for something more meaningful than convincing New Yorkers they need another luxury handbag."

"For what it's worth, I think you're going to be great at it. Both the inn and the consulting."

Watching her talk about her vision for helping local businesses, seeing the strategic mind at work behind those blue eyes—he could absolutely see her succeeding.

And that was exactly the problem.

Renee Bentley was brilliant. Accomplished. Sophisticated in ways that went far beyond the designer shoes currently spilling out of boxes in her bedroom. She'd built a career in Manhattan, earned awards, and commanded a salary that probably made Jake's annual income look like pocket change.

And here he was, a contractor who'd dropped out of college after losing his football scholarship. A man whose biggest professional achievement was building a reputation for quality work in a town of six thousand people.

What would someone like her ever see in someone like him?

"Jake?" Renee's voice pulled him from his thoughts. "You okay?"

"Yeah. Sorry. Just thinking." He forced a smile. "I should get back to the electrical work downstairs."

"Right. Of course. Thanks for bringing all these boxes up."

Jake headed toward the stairs, then paused at the landing. Renee was already kneeling beside another box, carefully pulling out books and stacking them on the coffee table. The late-morning light from the dormer windows caught her hair, turning it golden.

She belonged here; he realized. Not despite her Manhattan credentials, but because of them. She had the vision and skills to make the inn genuinely special. To help the community thrive. To build something that mattered.

And watching her build that future, being part of making it happen—that would have to be enough.

Even though a growing part of him wanted so much more.

Jake descended the stairs, and when he reached the main floor, Dawson was waiting, leaning against the bannister with that knowing expression Jake had learned to dread.

"Don't start," Jake warned.

"Wasn't going to start anything."

"Good."

"You were up there for twenty minutes."

Jake brushed past his brother, heading toward the junction box that needed finishing. "We were talking about her business plans."

"Uh-huh." Dawson followed. "And that required twenty minutes?"

"She showed me her portfolio. It's impressive work."

"I bet. She's impressive. And you're smitten."

"I'm a professional," Jake corrected, picking up his wire strippers with more force than necessary. "There's a difference."

"Sure there is. That's why you volunteered the entire crew to move boxes on company time."

"We were due for a break, anyway. Just thought offering a helpful hand was the right thing to do."

"Right." Dawson clapped him on the shoulder.

"She's a client. A client who lives in an entirely different world than I do. A world of designer shoes and marketing awards."

"And yet she's here. Renovating an inn and wanting to help us and learn about what we do for a living and choosing to build a life in Mistletoe Falls." Dawson's voice lost its teasing edge. "Maybe you're not as far apart as you think."

Jake wanted to believe that. Wanted to think that the differences between them—education, background, and the paths their lives had taken—didn't create a gap too wide to cross.

But he'd seen those shoes. That portfolio. The evidence of a life lived at a level he couldn't even imagine.

And believing in possibilities that didn't exist was a good way to get his heart broken.

"Back to work," Jake said firmly. "This junction box won't wire itself."

Dawson raised his hands in surrender and wandered off toward the kitchen. Jake focused on the wiring in front of him, losing himself in the familiar routine of connecting circuits and ensuring proper grounding.

But even as he worked, his mind kept drifting upstairs to where Renee was unpacking a life that fit in forty-two boxes.

And wondering what it said about him that he'd gladly carry a hundred more if it meant spending another twenty minutes in her presence.

Chapter 9

The brass bell above the door announced Renee's arrival with a cheerful jingle that echoed through Morrison's Hardware Store. She stepped inside and paused as her eyes adjusted to the bright lighting.

Overhead, the tin ceiling tiles gleamed, and the ceiling fans turned in lazy circles. To her left, a pot-bellied stove radiated warmth, surrounded by mismatched chairs that had clearly seen decades of use. An old checkerboard sat on a small table between two of the chairs, a game paused mid-play.

Renee turned slowly, taking in the sheer scope of the place. Long aisles stretched toward the back, lined floor-to-ceiling with tools, fasteners, and supplies she couldn't begin to name. Wooden drawers with brass label plates held screws and bolts organized by size. Hand tools hung on pegboard walls in neat rows.

This was nothing like the sleek home improvement stores she'd visited in Manhattan, where everything was color-coded and clearly labeled for people who didn't know what they were doing.

"Renee Bentley?"

She turned toward the voice and watched as Betty Morrison emerged from behind the front counter, her silver-streaked brown hair pulled back in a practical bun. She wore comfortable jeans and a flannel shirt, and her blue eyes held the same warmth Renee remembered from childhood.

"Mrs. Morrison." Renee crossed to meet her, and Betty pulled her into a hug.

"Oh, honey, it's just Betty. Mrs. Morrison makes me feel ancient." She pulled back, keeping her hands on Renee's shoulders as she studied her face. "Look at you. All grown up and back home. I heard you bought Holly's Inn. That's wonderful news."

"Thank you. It's good to be back."

"Tom!" Betty called toward the back of the store. "Come say hello to Renee!"

A moment later, Tom Morrison appeared from one of the back aisles, carrying a clipboard and wearing a blue flannel shirt and dark work pants. His gray hair was neatly combed, and when he saw Renee, his weathered face broke into a genuine smile.

"Renee. Welcome home." He extended his hand, and his handshake was firm and warm. "Heard you're tackling the Jingle Bell Inn. That's a big project."

"It is," Renee admitted. "Jake and Dawson have been great. They started demo work this past week."

"Those boys know what they're doing," Tom said with unmistakable pride. "You're in good hands."

"I can tell." Renee shifted her purse strap on her shoulder. "I have to be honest; I need some help. I need some supplies for my living space on the third floor. But I have to admit, I'm a little out of my element. I'm not sure where to even start."

Betty's expression turned to understanding. "What are you looking for?"

"Paint, definitely. I want to start planning colors for my rooms up there. And I'd like to look at bathroom fixtures, maybe kitchen fixtures too, just so I can actually see the finish instead of just looking at pictures." She paused. "Oh, and something to remove wallpaper. That's my weekend project. I can't stand looking at that peeling floral pattern anymore."

Betty nodded knowingly. "Wallpaper can be stubborn, but we've got what you need. Paint samples are in aisle three." She pointed towards the right side of the store. "Paint chips are all organized by brand and color family. Take your time browsing. The wallpaper stripping supplies are on the same aisle, bottom shelf. For fixtures, you'll want to go to the plumbing section in the back corner. We've got catalogs there too if you want to see more options than what we have in stock."

"Thank you so much."

"You need any help, you just holler," Tom said.

Renee made her way toward the paint aisle. The store was quiet except for the soft hum of a radio playing country music somewhere in the back. A few other customers browsed other sections, but the place had the peaceful feel of a Saturday morning when everyone moved at their own pace.

The paint aisle opened before her like a wall of possibility. Paint chips were displayed in vertical strips, organized by manufacturer and then by color family. Blues ranged from pale sky to deep navy. Greens went from soft sage to rich forest. Warm tones included everything from cream to deep rust.

Renee pulled a few chips from the display, studying them. She wanted her living space to feel like a sanctuary. Something warm and inviting. Something that felt like a cozy home.

She selected a soft sage green. Then, there was a cream that had just enough warmth to feel cozy without being yellow. A blue-gray that looked like mountain mist. She fanned them out in her hand, trying to imagine how they'd look on her walls.

"That sage is nice."

Renee looked up to find an elderly woman with white curls studying the paint chips in her hand.

"Thank you. I'm trying to decide on colors for my bedroom."

"Sage is restful. Good choice." The woman selected her own paint chips and continued down the aisle.

Renee added a few more options to her collection, then moved down to examine the wallpaper stripping supplies on the bottom shelf. Bottles of solution, spray bottles, scrapers, and various other tools. She had no idea what any of these things did.

She was reading the back of a wallpaper stripping solution bottle when footsteps approached.

"Planning to tackle wallpaper removal today?"

The voice was familiar, and Renee's pulse kicked up a notch. Jake was walking toward her down the aisle, wearing jeans and a gray henley that fit perfectly across his shoulders. His dark hair looked slightly damp, as if he'd just showered, and he carried a small list in one hand.

"Jake, hi." She straightened, suddenly very aware that she was crouching on the floor surrounded by paint chips and wallpaper supplies like someone who had no idea what they were doing. Which, to be fair, was accurate. "I didn't expect to see you here."

"Could say the same." His mouth curved in a slight smile. "Wallpaper giving you trouble?"

"All the wallpaper in my living space is making me want to tear my hair out. I thought I'd try to strip it myself this weekend." She held up the bottle. "But I'm not entirely sure what I'm doing."

Jake stepped closer and took the bottle from her hand, reading the label. His fingers brushed hers briefly in the transfer, warm and work-roughened. "This one's good, but you're going to want the gel formula for older wallpaper. Clings better to vertical surfaces and gives you more working time." He set the bottle back on the shelf and selected a different one. "This is what you want. Use it with a scoring tool first to perforate the paper, then apply the gel and let it sit for a few minutes before you start scraping."

"Scoring tool?"

Jake crouched beside her and grabbed one of the scoring tools. "This. You roll it over the wallpaper before you apply the stripper. It creates little holes that let the solution penetrate better."

"That makes sense." She took the tool from him, turning it over in her hands. "See, this is why I need help. I would have just started spraying and hoping for the best."

"You might have gotten it off, eventually." His eyes held amusement. "It would have taken longer and been more frustrating, but you'd have figured it out."

"That's generous." Renee gathered her supplies and stood, and Jake rose with her. He was tall enough that she had to look up to meet his eyes, and standing this close in the narrow aisle, she noticed details she'd missed during their work conversations. The small scar through his left eyebrow gave his face character. The way he smelled of soap and something woodsy, clean, and entirely masculine.

She took a half step back, needing space to think clearly. "What else am I missing?"

Jake surveyed her collection. "Drop cloth to protect your floor. Good putty knife for scraping. Sponges for cleanup. Bucket for water." He paused. "How about I help you gather everything?"

"You don't have to do that. I'm sure you have your own shopping to do."

"My list can wait." He was already reaching for a drop cloth from a nearby shelf. "What else are you looking for today besides wallpaper supplies?"

Renee held up her fan of paint chips. "Paint colors. And I wanted to look at bathroom and kitchen fixtures. I want to see the actual finishes and get a better idea of what I want."

Jake took the paint chips from her hand, studying them one by one. "Good choices. This sage would look nice in a bedroom. The blue-gray would work well in a bathroom." He handed them back. "The fixtures are in the back corner. We can head there after we get you squared away with the wallpaper supplies."

They spent the next ten minutes gathering everything Renee would need. Jake explained the purpose of each item, demonstrating techniques with his hands or showing her packaging diagrams. He added things she wouldn't have thought of: painter's tape for protecting trim, trash bags for the stripped wallpaper, and even a small stepladder because her ceilings were higher than she'd be able to reach easily.

"This is way more complicated than I thought," Renee said as they loaded everything into a shopping cart Jake had grabbed from the front.

"First time doing it always is. But once you understand the process, it's just repetitive work. Tedious but not difficult." He pushed the cart toward the back of the store. "You plan on removing all the wallpaper on the third floor?"

"You better believe it; whoever decorated that floor sure did love floral patterns."

Jake's laugh was quiet but genuine. "The nineties were an interesting time for interior design."

They reached the plumbing section, and Renee stopped short. The entire back corner was filled with fixtures: faucets, sinks, toilets, showerheads, and tub hardware. Everything gleamed chrome, brass, and brushed nickel under the overhead lights. Thick catalogs sat on a shelf nearby, their pages marked with sticky notes and dog-eared corners.

"I don't even know where to start," Renee admitted.

"Remind me again... what's wrong with your bathroom now? Besides the tile color."

"Everything. The sink is one of those little pedestal ones that doesn't have any storage. The faucet drips. The shower has terrible water pressure, and the showerhead looks like it's from 1985. The whole space just feels horrible and outdated."

Jake picked up one of the catalogs and flipped it open to a marked section. "I remember now. What style are you going for? Traditional, modern, or somewhere in between?"

Renee moved to stand beside him, looking at the glossy photographs of bathrooms that ranged from sleek contemporary to vintage farmhouse. "I like the idea of blending traditional and modern. Keep the character of the house but update the functionality."

"Makes sense." He turned a few pages, then pointed to a bathroom that featured a white subway tile shower, vintage-style fixtures in brushed nickel, and a vanity with traditional lines. "Something like this?"

"Yes, exactly like that." Renee leaned closer to study the details. She was acutely aware of how close he was and the warmth radiating from him.

She cleared her throat and straightened slightly. "The fixtures are beautiful. Classic but not fussy."

"Brushed nickel wears well and doesn't show water spots as much as chrome." Jake pulled a small notebook from his pocket and wrote down a few numbers from the catalog. "These are the model numbers for that faucet and showerhead. When you're ready to order, just give these to Mom or Dad, and they can get them for you."

"You're just writing those down from memory?"

"I've used these fixtures on other jobs. They're good quality and priced reasonably." He handed her the page from the notebook. "What about your kitchen?"

"The kitchen is so tiny, which is probably okay. I can use the kitchen downstairs for major cooking. But the sink is small, there's barely any counter space, and there's a two-burner stove that I'm pretty sure is a fire hazard. I'd like to make it more functional, but I'm not sure how much I can do with the space I have."

Jake closed the catalog and returned it to the shelf. "Well, on Monday, while the crew is working downstairs, if you like, you and I can work on a layout for your kitchen on the third floor."

"That would be wonderful." Renee paused, an idea forming. "Actually, I was going to order pizza for lunch today. Would you want to come to the inn? You could look at my kitchen and bathroom, maybe give me your thoughts on what's possible."

Jake's expression shifted. His eyebrows drew together slightly, and he looked down at the list in his hand, then back at her. The pause stretched long enough that Renee felt her stomach tighten.

"It's your day off," she said quickly. "If you have other things to do, I understand. I just thought since you were offering to help, and I was planning to eat anyway, we could multitask."

"No, it's not that." Jake folded the list and tucked it into his back pocket. "I don't have plans. Just errands and laundry. I can come over."

"You're sure? I promise this isn't me trying to work you for free. I legitimately need to figure out what I want to do with my space, and you know what you're talking about. Plus, I owe you for helping me shop today."

"I don't mind helping."

"So come have lunch. Help me figure out my kitchen and bathroom situation. I'll even let you pick the pizza toppings." She smiled, hoping she looked casual and not like her heart was beating faster than it should over what was essentially a working lunch.

Jake's mouth curved slightly. "What if I have terrible taste in pizza?"

"Then I'll know never to trust your design advice." The words came out before she could stop them, and she felt her cheeks warm. "That sounded sarcastic. I meant it as a joke."

"I know." His smile widened a fraction. "All right. Lunch at the inn. Whatever pizza toppings you like, I eat anything. What time?"

"Noon?"

"Noon works."

"I'll leave the front door unlocked, so just come on in."

"Door unlocked, got it." Jake glanced at her cart. "Do you need help finding anything else?"

"No, I'm good, thanks to you."

"Come on. I'll help you get checked out, and then I need to grab my supplies before Dad puts me to work stocking shelves."

They made their way back to the front counter, where Betty was helping another customer. Tom was restocking a display of work gloves nearby, and he looked up as they approached.

"Find everything you needed?" he asked Renee.

"I did. Jake helped me."

"That's my boy. Always willing to lend a hand."

She and Jake started unloading her cart onto the counter while Betty finished with her customer.

Betty rang up each of her items next, her fingers flying over the register keys. "Looks like you're taking on quite a project," she said, glancing at the wallpaper supplies.

"The entire third floor of the inn—it's a lot of wallpaper, and apparently it requires more equipment than I anticipated."

"First time stripping wallpaper?"

"That obvious?"

Betty laughed. "Honey, I've seen every first-time home improvement project walk through that door. You have the right supplies, though. That's what matters."

The total came to just over a hundred dollars, and Renee handed over her credit card without flinching. Her Manhattan self would have balked at spending money on DIY supplies when she could have hired someone. Her Mistletoe Falls self understood that learning to do things with her own hands had value beyond the monetary savings.

Jake helped her load everything into her SUV, arranging the supplies carefully in the back so nothing would shift during the drive.

"Thanks again for the help," Renee said as Jake closed the hatch. "I really would have been lost in there without you."

"Anytime." He stepped back, hands in his pockets. "See you at noon."

"See you at noon."

Chapter 10

Jake sat in his truck in the parking lot of The Jingle Bell Inn, the truck door half-open, trying to figure out why his palms felt damp. This was just lunch. Renee needed help figuring out her living space. Simple. Professional. Nothing to be nervous about.

Except he was nervous.

He grabbed his notebook from the passenger seat and climbed out.

The front door was unlocked, as she'd said it would be. He stepped into the foyer, and the silence of the building wrapped around him. No crew noise today, no saws or hammers, or Billy's radio playing classic rock.

"Renee?" he called out.

"Up here!" Her voice floated down from the third floor. "Come on up!"

Jake started climbing. His boots made soft thuds with each step, and he found himself aware of every sound he made.

"Two flights of stairs is no joke; I feel for you if you have tons of groceries or things to bring up here," he said as he took the last few steps.

"Tell me about it. I'll be getting my cardio whether I want it or not."

He stepped into her living space. Renee was standing near the small dining table by the windows. She'd changed from the clothes she'd worn to the hardware store into jeans and a soft blue sweater that brought out the color in her eyes. Her hair was pulled back in a ponytail, casual and easy.

"Good timing," she said, gesturing to the pizza boxes. "I just got back a few minutes ago."

Jake set his notebook on the table and glanced around the space. Many of the boxes they'd brought up on Friday were still stacked in various places, but it appeared she'd made progress unpacking. Books lined a small shelf. A few framed photos sat on a side table. A throw blanket was draped over the arm of the sofa.

"You've made progress up here," he said.

"A little. It's hard to get motivated when the floral wallpaper is driving me batty up here." She said as she handed him a plate. "Help yourself. I got a pepperoni and a veggie."

"Both work for me." Jake took a pepperoni slice and bit into it. The cheese was still hot, and he had to be careful not to burn the roof of his mouth. "This is good."

"Rosa's, my sister swears by it." Renee took a slice of the veggie and set it on her plate. "So, where do you want to start? Kitchen or bathroom?"

"The kitchen's fine."

They carried their plates toward the tiny kitchenette tucked into one corner of the main living area. Jake had seen it during the walk-through, but he hadn't really studied it too hard. Now, standing in the small space with Renee beside him, he could understand how inadequate it was.

The counter ran maybe three feet along one wall. A two-burner stove sat at one end, looking like it belonged in a college dorm room. The sink was barely big enough to wash a dinner plate. A few upper cabinets provided minimal storage, and that was it. No room to prep food, no space that would make cooking even remotely easy.

"This is rough," Jake said.

"That's putting it kindly." Renee set her plate on the narrow counter and gestured at the stove. "That thing wobbles if you look at it wrong. I'm pretty sure it's a fire hazard. And the sink is so small I can barely rinse a pot."

Jake opened the cabinet under the sink and checked the plumbing. "This is all original. I'd suggest replacing it all."

"I want it replaced. Now, talking in general, can you think of a way to make this whole kitchen area a little bigger?"

"Well, we could borrow a little space from the living area." Jake grabbed his notebook and flipped to a clean page. He drew a quick rectangle representing the current kitchenette, then extended it. "If we push the counter out about two feet in this direction, you'd gain usable workspace. Put in a real sink, replace the stove with a proper four-burner, and add some open shelving above for dishes."

Renee leaned in to look at his sketch, close enough that he could smell whatever soap or shampoo she used. Something clean and floral.

Jake stepped back slightly, giving himself breathing room. "You'd lose a few feet of living room space, but you'd gain a kitchen that's actually functional. You could add a rolling cart for extra prep space too. Something you can move around as needed."

"That would be wonderful." She pulled her phone from her pocket and took a photo of his sketch. "What about storage?"

"Lower cabinets here, drawers here." He pointed with his pencil. "Then the open shelving above for things you use often. Keeps it from feeling too closed in."

"A larger stove would go here?" She pointed to his sketch.

"Yeah. We'd need to run a gas line if you want gas burners or upgrade the electrical if you go with electric or induction. Either works, just with different considerations."

"Which would you recommend?"

"Depends on how you enjoy cooking. Gas gives you immediate temperature control and works if the power goes out. Electric is typically cheaper to install and gives you a flat surface that's easier to clean. Induction is the most energy-efficient but requires specific cookware."

Renee bit her lower lip, thinking. "I'm used to gas."

"Gas it is." Jake made a note. "Now let's look at the bathroom."

They walked across the living area to the small bathroom tucked in the corner. Jake had to duck slightly to avoid hitting his head on the low doorframe. The space was even more cramped than he remembered.

And pink. So incredibly pink.

The tile covered every surface in various shades of rose and burgundy that clashed with each other in a way that could only have been intentional in some distant decade when this had been considered stylish. The pedestal sink was tiny, with no counter space and no storage underneath. A narrow medicine cabinet above it provided the only storage in the room.

But what caught Jake's attention were the products lined up on a small shelf near the sink. Expensive products, from what he could tell. Sleek bottles and jars with minimalist labels and French names he couldn't pronounce. The kind of stuff that probably cost more than his monthly grocery budget. A fancy electric toothbrush sat on a charging stand. Thick, fluffy towels hung on the rack, the kind that most likely felt like clouds.

This was the bathroom of someone who appreciated quality. Someone used to a certain level of comfort and luxury.

He suddenly felt uncomfortable. This was her personal space. Her private bathroom. And he was standing here noting her expensive products and the fact that she apparently used some kind of special face cream at night.

He cleared his throat and focused on the tile. "So. Pink and burgundy."

"I know." Renee leaned against the doorframe, arms crossed. "It's like someone wanted to live inside a Valentine's Day card."

"The tile's in good condition, though. No cracks, no water damage that I can see." Jake opened the medicine cabinet, checking for any signs of moisture or mold. "A complete re-tile would cost a couple thousand dollars, but you can paint tile. Special primer and paint, proper prep work. You could go from this to white or gray for a few hundred dollars instead."

"Really? I didn't know you could paint tile."

"Not everyone does." He tested the shower fixtures, turning the handles. The water pressure was weak, and the showerhead looked original to the house. "These fixtures need to be replaced, and I guarantee the plumbing needs to be upgraded. And if I were you, I'd put in a vanity and get rid of the pedestal sink."

"So not a complete gut job?"

"Nah. This is cosmetic stuff." Jake closed his notebook and tucked the pencil behind his ear. "Actually, I could start work up here on Monday if you want."

The crew could handle the first floor demo and rough-in work without him hovering over every detail. Dawson was more than capable of managing the team. And if it meant Renee could have at least one finished space to retreat to while the rest of the renovation chaos continued downstairs, that seemed worth doing.

"Monday? Seriously?"

"Sure. The crew's got a good rhythm going on the first floor. They don't need me micromanaging every step." He met her eyes. "You'd have to use one of the bathrooms on the second floor for a few days, but you'd end up with a space that doesn't drive you crazy."

"That would be incredible." Renee's face lit up, and before Jake quite registered what was happening, she'd grabbed his forearm with both hands. "Are you serious? You'd really do this?"

She was standing close enough that he could see the flecks of darker blue in her eyes. Her smile transformed her whole face from pretty to something that made his chest tighten.

"Yeah," he said, his voice coming out rougher than he'd intended. "I'm serious."

"Oh, thank you." She squeezed his arm once more, then let go and stepped back. "You have no idea how much this means. I was about to just close this bathroom door and use one of the bathrooms on the second floor to avoid looking at this tile."

Jake's arm felt weirdly cold where her hands had been.

"Come on," Renee said, already heading back to the main living area. "Let's sit down and eat before the pizza gets cold. We can go over the details."

Jake followed her to the small dining table. They settled into chairs across from each other, and he picked up his pizza, grateful to have something to do with his hands.

"So tell me about the tile paint," Renee said after finishing her first slice. "How does it work?"

Jake explained the process. The cleaning and sanding required to prep the surface. The special bonding primer which helped the paint adhere. The multiple thin coats that were needed for even coverage. The sealer which protected everything once it cured.

"It sounds tedious," Renee said.

"It is. Just requires patience and attention to detail."

"Those I can do. The marketing world required lots of patience and attention to detail."

"You've always been good at that... details and patience," Jake said, reaching for another slice. "I remember you being the only person in our graduating class who actually enjoyed Mrs. Phillip's senior history project. Everyone else was complaining about the fifty citation requirements, and you were color-coding your note cards."

Renee's eyes widened. "You remember that?"

"Hard to forget. You had this whole system worked out. Different colors for different source types." He shook his head, smiling at the memory. "I spent three days on my bibliography alone and still got points taken off for using the wrong font."

"Mrs. Phillips and her font requirements." Renee laughed. "I spent three weeks on a paper about the Scottish settlers. She took off points if your margins were wrong by even an eighth of an inch."

"I wrote mine about the Civil War battles in the Smoky Mountains. Got a B-plus because I used the wrong font." Jake shook his head at the memory. "I was so mad. Spent all that time on research and lost points over Times New Roman versus Arial."

"I think Mrs. Phillips cared more about format than content." Renee finished her slice and reached for another. "I remember seeing you in the library sometimes while we worked on those projects. You were always at one of the back tables with half the football team, and I was usually up front with the newspaper staff."

"Different worlds," Jake said.

"Different worlds," Renee agreed. "We existed in the same space but might as well have been in separate buildings."

Jake finished his slice and wiped his hands. "It's strange being back here with you after all this time. We knew each other growing up, but we weren't exactly friends."

"We ran in different circles," Renee said without any judgment in her voice. "You had football; I had cheerleading, student council, and the newspaper. We said hi in the hallways sometimes, but that was about it."

"You were always surrounded by people. I remember that about you. Everywhere you went, there was this group around you."

"That's one way of putting it." Renee's expression shifted slightly, becoming more thoughtful. "I was so focused on being involved in everything, being the person everyone knew. I thought that mattered. That being popular was the same thing as being happy. I had lots of friends but not many people who actually knew me. Does that make sense?" She traced the rim of her water glass. "It wasn't until I got to college and met people who didn't care about high school hierarchies that I started figuring out who I actually was versus who I thought I was supposed to be."

Jake understood that more than he wanted to admit. He'd been the quarterback, the guy everyone expected to go places. The golden boy who couldn't do wrong. Until he did. "High school was weird. Everyone tried so hard to fit into whatever box they thought they were supposed to occupy."

"I agree." Renee looked at him with an intensity that made his pulse kick up. "You were the football star. I was a cheerleader and overachiever who joined every club. We were both playing roles."

"And now?"

"Now I'm renovating an inn in my hometown and learning how to strip wallpaper from YouTube videos." Her smile returned, self-deprecating but warm. "Not exactly the trajectory anyone predicted for me during our senior year."

"I don't know. You were voted Most Likely to Succeed. Seems like buying and renovating a historic inn counts as success."

"I forgot about those senior superlatives." Renee laughed. "What were you? Most Athletic?"

"Most Likely to Be Famous." Jake felt his face heat. "Which did not age well."

"Hey, you're Morrison's Construction. That's pretty well known around here."

"Not quite the same as NFL fame."

"No, but maybe better. You're actually here, part of the community, building things that last. That matters more than being on TV for a few years and then being forgotten."

Jake looked down at his plate, uncomfortable with the praise but also oddly pleased by it. "What about you? Most Likely to Succeed turned inn owner. Think the cheerleading squad or the yearbook committee would be surprised?"

"Probably." She paused. "Do you ever see anyone from high school?"

"A few people. Landon Webb owns the hardware store in Gatlinburg now. Sabrina Williams teaches at the elementary school. There are others we graduated with who stayed here, but there are several who left for good after graduation. Went to Knoxville or Nashville or further."

"Do you ever wish you'd not come back here after you left college?"

"Sometimes I wonder what it would have been like," he said honestly. "But this town, this work, it fits me. And when you grow up somewhere like this, you either love it or you can't wait to escape. I guess I'm the first kind. I like it here and have no desire to live in a big city at all."

"I thought I was the second kind. I couldn't wait to leave. I thought Mistletoe Falls was too small, too limiting. And then I spent years in a city of eight million people and felt more trapped than I ever did here."

"What changed?"

"I did. I finally got honest about what I actually wanted versus what I thought I should want." She met his eyes. "Coming back feels like the first good decision I've made in a long time."

The afternoon light had shifted, coming through the windows at a lower angle that made everything in the room look golden. Renee's face was lit from the side, highlighting the curve of her cheek and the small smile playing at her lips.

Jake's throat felt tight. She was talking about good decisions, about figuring out what mattered, and he was sitting here trying not to notice how pretty she looked or how much he enjoyed just talking to her about nothing important.

He cleared his throat and reached for his water bottle. "Your aunt would be happy. Seeing you here, fixing up the inn. She loved this place."

"She did. I remember spending weekends here when I was little, helping her make beds, fold linen napkins, and bake cookies. She made everyone feel special. Even folding napkins was fun when Aunt Holly was teaching me. I want to do that. Make this place feel the way she made it feel."

"You will."

"Anyway," Renee said, changing the subject. "If you start work up here on Monday, what's the timeline look like?"

Jake pulled out his notebook and flipped to his notes from earlier. "Bathroom first. I'll paint the tile, replace the fixtures, and install a vanity with storage. That's probably three days of work once we account for drying time on the paint. Then we'll tackle the kitchenette. Extend the counter, install a new sink and stove, and add shelving. Another three or four days for that."

"So about a week?"

"Give or take. It depends if you choose stock fixtures, cabinets, and a vanity. It depends on whether we hit any surprises, too."

"Well... it sounds like I better not waste any time deciding on the fixtures and the cabinetry I want," she said as she stood and gathered the paper plates, carrying them to a small trash can near the kitchenette. When she came back, she didn't sit down. Instead, she rested her hands on the top rung of the chair. "Can I ask you one more favor?"

"Sure."

"The wallpaper supplies. Would you mind explaining again exactly how to use them? I was watching a YouTube video before you got here, but I'm still not entirely sure what order to do things in."

"YouTube can be hit or miss with home improvement advice," he said as he stood and walked to where the bags from the hardware store were sitting. "Let's go through it step by step."

He pulled out the scoring tool and held it up. "This first. You roll it over the wallpaper in overlapping passes. You don't want to press too hard, or you'll damage the wall underneath, but you need enough pressure to actually perforate the paper."

"How do I know if I'm pressing too hard?"

"You'll see gouges in the wall. If that happens, back off the pressure." He set down the scoring tool and picked up the gel stripper.

"After you've scored a section, you apply this. Brush it on generously, and let it sit for a few minutes."

Renee was watching him intently, nodding along. "Got it."

"Then you take the scraper and start working the paper off. It should come off in strips if the stripper's done its job. If it's not coming off easily, don't force it. Apply more stripper, wait a few more minutes, and try again."

"What about the sponges?"

"Those are for cleanup after. Once the paper's off, you'll have adhesive residue left on the walls. Sponge with warm water, and wipe it clean. Might take a few passes to get it all."

"That doesn't sound too terrible."

"It's not. Want me to help you get started?"

The offer came out before he'd thought it through. Apparently his mouth had decided to work independently of his brain today, committing him to things without consulting his common sense first.

"Would you? I don't want to take up your whole Saturday, but if you have time, that would be so helpful."

"I have time." He did have laundry waiting at home, but laundry could wait. And if he was being honest with himself, he'd rather spend the afternoon here helping her strip wallpaper than folding socks.

"Are you sure?" Renee asked. "I don't want you to feel obligated just because I'm your client."

"I don't feel obligated. I'm offering because I can and because it'll go faster with someone showing you the technique rather than you trying to figure it out from a YouTube video." He met her eyes. "Besides, we're friends, right? Friends help each other out."

"We are friends. Let's do this."

Renee gathered the hardware store bags and carried them to the table, setting everything out in neat rows. The scoring tool. The gel stripper. The scrapers in three different sizes. The sponges. The drop cloth. The bucket is for water.

Jake stood at the table, looking at the supplies spread out like surgical instruments before an operation.

What had he gotten himself into?

He'd come here for a working lunch. To help Renee figure out her kitchen and bathroom plans, take some notes, eat some pizza, and head home. Simple. Professional.

Instead, he'd committed to starting work on her personal living space on Monday. He'd offered to help get her started stripping wallpaper on his day off. And he was standing in her home on a Saturday afternoon, very aware that they were alone and that she kept looking at him like he was someone worth looking at.

Which was ridiculous. She was Renee Bentley, a former Manhattan marketing executive with expensive skincare products and fancy shoes. And he was Jake Morrison, a small-town contractor who'd lost his shot at the big time.

She was out of his league in ways that had nothing to do with their respective bank accounts and everything to do with the fact that she was smart and accomplished and could have anyone she wanted.

Jake picked up the scoring tool and turned it over in his hands, testing the weight.

Spending more time with Renee Bentley was going to be interesting.

Very interesting indeed.

Chapter 11

Renee watched as another strip of faded floral wallpaper peeled away to reveal the wall beneath. Her shoulders ached in a way that reminded her she'd been at this for over two hours, but the satisfaction of seeing progress kept her going.

She stepped back to look at the bare wall. "This is going to look so much better once it's painted."

"Have you decided on a color yet?" Jake asked from his position near the window.

Renee set down her scraper and crossed to the coffee table where she'd left the stack of paint chips. She picked up two and held them side by side. "I was thinking either this deep cream or this warmer tan for here in the living room."

He walked over, wiping his hands on a rag tucked into his back pocket. "What look are you going for?"

"Something neutral. I want to be able to change the decor whenever I need a refresh without having to repaint. Which one reads more inviting to you?"

Jake studied both chips, his brow furrowed slightly. "The tan. The cream's nice, but it might look too stark once you've got more furniture in here. The tan has a warmth to it."

"That's what I was thinking. Warm but not trendy. Something that'll feel welcoming in any season."

"Smart. You're thinking long term."

"Trying too. I cannot wait to get some different furniture in here. This couch has got to go."

"What's wrong with it?" Jake's tone held amusement.

Renee gestured at the sagging floral monstrosity that dominated the room. "Besides everything? It's older than I am, the springs are shot, and I'm pretty sure something is living in the cushions."

"Fair points." Jake grinned.

"Where's a good place around here I can shop for furniture?"

"Miller's Home Furnishings over on Cranberry Court has decent stuff at reasonable prices. But if you're looking for more selection, there's a large furniture store in Gatlinburg."

"Gatlinburg... I can handle that drive for a bigger selection."

"They've got everything from rustic cabin style to contemporary. Good quality, and they deliver." He said as he went back to work on the wall he'd been working on near the window. "Dawson and his wife just got their living room furniture from there."

"I didn't know Dawson was married."

"Two years now. Laura's great. They're renovating the house they bought last spring, doing most of the work themselves. They've turned it into a weekend project they work on together."

"That sounds nice." Renee returned to her section of wall and resumed scraping.

"They seem to enjoy their weekends together. I rarely hear from Dawson until it's time to work again on Monday. He and his wife... they're good for each other."

They worked in silence for several minutes, and Renee let her mind wander. The scraper moved almost automatically now, the rhythm familiar enough that she didn't have to think about what she was doing.

"So why aren't you married?"

Jake's scraper stopped mid-stroke. He turned slowly to face her. "I'm sorry, what?"

"I shouldn't have just blurted that out." Heat crept up Renee's neck. "But you seem like a great guy. You're attractive, you have your own successful business, and you seem settled in life. So why aren't you married?"

He blinked at her. Once. Twice. Then he let out a laugh that sounded somewhere between surprised and nervous. "Well. You certainly know how to throw out questions that catch a guy completely off guard."

"I'm sorry. Too personal?"

"No, it's fine. Just unexpected." Jake set his scraper on the windowsill and crossed his arms. "The honest answer is, I just haven't found the right person. I've dated. Some relationships lasted a few months, but nothing ever felt right."

"Why not?"

"I don't know. Timing, maybe. Or just waiting for someone who wants the same kind of life I do. What about you? Why isn't a Manhattan executive wearing your ring?"

Renee resumed scraping, grateful to have something to do with her hands. "I dated. Some relationships were serious, or at least I thought they were at the time. But nothing stuck. Men in Manhattan were focused on work and achieving success. Climbing the ladder, making partner, and building their brand. And honestly? So was I. There wasn't room for anything real in that equation."

"But you'll want that someday. Something real."

"Someday. I'd like to get married. Maybe have a family." She paused, considering how much to share. "I want what my parents have. A soulmate. Someone who actually gets me, who I can talk to about anything. A close, loving relationship where we're partners in everything."

Jake was quiet for a moment. When she glanced at him, his gaze was steady and thoughtful. "That's what I want too. I look at my parents, at what Dawson and Laura have, and I envy it. Not in a bitter way, just in a way that makes me hope I'll find something like that for myself."

"You will. You're the kind of man women hope exists."

His eyebrows rose. "That's quite a statement from someone who's only known me for a week... well, besides high school."

"A week of watching how you work, how you treat your crew, and how you explain things with patience even when I'm asking basic questions for the third time. Character shows itself pretty quickly if you're paying attention."

"I could say the same about you."

Renee's hands stilled. "What do you mean?"

"You're smart and driven, but you're not too proud to admit when you don't know something. You treat my crew like people, not hired help. You're trying to honor your aunt's legacy while making this place your own. That takes character."

For a moment, Renee didn't quite know how to respond. She'd received plenty of praise in her corporate life, but it had always been about her output, her results, or her performance metrics. This felt different. Personal.

"Thanks," she managed.

"Just being honest."

They returned to work, but the atmosphere in the room had shifted. The silence between them wasn't awkward exactly, but it carried a weight it hadn't before. Renee's mind spun with questions she didn't quite know how to voice. About why Jake had really stayed single all these years. About what kind of woman he pictured when he imagined a future. About whether he ever thought about someone like her in that way.

She shook her head slightly, trying to dislodge the thoughts. This was hardly the time to be wondering about his romantic ideals.

"Last section," Jake announced, pointing to the remaining strip of wallpaper in front of him. "Want to do the honors?"

"Absolutely. I can't believe how much better this room looks already."

She worked the scraper beneath the loosened edge and then pulled. The paper came away in one long, satisfying strip, and she held it up like a trophy. "Done."

Jake's smile reached his eyes. "Nice work. You're officially qualified to strip wallpaper."

"I'll add it to my resume. Former marketing executive, current wallpaper removal specialist."

He laughed, then glanced at his watch. The movement was casual, but his expression shifted into something more reserved. "I should probably get going."

Renee studied his face. His jaw had tightened just slightly, and he wouldn't quite meet her eyes the way he had been moments ago. "Did I make you uncomfortable? With the marriage question?"

"You kind of threw me off, yeah." His honesty was refreshing. "But I honestly do need to go. I wasn't just making an excuse."

"Okay." She walked him toward the stairs. "Thanks for helping me."

"Happy to help." He paused at the top of the landing. "See you Monday morning?"

"Bright and early."

She followed him down to the main floor and watched through the front window as he climbed into his truck.

What was it about Jake Morrison that made her so curious? He wasn't flashy or overtly charming. He didn't try to impress her or win her over with grand gestures. He just showed up, did excellent work, treated her with respect, and occasionally said things that made her want to know even more about him.

She thought about his answer to her question. About waiting for someone who wanted the same kind of life. About hoping to find a partnership like his parents had, like his brother had.

What kind of life did she want?

Her phone buzzed in her pocket, and she pulled it out to find a text from her mother asking about dinner plans for tomorrow. Real life asserting itself. Good. She needed to focus on practical matters. On getting the inn ready. On building a business and a new life here.

Not to wonder what Jake Morrison looked for in a partner.

Not on imagining what it would be like to be the person who caught his eye.

She typed a response to her mother and headed back upstairs to clean up the wallpaper scraps. Work. That's what she needed. Work had always been her answer, her anchor. And right now, she had an entire inn that needed her attention.

Jake Morrison would be back Monday morning to continue the renovations. They'd work together, maintain their professional relationship, and she'd keep her curiosity in check.

Even if part of her really, really wanted to know more about what made him tick.

Chapter 12

The screen door creaked the way it always had—a sound Renee knew by heart from eighteen years of running in and out of this house. She stepped onto the familiar front porch, a bottle of Pinot Noir tucked under her arm, and through the kitchen window she could see her mother at the stove, wooden spoon in hand. Steam rising from whatever was simmering on the burner.

Renee opened the door, and the smell hit her immediately—pot roast.

"Mom, I'm here," she called, closing the door behind her.

"In the kitchen, honey."

Michelle stood at the stove wearing jeans and a burgundy sweater, her salt-and-pepper hair pulled back with a clip. She turned when Renee entered, and her entire face lit up.

"There's my girl." Michelle set down the spoon and pulled Renee into a quick hug. "I'm so glad you came."

"Me too." Renee held up the wine. "Where do you want this?"

"Counter's fine. Your father will open it in a minute."

Renee set the wine on the counter and walked through the kitchen into the living room. The space hadn't changed since she was a teenager—same cream-colored sofa, oak coffee table, and stone fireplace where her father knelt, adding another log.

"Hey, Dad."

Carter looked up and grinned, brushing wood debris from his hands. "Hi, honey." He stood and pulled her into one of his solid, fatherly hugs. "How's the inn?"

"Loud. Dusty. Full of construction workers." She smiled. "It's perfect."

"That's the spirit." Carter gestured toward the dining room. "Your sister's in there setting the table if you want to help her."

Renee found Heather in the dining room, placing cloth napkins beside each plate. Her hair fell in loose waves over her shoulders, and she'd paired her jeans with a forest green sweater that made her eyes look impossibly bright.

"Need help?" Renee asked from the doorway.

Heather glanced up and smiled. "You can put out the water glasses."

Renee retrieved four glasses and brought them to the table. They worked together without needing words—Heather adjusting silverware, Renee filled glasses from the pitcher, both moving around each other with the simple rhythm of people who'd done this a hundred times.

"So," Heather said after a moment. "How's life in the construction zone?"

"Chaotic. Noisy." Renee set down the last glass. "I've learned more about plumbing in the past couple of days than I ever thought I'd need to know. Jake and his crew know what they're doing. I'm glad I hired them."

"Jake." Heather's mouth curved slightly. "He's the younger brother, right?"

"Yeah. He's handling most of the direct work with me."

"And Jake's the one teaching you about plumbing?"

"Among other things. Yesterday he showed me how to strip wallpaper. We did the entire living room." Renee moved back toward the kitchen. "I should see if Mom needs anything."

Michelle was pulling dinner rolls from the oven, and the smell of yeast and butter added another layer to the already overwhelming comfort of being home. Carter appeared with the open wine bottle and started pouring glasses.

"How much longer, hon?" he asked Michelle.

"It's ready. Why don't you all sit down? I'll bring everything out."

"I'll help you, Mom." Renee reached for potholders.

Together they carried dishes to the dining room—the pot roast on its platter, carrots and potatoes glistening with herbs, the basket of rolls, and a bowl of green beans.

They settled around the table, the same seats they'd occupied for years. Carter at the head, Michelle to his right, Heather across from her mother, and Renee beside her sister.

"All right, Renee. Tell us about this inn project. Your mother's been dying to hear details all week," her father said as he reached for the pot roast.

"Well, the first floor is progressing faster than I expected. The kitchen's completely gutted—walls opened up, all the old plumbing and electrical removed. Jake said the pipes were original to the house and completely corroded. He's really patient in explaining things to me."

"That's good of him," Carter said.

"Jake's been great about letting me help with things." Renee passed the green beans to her mother. "I know I'm paying them to do the work, but I want to learn. He could've just said no and had his crew handle everything, but he takes time to show me the right way to do stuff."

"What kind of stuff?" Michelle asked.

"How to use a scoring tool for wallpaper. How to identify load-bearing walls versus partition walls. The difference between copper and galvanized pipes." Renee smiled, remembering Jake's patient explanations. "He's got a way of teaching that doesn't make you feel stupid for not knowing things."

"Sounds like a good teacher," her father said.

"He is. And he's smart about design choices too. I was worried about losing the inn's character during renovation, but Jake gets that balance between modern functionality and historic charm."

Heather took a sip of wine, her eyes dancing with amusement over the rim of her glass. "You mention Jake a lot."

Renee paused with her fork halfway to her mouth. "I do?"

"You've probably said his name ten times since we sat down."

"I have not."

"You absolutely have." Heather's grin was pure mischief.

Heat crept up Renee's neck. "He's my contractor. We talk about renovation stuff all the time."

"Apparently," Heather said.

Michelle hid a smile behind her napkin, and Carter focused intently on cutting his pot roast, but Renee caught the knowing glance her parents exchanged. That parent telepathy that needed no words.

"Okay, fine. I talk about him because I'm working with him every day. He's just... he's interesting. He's a nice guy. One of those people you want to be around and get to know better."

"There's nothing wrong with that," Carter said.

"How's the crew treating you?" Michelle asked. "Are they respectful? Professional?"

"Completely. They're all great—Billy, Sam, Levi, all of them. And they're fast. The kitchen's going to be ready for drywall by next week as long as they don't run into any issues."

"That's impressive," her father said. "What's the timeline looking like?"

Renee launched into details about the schedule—eight to ten weeks total, with the main floor prioritized so she could potentially open by early January if everything went smoothly. She talked about the new appliances she'd selected, the subway tile backsplash, and the island Jake had designed for the space.

And there it was again. Jake's name. In every other sentence.

She was doing exactly what Heather had accused her of.

She tried to focus on eating, but her mind kept circling back to yesterday. The way Jake had patiently walked her through wallpaper removal. The conversation they'd had about marriage and relationships.

The way he'd looked at her when she'd asked why he wasn't married. That brief moment of surprise before his honest answer. *I just haven't found the right person.*

"Renee?"

She blinked and looked up. Her mother was watching her with those knowing hazel eyes that had always seen more than Renee wanted them to.

"Sorry. What?"

"I asked if you'd decided on paint colors yet."

"Oh, yeah, mostly." Renee cleared her throat. "Jake helped me narrow down the options yesterday when we were working on the wallpaper. He's got a good eye for what works in older houses."

Heather coughed delicately into her napkin, and Renee shot her a look.

They finished dinner with the conversation drifting to other topics—Heather's upcoming wedding orders, Carter's plans to expand the diner's menu for the holiday season, and Michelle's book club drama over their latest selection. Easy family talk that required no examination of why Renee kept bringing up her contractor.

When the plates were empty, and the wine glasses drained, Michelle started stacking dishes. "Girls, you're on cleanup duty. Your father and I cooked."

"That's fair," Renee said, standing. She and Heather gathered everything while Carter and Michelle moved to the living room with fresh cups of coffee.

The kitchen was warm and bright, and through the window above the sink, Renee could see full darkness had settled over the neighborhood. Heather ran hot water and squeezed dish soap into the stream, creating a mountain of bubbles. Renee grabbed a dish towel and positioned herself beside the drying rack.

"So," Heather said, scrubbing at a stubborn bit of gravy on a plate. "Jake Morrison."

"What about him?" Renee kept her eyes on the plate she was drying.

"He's your contractor. But you don't talk about him like he's just your contractor."

"How do I talk about him?"

"Like you're interested in him." Heather handed her another dish.

Renee dried the plate with more attention than necessary, running the towel over every inch of ceramic. The dish was perfectly dry, but her hands needed something to do while her brain caught up with what Heather was saying.

"I am interested in him."

Heather's hands stilled in the soapy water. She turned to look at Renee directly. "Really?"

"Yeah."

Heather grinned. "Tell me more."

"He's handsome. Confident but not cocky. Capable." Renee picked up another plate to dry. "And he's so settled. He knows who he is and what he wants. There's no pretending with him. No performance."

Heather handed her a serving bowl. "What else?"

"There's something mysterious about him. Like there's a depth I haven't seen yet. He's careful about what he shares, but when he does open up, it matters. Yesterday we talked about relationships and what we want from life, and he was so honest. So genuine."

"And?"

"And I'm attracted to him. More than I've been attracted to anyone in years. Maybe ever."

"Wow, good for you."

"I have no idea what to do about it, though." Renee set down the bowl and leaned against the counter. "I came back here to rebuild my life. To figure out who I am. I wasn't planning on falling for my contractor."

"Plans change."

"But what if I'm just lonely? What if I'm confusing gratitude for his good work with actual interest?"

"Are you?" Heather pulled the plug and let the soapy water drain. She dried her hands on a towel and turned to face Renee fully. "Does it feel like gratitude, or does it feel like something else?"

Renee thought about yesterday. The way her pulse had jumped when Jake arrived. She'd watched his hands while he demonstrated the wallpaper scraper, noticing the competence and care in every movement.

"It sure feels like something else," she admitted.

"Then it probably is. What do you know about him? Besides the work stuff."

"Not much. He has a workshop at his house where he does custom woodworking. He's close to his brother Dawson. He lost his football scholarship in college and came home." Renee picked up another glass. "He wants what his parents have—that kind of partnership where your equals and best friends and in it together."

"That's a good thing to want."

"It is. But I don't know much else. Does he date? Has he had serious relationships? What's he like outside of work?" Renee looked at her sister. "What do people say about him around town?"

Heather considered this while drying a plate. "From what I've seen, he's well-respected. People trust Morrison's Construction because they do quality work and treat customers fairly. Jake specifically has a reputation for being patient and detail-oriented. Quiet but friendly."

"What about relationships?"

"I don't know much about his personal life." Heather stacked the dried plate with the others. "But I've never seen him with anyone. Not at community events, not around town. Women have tried—I've watched it happen at the Christmas market and summer festivals. He's always polite but never interested."

"So he's single."

"Very single, from what I can tell." Heather handed Renee another glass. "Which might mean he's picky. Or it might mean he hasn't found the right person yet."

"Or it might mean he's not interested in dating at all."

"Does he seem uninterested?"

"No," Renee said slowly. "He doesn't seem uninterested."

"If he's spending extra time explaining things to you, being patient with your questions, helping you strip wallpaper on a Saturday when he could be doing anything else—that might mean something."

"Or it might mean he's helpful, professional... or bored."

"Contractors don't usually spend their Saturdays teaching clients how to remove wallpaper. I'm just saying, pay attention. See if he's making excuses to spend time with you. See if the conversations drift away from renovation topics. See if he looks at you differently than he looks at other people."

"He does," Renee said. "All of those things. Or at least I think he does."

"Then ask him to coffee. Or lunch somewhere that's not your construction zone. Give him an opening and see what happens."

"What if I'm reading this wrong? What if I make it weird and we still have eight more weeks of renovation?"

"Then you'll be professional adults who can work together despite a little awkwardness." Heather closed the silverware drawer and turned to face her sister. "But what if you're reading it right? What if he's interested too, and he's just waiting for a sign that you're open to it?"

The possibility sent something warm and nervous through Renee's chest. "I don't know if I'm ready for this."

"Nobody's ever ready. You just decide if it's worth the risk." Heather reached out and squeezed Renee's hand. "And from where I'm standing, a guy who's patient, respectful, talented, and makes you bring up his name multiple times at Sunday dinner? That seems worth exploring."

"Maybe."

"Maybe nothing, you know I'm right."

Chapter 13

"Renee? You up there?" Jake's voice carried up the stairwell, deep and familiar, and Renee smiled.

"Come on up," she called as she peeled away another strip of ugly wallpaper from her bedroom wall.

His footsteps grew louder, and then he appeared in the doorway of her bedroom, tool belt slung low on his hips, a canvas bag in one hand. He took in the scene—walls half-stripped, paper scraps scattered across the drop cloth, her ponytail coming loose from its elastic.

"You've been busy," he said.

"Couldn't sleep, so I figured I'd get a head start." She gestured at the walls. "This room is going to look so much better once all this floral nightmare is gone."

"It will. I'm gonna go work on your bathroom; holler if you need me."

"Can I help?"

He glanced at her, and his mouth curved slightly. "You sure you want to help? I can handle it if you want to keep working in here."

"I'm sure." She crossed her arms, meeting his gaze. "I told you I wanted to learn this stuff. The wallpaper can wait."

"All right. Let's get to work."

Renee followed him into the small bathroom, and she realized how close they'd be working.

Jake surveyed the space with the practiced eye of someone who'd seen hundreds of bathrooms in various states of disrepair. He opened the medicine cabinet, checked the mounting brackets, and then turned his attention to the shower fixtures.

"Here's the plan," he said. "I'm going to start removing the old showerhead and tub faucet. Those are straightforward but require some elbow grease. While I'm doing that, you can take down the medicine cabinet." He pointed to the mirrored cabinet mounted above the sink. "It's held in with screws inside the cabinet itself. You'll need to remove all of them, and then we'll lift it out together."

"Sounds simple enough."

"It is. Just be patient with it. Old screws can be stubborn." He pulled a screwdriver from his tool belt and handed it to her. "Phillips head. You'll need to open the cabinet and work from the inside."

Renee took the screwdriver and opened the medicine cabinet and peered inside. Sure enough, four screws were visible along the interior frame, one in each corner. The first screw was in the top left corner, partially obscured by the shadow of the cabinet's interior. She fitted the screwdriver into the slot and turned. The screw resisted at first, then began to move with a faint squeak of metal against metal.

Behind her, Jake grunted softly as he worked on the showerhead. She heard the screech of old threads giving way, then the clatter of something hitting the tub floor.

"How's it going over there?" she asked, not taking her eyes off the screw she was removing.

"Showerheads off. Faucet's next. How about you?"

"First screw is out." She moved to the top right corner and started on the second. This one came more easily. "Two down, two to go."

The third screw came out smoothly. She moved to the bottom-right corner for the last one.

"Almost done."

"This faucet's fighting me."

Renee positioned the screwdriver against the final screw and turned. It moved easily at first, then caught. She adjusted her angle and tried again. The screw turned another half rotation, then stopped completely.

"Come on," she muttered.

"Stuck?"

"A little. But I've got it."

She braced her other hand against the cabinet frame and applied more pressure. The screw groaned and then suddenly gave way, turning freely. She backed it out the rest of the way and pulled it from the hole.

"Done!" She held up the last screw triumphantly. "All four are out."

Jake set down his wrench and climbed out of the tub. "Good. Now we lift it out together. These old cabinets can be tricky; sometimes there's caulk behind them as well."

He moved to stand beside her, so close she could smell the faint scent of soap. They both reached for the cabinet, his hands at the top corners, hers near the bottom.

"On three," Jake said. "One, two, three."

They pulled, and the cabinet came out of the wall with surprising ease.

She adjusted her hands, one at the top of the cabinet and one at the bottom. "I got this."

Jake stepped back, and Renee turned to carry the cabinet out of the bathroom.

The cabinet was heavier than she'd expected and awkward to balance. She made it through the bathroom doorway and into the main living area, heading toward the pile of garbage bags filled with wallpaper debris near the stairs.

She shifted her grip as she lowered the cabinet to the floor, and the edge of the metal frame bit into her thumb. Pain flared, sharp and immediate. She dropped the cabinet, jerked her hand back, and looked down to see blood welling from a cut across the pad of her thumb. Not deep, but enough to hurt, enough to bleed.

She pressed her other hand over the cut, applying pressure, and she heard him come up behind her. "What happened?"

"The edge of the cabinet." She turned to face him. "I'm fine. It's not that bad."

Jake crossed the space between them in two strides. He took her wrist gently, moving her other hand aside so he could see the injury. His brow furrowed as he examined the cut.

"It's not terrible, but it's bleeding pretty good. Come on." He guided her toward the small dining table near the windows. "Sit."

"Jake, it's really not—"

"Sit."

He disappeared back into the bathroom and returned moments later with his canvas bag and took out a first aid kit. He set it on the table and pulled out supplies—antiseptic wipes, gauze, medical tape, and a small tube of antibiotic ointment.

Jake pulled a chair close and sat facing her, then took her hand in his.

His hands were warm and rough with calluses, but his touch was surprisingly gentle as he cleaned the blood away with a gauze pad. The cut ran across her thumb pad at an angle, maybe an inch long. Not deep enough to need stitches, but definitely enough to be annoying for the next few days.

"You're officially a real renovator now," Jake said without looking up from her hand. "First injury is a rite of passage."

"I was hoping to avoid this particular rite of passage."

"Nobody does." He tore open an antiseptic wipe. "This is gonna sting."

It did sting—a sharp, burning sensation that made her wince. But Jake's hold on her hand remained steady, and he worked quickly, cleaning the wound.

"Sorry," he said.

"It's fine."

He dabbed antibiotic ointment along the cut, then reached for a bandage. His head was bent over her hand, his dark hair falling forward slightly. This close, she could see the details she'd missed before. The fine lines at the corners of his eyes came from years of smiling. The shadow of stubble along his jaw. The way his eyelashes were darker than his hair.

He wrapped the bandage around her thumb, securing it with medical tape, then checked his work. Satisfied, he released her hand.

"How does it feel?" he asked.

"Better, thanks." She flexed her thumb. "You're pretty good at this."

"Years of practice," he said as he picked up the garbage after treating her wound. "Construction sites see their share of minor injuries. You should probably give that hand a rest for a bit."

"I can still help—"

"Renee." He met her eyes. "Take a break. Doctor's orders."

"You're not a doctor."

"Contractor's orders, then." He stood and walked to the garbage can near her small stove. He gestured toward her coffeemaker on the counter. "Besides, I could use some coffee. I'm curious which seventy-dollar bag you chose to make this morning."

The teasing in his voice made her smile despite the dull ache in her thumb. "It's actually a sixty-dollar bag, thank you very much. Guatemalan Antigua. And it's delicious."

"Sixty dollars." Jake shook his head, but he was grinning. "You could buy a lot of groceries for sixty dollars."

"Or I could buy coffee that actually tastes good instead of whatever generic brand you probably drink straight from a can."

"Hey, my coffee is perfectly adequate."

"Adequate." She stood and moved to the kitchenette. "That's the saddest word I've ever heard used to describe coffee. Coffee should never be just adequate. It should be an experience."

"An experience." He leaned against the counter while she pulled two mugs from the cabinet. "Is that what they teach you in Manhattan? How to make coffee pretentious?"

"It's not pretentious to have standards." She poured coffee into both mugs, the rich aroma filling the small space. "Here. Try it before you judge."

Jake accepted the mug she offered and took a sip. His eyebrows rose slightly.

"Okay," he admitted. "That's actually pretty good."

"Told you. Guatemalan Antigua has chocolate and spice notes that regular coffee just doesn't have. And it's smooth—no bitterness."

"It is smooth," Jake agreed. "I still think sixty dollars is ridiculous. But it's good coffee."

"Progress." She carried her mug to the dining table and sat, and after a moment Jake joined her.

"How many of those fancy coffee bags did you ship here?"

"Maybe forty bags total?"

"Forty bags." He stared at her. "How long is that going to last you?"

"Probably nine months. Maybe ten if I'm disciplined. I know it sounds excessive. But coffee is just my thing. It's something I splurge on, and I feel no guilt."

Jake was quiet for a moment, his gaze thoughtful. "I get it."

"So... what's your thing?"

"Fishing. Early morning, out on the water before anyone else is awake. Just me, the quiet, and whatever I catch." He smiled. "And the coffee in my thermos is definitely not sixty-dollar Guatemalan."

They drank in comfortable silence for a few minutes. Renee could hear the sounds of the construction crew downstairs, country music playing and chatter between the men, though she couldn't make out what they were saying.

"What was I like in high school? From your perspective." Renee set her mug down, tracing the rim with one finger.

Jake's eyebrows rose. "You're really good at tossing out random questions."

"I know. Come on, answer the question."

"We barely knew each other back then."

"Exactly. We existed in entirely different worlds. But we saw each other in the hallways, in classes, and at games and events. You must have had some impression." She leaned forward slightly. "I'm curious about what it was."

Jake set his mug down and leaned back in his chair, arms crossed. His expression shifted to something more guarded, and she wondered if she'd pushed too far.

"You were the girl who had it all together. Cheerleader, honor roll, student council, newspaper staff. Always surrounded by people, always smiling, always seemed to know exactly where you were going and how you were going to get there." He paused. "Honestly? You were intimidating."

Renee blinked. "I was intimidating?"

"Completely. You were smart and pretty, and confident, and you seemed untouchable. Like you existed on a different level from the rest of us." He picked up his mug again, but didn't drink, just held it. "I remember seeing you in the library during that senior history project we talked about the other day. You had that whole system worked out with color-coded note cards, and I was just trying to cobble together enough research to pass. You were in the front, I was in the back, and it felt like we were in different buildings even though we were in the same room."

She tried to reconcile his description of how she'd felt at eighteen—desperate to be liked, terrified of failing, performing constantly to maintain the image everyone expected. "I wasn't confident. I was performing."

"Maybe. But from the outside, you looked like you had everything figured out."

"I didn't. I was so focused on being the person I thought I was supposed to be. Popular, accomplished, always in control. But I was lonely. I had lots of friends, but nobody really knew me. Not the real me."

Jake studied her across the table, and something in his expression had softened. "What about me? What did you think when you saw me in those hallways?"

Renee took a breath, considering how honest to be. But they'd come this far. "You were the golden boy. Star quarterback, full ride to UT, life of the party. Everyone loved you. You always seemed to be laughing, always surrounded by the football team. You always had a girlfriend. You had this confidence that I envied—like nothing could touch you, like you knew you were going somewhere and nothing was going to stop you."

"You thought I was confident." Jake's laugh was quiet and held no humor. "That's funny."

"You weren't?"

"I was arrogant. There's a difference." He set his mug down and ran a hand through his hair. "I thought I was invincible. I thought the rules didn't apply to me because I was good at throwing a football. I spent more time at parties than studying and more time proving I was fearless than actually being responsible. And I got away with it for a while because the coaches wanted me on the field and the school wanted another championship."

"What changed?"

His jaw tightened almost imperceptibly. "College. I got to UT, and suddenly I wasn't special anymore. Everyone I hung around with had been a star in high school. Everyone was talented and fast and used to being the best. And I wasn't prepared—not academically, and definitely not emotionally. I partied too much, skipped too many classes, and thought I could coast the way I had in high school. Failed out after one semester."

Renee watched him carefully. There was something in his voice, in the way he'd gone very still, that suggested there was more to his story.

"Coming home after that was humbling," he continued. "I'd left as this golden boy headed for greatness, and I came back as a failure who'd blown his one shot. I had to face everyone who'd believed in me and admit I'd screwed it all up."

"But you didn't stay a failure."

"No. It took a while. I got my head straight and started taking things seriously. Dawson was already working in construction, and he brought me on. Turned out I was good at it. Better than I'd ever been at football."

"Because you cared about it more."

"Maybe. Or because it felt real in a way football never did. Building something with my hands, seeing the result of the work—that mattered. Touchdowns were just points on a board that nobody would remember a week later."

Renee reached across the table and covered his with hers. "I think you became exactly who you were supposed to be. And I like what I see."

Jake's eyes met hers, and he turned his hand beneath hers, his palm warm and rough, and for a moment neither of them moved.

Then he cleared his throat and pulled back gently, reaching for his coffee. "What about you? Tell me more about when you figured out the Manhattan dream wasn't what you wanted?"

"I knew for a while, but I was too stubborn to admit it. I'd worked so hard to get there, to build that career. Admitting I wasn't happy felt like admitting failure."

"But you left anyway."

"I got pushed. The buyout forced my hand, and I had to decide whether to find another corporate job or do something different. And once I gave myself permission to consider differently, everything fell into place pretty quickly."

"And you don't miss any of it?"

"I miss the energy a little. It's hard to go from such a fast-paced life, always being on the go. But I'm learning to live at a slower pace again, and I like it a lot more. But I don't miss the emptiness. The constant pressure. The feeling that regardless of what I accomplished, it was never quite enough."

"That's how I felt about football. Except I was chasing something that didn't even belong to me—it was everyone else's dream that I'd adopted because it was easier than figuring out what I actually wanted."

Renee smiled. "Look at us. Both of us spent our twenties living up to other people's expectations."

"And now?"

"Now I'm stripping wallpaper in a Victorian inn and learning how to remove bathroom fixtures. And that feels more real than anything I did in Manhattan."

"That's because it is real." Jake finished his coffee and stood, carrying the mug to the kitchenette. "You're building something that's yours. Not performing for someone else or chasing someone else's definition of success. That matters."

She followed him with her own empty mug, rinsing it in the tiny sink. "So what's next for the bathroom?"

"Next, I'll finish removing the tub faucet, then I'll start sanding the tile for the primer. But—" He nodded toward her bandaged thumb. "You should probably give that hand a rest. Why don't you head down to the hardware store and order your vanity and fixtures?"

"Are you trying to get rid of me?"

"Yeah, I'm trying to keep you from doing more damage." His tone was teasing, but his eyes were serious. "You need a vanity that'll fit the space, and my dad can help you pick the right size. Plus, you'll need to special order your fixtures if you don't like what he has in stock."

He pulled a folded piece of paper from his pocket and handed it to her. She unfolded it to find a sketch of the bathroom with dimensions noted in the margins, along with a list of what she needed: vanity, sink faucet, tub fixtures, towel bars, and toilet paper holder.

"You already wrote this up."

"Figured you'd need it eventually. Might as well be today." He tapped the paper. "Give that to Dad. He'll walk you through everything and make sure you get pieces that'll work together."

Renee studied the list, then folded it carefully and tucked it into her pocket. "You're well-organized for someone who works with power tools and demolition."

"Organization is how you keep projects on schedule and under budget. Chaos might look impressive on TV, but it's terrible for business."

"Spoken like a true professional."

"I try. Go. Order your stuff. I'll keep working here."

"Are you sure you don't need help?"

"I'm sure. Give your hand a rest. Doctor's orders."

"Still not a doctor."

"Contractor's orders with medical training from years of job site injuries." He was already heading back to the bathroom, and she heard the clatter of tools being picked up.

She grabbed her purse and keys, then walked to the bathroom. Jake was back in the tub, wrench in hand, working on the stubborn faucet. He looked completely at ease and in his element.

"Jake?"

"Yeah?"

"Thanks. For the first aid. And the coffee break. And—" She gestured vaguely. "Everything."

He looked at her and grinned. "Anytime."

She left before she could say anything else, before she could examine too closely why her heart was beating faster than it should.

The stairs creaked under her feet as she descended to the main floor. The renovation work downstairs had transformed the first floor into what looked like a disaster zone—plastic sheeting, tools, and building materials stacked and labeled. But she barely noticed. Her mind was still upstairs, replaying the conversation.

You were kind of intimidating.

She'd thought the same about him. They'd existed in parallel worlds, each assuming the other had everything figured out, neither realizing they were both just trying to survive high school without revealing how uncertain they felt.

And now, years later, they were here. Working together. And every day she found herself more curious about the man he'd become—not the golden boy she'd watched from a distance, but the steady, patient, thoughtful person who bandaged her thumb with surprising tenderness.

Get a grip, girl, she thought. *You're falling hard and fast.*

Chapter 14

Renee worked the scraper carefully beneath the edge of the wallpaper. The floral pattern—cabbage roses the size of dinner plates against a cream background—had been mocking her all morning. She'd conquered the living room and her bedroom. This second bedroom, her future office, was the last holdout.

Eventually, the paper pulled free in a long, satisfying strip. She dropped it onto the growing pile at her feet and started on the next section.

Footsteps made her glance toward the door as Jake appeared, wiping his hands on a rag tucked into his tool belt.

"First coat's done on the bathroom tile."

"Really?"

He tucked the rag back into his belt. "Needs several hours to dry before I can do the second coat. I'm going to start gutting the kitchenette next."

"I have to see it."

"It's just paint," he said.

She heard his soft laugh behind her as she rushed to the bathroom.

The tile gleamed soft white, transforming the space entirely. The first coat wasn't perfect—she could see slight variations in coverage where the paint hadn't quite obscured the original color—but it was beautiful. Clean. Fresh. A bathroom she could actually imagine using every day without wanting to close her eyes.

"Jake." She turned, finding him standing just behind her in the narrow hallway. "No more pink and burgundy, I'm so excited!"

"Still needs another coat, maybe two more."

She threw her arms around him and felt him stiffen, his hands coming up automatically as he took a half-step back to keep his balance. For one brief moment his arms were around her, steadying them both.

Then he was pulling back, creating a space between them, his hands dropping to his sides.

"Sorry." She laughed, slightly breathless. "I'm just really excited."

"It's fine." His voice came out rougher than usual. He cleared his throat. "Glad you're happy with it."

"I'm going to make a pot of coffee before you shut off the water in the kitchen." She was already moving past him toward the kitchenette.

He walked toward the stairs. "I need to grab some tools from downstairs."

Renee grabbed a bag of coffee beans from the box and measured out enough for a full pot. The grinder whirred, filling the small space with the rich scent of fresh coffee. She added the grounds to the filter, then picked up the carafe and moved to the sink.

The faucet handle turned smoothly under her palm.

Then came the sound—a sharp metallic groan from beneath the sink, followed immediately by a spray of water that hit the cabinet door from inside.

"No, no, no." She dropped to her knees, yanking open the cabinet door.

Water sprayed from the pipe connection, hitting her square in the chest. She reached into the cabinet, feeling for the valve. Her fingers found it, but it wouldn't budge.

She tried again, putting her weight into it, water soaking through her flannel shirt and into her jeans.

"JAKE!"

She heard him take the stairs. Fast. His work boots pounded up the first flight, then the second. The crew's voices followed—Billy asking what was wrong, Sam saying something she couldn't make out over the sound of rushing water.

Jake burst into the room. His eyes went from her to the cabinet to the water spreading across the floor in about two seconds. He moved toward her quickly. When his boot hit the water, he slid a little and caught himself with one hand on the counter.

"The valve won't turn!"

He reached past her into the cabinet, his shoulder pressing against hers as he wrapped both hands around the valve. His jaw tightened. The valve didn't move.

"Dawson!" He twisted to look over his shoulder at the doorway where his brother and half the crew had appeared. "Wrench!"

Dawson hustled toward them, pulled the wrench free from his tool belt, and handed it to Jake.

The valve groaned. Shifted. Turned.

The water stopped.

Jake sat back on his heels, the wrench still in his hand. His flannel shirt was soaked through on one side, his jeans dark with water from the knee down.

Renee looked down at herself. Her shirt clung to her like a second skin. Water dripped from her hands. Her jeans were soaked from waist to ankle. A puddle of water all around her.

She looked at Jake.

He looked at her.

The laugh started somewhere in her chest and came out before she could stop it. Not a polite chuckle but a real, gasping laugh that made her shoulders shake.

Jake's mouth twitched.

"Well," Billy said with a chuckle, perfectly dry and deeply amused, "I'll head to the basement and shut off the main water line."

His comment made her laugh harder. She pressed her hand over her mouth, trying to compose herself, but every time she looked at Jake—soaked and still holding the wrench like it was a weapon—the laughter bubbled up again.

"It's not funny." But his mouth was pulling into a smile despite his words.

"It is funny." She wiped her eyes, though she couldn't tell if the moisture was tears from laughing or water from the pipe. "I just wanted coffee."

He set the wrench down and pushed himself to his feet, then offered her his hand. "I'd say that pipe was definitely corroded on the inside. You turned on the water; the pressure was enough to blow it."

She took his hand, and he pulled her up. They stood in the middle of the puddle, both dripping, close enough that she could see water droplets caught in his hair.

"I must look ridiculous right now."

His eyes moved over her face—her wet hair, the water dripping from her chin, and her completely soaked flannel shirt.

"Most people don't make flannel look that good."

Her laugh died, and she stared at him.

He seemed to realize what he'd said at the same moment she did. His jaw tightened, and he took a step back, nearly slipping again on the wet floor before he caught himself.

"I should—" He gestured vaguely toward the stairs. "I need to change. Got spare clothes in the truck."

"Right, yeah." Her voice came out steadier than she felt. "I should change too."

"Water's going to be off for a few days while we gut this kitchen anyway." He was moving toward the stairs now, not looking at her. "You'll need to use the second floor for water."

"I know."

He paused in the doorway. "Where's your mop?"

"Second floor. First bedroom on the right. Can you grab all the extra towels from that bathroom too?"

He nodded and disappeared.

Renee looked down at her flannel shirt.

Most people don't make flannel look that good.

She stood there, sopping wet, and smiled.

Chapter 15

Jake's arms burned as he climbed the second flight of stairs, the bathroom vanity's weight distributed between him and Dawson. The dark gray cabinet wasn't particularly heavy—maybe sixty pounds—but navigating the stairs required careful maneuvering.

Dawson adjusted his grip. "This thing better fit in that bathroom."

"It'll fit..." Jake said as they reached the third-floor landing.

They carried the vanity into Renee's living space and set it down against the wall near the kitchenette. Jake straightened, rolling his shoulders to work out the knots. The apartment felt different without Renee in it—quieter, emptier. He'd spent yesterday applying another coat of paint in her bathroom, and then she helped him gut the kitchenette. This morning he'd applied a coat of sealer to the bathroom tile.

Dawson wiped his hands on his jeans and looked around. "Where is she?"

"Went to buy groceries and paint for the living room."

Jake walked to where he'd left the bag of new electrical outlets and light switches earlier that morning. "I'm upgrading all the outlets and switches up here today. Installing the light fixtures she bought too, plus a ceiling fan combo for the living room."

"Need help?"

Jake glanced at his brother, surprised. Dawson had his own work to oversee downstairs. "You don't have to. I can handle it."

"I know. I'm offering anyway."

"Yeah, all right. Thanks."

They started with the outlets in the living room. Jake cut the power on the third floor at the breaker box, then returned with his voltage tester to confirm everything was dead. The old outlets were yellowed with age. He pulled the first one from the wall and disconnected the wires.

"Hand me a new outlet."

Dawson pulled one from the bag and passed it over. They worked in companionable silence for a few minutes—Jake rewiring, Dawson preparing the next outlet, both of them falling into the rhythm they'd developed over years of working together.

Then Dawson broke the silence. "So. Wednesday."

Jake's hands stilled on the wire he was wrapping around the terminal screw. "What about it?"

"Most people don't make flannel look that good." Dawson's voice was pure amusement.

"It slipped. Drop it."

"Nope. The whole crew's been talking about it." Dawson leaned against the wall, arms crossed. "You should've seen Billy's impression. He's got your tone down perfectly."

"Billy needs to find a hobby."

"Billy's hobby is giving you grief. Always has been." Dawson watched him work for a moment. "Talk to me."

Jake fitted the outlet back into the box and reached for the screwdriver to secure the cover plate. "Nothing to talk about. She's a client."

"She's more than that, and you know it."

"Dawson—"

"Just ask her out already."

The screwdriver slipped, nearly gouging the wall. Jake caught himself and set the tool down. He turned to face his brother. "I'm way out of her league."

Dawson's expression shifted from amusement to something more serious. "What are you talking about?"

"You know exactly what I'm talking about." Jake picked up the screwdriver again, needing something to do with his hands. "She spent ten years in Manhattan. She ran marketing campaigns for major companies. She probably made more in one year than I do in two. And I'm—" He gestured vaguely at himself. "I'm a guy who barely made it through high school and blew his one shot at college. I spend my days hanging drywall and installing toilets."

"You run a successful business."

"We run a successful business. And it's good work, honest work, but it's not the same as what she did. What she could still be doing if she wanted. She could go back to New York tomorrow. Get a job that pays six figures. Live in some nice apartment with a doorman and a view of Central Park."

"She's here now."

"Until she decides small-town life isn't what she thought it would be. Until she realizes running an inn is harder than it sounds. Until—" He stopped, the words catching in his throat.

"Until what?" Dawson pushed off the wall and crossed to where Jake knelt by the outlet. He crouched down, forcing Jake to meet his eyes. "Listen to me. You're talking yourself in circles. You're one of the best men I know. You're honest and dependable and kind. You rebuilt your entire life after it fell apart, and you did it without complaint or excuses. That counts for something."

"Not enough."

"Says who? You? Jake, you've been carrying this thing around since you failed out of UT, like you've got to prove to everyone that you're not that stupid kid anymore. But nobody thinks that except you."

"Renee's different. She's—"

"She's a woman who bought a run-down inn. She's working her tail off to make it into something special. She's a woman who laughs when a pipe bursts and soaks her to the skin." Dawson smiled slightly. "She's not some untouchable Manhattan princess. She's a person trying to figure out her life, the same as you did when you came back here."

Jake disconnected the old outlet and stared at the wires in his hand. Black, white, and copper ground. Simple. Straightforward. Not like people.

"She's just being nice? I'm reading too much into this."

"Nope, you're not."

"Let's just drop it, Dawson."

Dawson stood and offered Jake his hand. Jake took it and let his brother pull him to his feet. "There's something between you two, Jake. Don't doubt that. I can see it, and I'm sure you do as well."

"I don't want to make things awkward. We've still got at least a month and a half of work left on this place."

"Jake, just ask her out."

He turned to work on another outlet, threading wires through the new box. His hands moved automatically, muscle memory from thousands of installations. But his mind was somewhere else—replaying Wednesday, the feel of Renee's arms around him when she hugged him, and the surprise and warmth of it. The way she'd laughed after the water pipe burst, completely unselfconscious. The moment she'd looked down at herself, soaking wet.

Dawson clapped him on the shoulder. "Look, I'm not saying you have to propose tomorrow. Just do yourself a favor and stop assuming you're not good enough. Let her make that call. Give her some credit."

They moved through the apartment methodically, replacing outlets and switches in every room. The work was mindless enough that Jake's thoughts could wander. He thought about the way Renee asked questions—genuinely interested, wanting to understand rather than just observe. The way she'd grabbed his forearm with both hands, excited about the bathroom progress.

He thought about her laugh. The one that made her entire face light up.

By the time they finished the outlets, it was nearly eleven.

"I can handle the rest," Jake said. "You should get back downstairs."

"You going to think about what I said?"

"Yeah."

"Good." Dawson headed for the door, then paused. "For what it's worth, I think she'd be lucky to have you. And I think you'd be lucky to have her. Sometimes, lucky finds lucky, you know?"

Chapter 16

Renee set down both gallons of paint and her bag of groceries when she entered her living room. Jake stood on a ladder in the middle of the room, his arms raised as he worked on her ceiling fan.

"Did you get everything you needed?" He asked without turning around.

"I did," she said as she crossed the room, stopping a few feet from the ladder.

He climbed down, screwdriver still in hand, and stepped back to look at his work. The ceiling fan hung perfectly centered, its brushed nickel finish catching the afternoon light. The wooden blades were a warm honey color that complemented the room's original wood trim.

"Well?" He glanced at her. "What do you think?"

Renee tilted her head back, studying the fan. She'd spent almost an hour in Morrison's Hardware Store last week choosing it, weighing options, and reading reviews on her phone while Tom patiently answered her questions.

"I love it." She walked closer, standing directly beneath it. "Better than I imagined, actually."

Jake pulled the chain, and the fan hummed to life, blades turning smoothly. "Quiet motor. Good choice. Should last you twenty years if you treat it right."

"Which means not using it as a jungle gym?"

His mouth quirked. "Generally recommended, yes."

She watched the blades rotate for a moment, then noticed the new light switch cover by the door. Cream-colored and modern, nothing like the yellowed plastic that had been there yesterday. "You replaced all the switches too."

"And the outlets." He tucked the screwdriver into his tool belt. "Everything's up to code now."

"Wow, you really did a lot while I was gone."

"I put the first coat of sealer on the bathroom tiles also."

"Are you hungry? I bought bagels and cream cheese."

"I'll eat later. I'm gonna go ahead and start working on running your new water lines."

"After you eat." She pulled out the bagels—everything, plain, and cinnamon raisin—and set them on the small dining table. "I'm not going to be responsible for you passing out from low blood sugar while you're working in my home."

Jake picked up the ladder and carried it toward the hallway. "Yes, ma'am."

"Don't 'yes ma'am' me. I'm thirty-two, not seventy."

He pulled out one of the dining chairs and sat, watching as Renee opened the cream cheese and grabbed a plastic knife from a Ziploc bag on the table.

"I picked out the cabinets for the kitchenette—unfinished natural oak. And the fixture for the sink. Your dad said everything's in stock. You can pick it up whenever you're ready."

Jake reached for an everything bagel and tore it in half. "I'll grab it all on Monday morning. Should be able to start installing Tuesday, assuming the plumbing work goes smoothly this afternoon."

"Sounds good. Everything's moving right along."

He spread cream cheese on his bagel. "I should be able to install your vanity and fixtures in the bathroom next week too."

Renee picked up a cinnamon-raisin bagel and pulled it apart. "Perfect. Using the second-floor bathroom is getting old. Too many stairs for a midnight trip."

"Fair point. Speaking of the kitchenette—did you find shelving?"

She paused with the cream cheese knife halfway to her bagel. "That's actually a problem."

"How so?"

"I looked at what your dad stocks. Went through a couple of the catalogs he had too." She set the knife down and gestured vaguely with one hand. "Everything was so... boring. Straight lines, hard corners, standard builder-grade stuff. Nothing wrong with it, exactly. Just not what I want."

"What do you want?"

"I don't know. Something different. Unique." She picked up the knife again and focused on spreading cream cheese. "The cabinets are natural oak? Unfinished, and I plan to just seal them to show the wood grain. I want the shelving to complement that but stand out. Something with character. Pizazz."

"Pizazz." Jake's tone was carefully neutral, but she saw the corner of his mouth twitch.

"Don't make fun of me."

"I'm not. Pizazz is a perfectly legitimate design term."

"Liar."

"Maybe a little." He finished his bagel and reached for the other half. "But I understand what you mean. You want something different. Maybe something custom. Something that feels intentional instead of picked out of a catalog."

"Exactly. I looked at floating shelves, bracket shelves, and corner shelves. All fine. All practical. All completely forgettable. And this is my kitchen. My home. I don't want forgettable."

Jake was quiet for a moment, his gaze distant in that way she'd noticed when he was thinking through a problem. His fingers drummed once against the table, then stilled.

"I might have an idea," he said.

"What kind of idea?"

He set down the bagel and leaned back in his chair, arms crossed. "Have you ever seen live-edge wood? Where they leave the natural edge of the tree instead of cutting it into a perfect rectangle?"

"I'm not sure… tell me more."

"It's got character. Organic lines, unique grain patterns. No two pieces are exactly the same. You could do floating shelves with a live edge—mount them with hidden brackets. Pair that with your natural oak cabinets, and you'd have something distinctive. Not catalog standard."

Renee tried to picture it. "Where would I find something like that?"

"I've made some. I do custom woodworking when I've got time. Mostly small projects. Gifts for family, furniture pieces, and shelving."

"Do you have pictures?"

"Better than pictures." His jaw tightened slightly, then relaxed. "Are you willing to take a ride with me?"

"Where?"

His mouth curved into a grin. "Don't you trust me?"

"I do, but I'm just curious where you want to take me."

"To my house. I want to show you some of the shelving I made and installed."

Renee set down what was left of her bagel. "Let's go," she said.

His eyebrows rose slightly. "Yeah?"

"Yeah. I'd like to see what you've made." She said as she stood up. "Give me two minutes to put the groceries away and grab my coat."

Chapter 17

Jake turned the F-150 onto Cedar Ridge Road, watching white flakes drift past the windshield. The snow had started a few minutes ago.

"It's really coming down," Renee said.

"First real snow of the season. It'll stick tonight. Ground's cold enough."

His house came into view at the end of the street—a modest single-story with cedar siding and a wide front porch.

He pulled into the driveway and cut the engine.

"This is it," he said.

"It's beautiful," she said as she unbuckled her seatbelt and opened the passenger-side door.

Jake came around the truck and led her up the porch steps. He unlocked the door and pushed it open, stepping aside so she could enter first.

The living room opened directly before them. Warm light from the windows fell across wide-plank oak floors that Jake had sanded and sealed himself. The stone fireplace dominated one wall, its river rock stretching floor to ceiling. Two leather chairs and a matching sofa faced it, positioned around a coffee table he'd built from reclaimed barn wood.

Renee stopped just inside the threshold as he closed the door, watching her take in the space. She walked forward slowly; her gaze moving from the fireplace to the hardwood floor to the shelving along the wall.

The live-edge shelves.

They ran the length of the wall beside the fireplace, mounted at staggered heights with hidden brackets so they seemed to float. The wood was walnut, its natural edge preserved—bark removed but the organic curve of the tree left intact. The grain swirled in patterns unique to each piece, dark and rich where he'd rubbed oil into the surface.

Renee crossed to the shelves and stopped a foot away, studying them as if they were art.

"You made these?" Her voice came out quiet.

"Yeah."

She reached out, her fingers hovering above the wood before making contact. She traced the natural edge, following the curve where the tree had grown. "They're incredible."

Jake stayed near the door, hands in his pockets. He'd built those shelves three years ago when he was remodeling his home, spending evenings in the workshop selecting the perfect slabs and sanding them smooth while leaving the character intact.

"Your home isn't what I expected," Renee said, turning to look at him.

"What did you expect?"

"I don't know. Bachelor pad furniture, maybe. A couch and a TV and not much else." She gestured at the room. "Your home is lovely and completely you."

The way she said it made Jake's chest tighten.

"It took me a few years to get it to this point," he said. "Gutted the place when I bought it. Replaced everything."

"You did all of this yourself?"

"Most of it. Dawson helped with some of the heavy lifting."

Renee walked to the coffee table, running her hand over the surface. "You made this too?"

"Barn wood from a property outside town. The barn was falling down, so the owner let me haul away what I wanted."

She looked at him, her eyes bright. "You have a gift, Jake."

He shrugged, uncomfortable with the praise. "It's just carpentry."

"It's not just anything." She moved toward the bookcase on the far wall—another piece he'd built, floor-to-ceiling with adjustable shelves and joints so tight you couldn't see the seams. "Every piece here tells a story. You can feel the care in it."

Jake cleared his throat. "Let me show you the kitchen. The shelves there are what I was thinking for your kitchenette."

He led her through the living room to the kitchen beyond. It opened into the space naturally, with no walls separating them. The cabinets were maple—pale and clean-lined with black hardware. The counters were butcher block, oiled until they glowed.

Above the counter, more live-edge shelves ran along the wall. These were lighter wood—maple, to match the cabinets—and shorter than the ones in the living room. They held everyday dishes, with mugs hanging from hooks beneath, and glass jars filled with coffee and sugar.

Renee stopped in the doorway, her hand going to her mouth.

"Oh," she said.

Jake watched her face. She moved closer to the shelves, studying the way they were mounted.

"This is what I want," she said. "Exactly this."

"I can do that. I've got slabs in the workshop that would work."

She turned to him, and the smile on her face made his heart beat a little faster. "Can I see your workshop?"

"Sure."

They walked through the kitchen to the side door that led into the attached garage. Jake flipped on the light, illuminating the two-bay space. His truck usually sat on one side, but today the spot was empty. On the other side, covered with a canvas tarp, sat his pride: a '69 Chevelle SS he'd been restoring for four years.

Renee stopped. "Is that a car under there?"

"Muscle car. I'm rebuilding it."

"Can I see?"

He hesitated, then crossed to the tarp and pulled it back.

The Chevelle gleamed even in the fluorescent light—black paint buffed to a mirror shine, chrome bumpers reflecting their images back at them. The interior still needed work, but the body was flawless.

"Jake." Renee's voice held wonder. "This is a beautiful car."

"It's a work in progress."

"How long have you been working on it?" She asked as she walked around it slowly, taking in every detail.

"Four years. Maybe five. Lost count."

"It's wonderful."

He replaced the tarp, feeling oddly exposed. The Chevelle was his indulgence, the thing he worked on when he needed to clear his head or think through a problem. Not many people knew about it.

"The workshop's back here," he said, leading her toward the rear of the garage.

Another door opened into the space he'd built himself—an extension off the back of the garage, insulated and heated with bright overhead lights. The scent of sawdust and wood oil filled the air.

Renee stepped inside and went still.

The workshop stretched before them, organized and purposeful. Long workbenches lined the walls, their surfaces scarred with use but clean. Tools hung in neat rows—saws, chisels, planes, each one in its place. Along one wall, slabs of wood leaned upright: walnut, cherry, and maple, their grain patterns visible even in their raw state.

In the center sat a massive oak worktable, its surface marked with years of cuts and sanding, every scratch a record of something created.

Renee walked forward slowly, her gaze moving from the tools to the wood to the projects in progress. A bookcase stood half-finished near the window, its joints clamped tight. Two live-edge shelves gleamed on a smaller table where he'd just started oiling them.

She moved to the wall where antique tools he'd collected over the years were displayed, each one cleaned and oiled and arranged like they mattered.

"Do you collect these?"

"Some I found at estate sales. Some were my grandfather's. A few I restored myself."

Renee turned, taking in the entire workshop. "I could spend hours in here just looking at everything."

"Most people find it boring."

She walked to the slabs of wood leaning against the wall, studying them one by one. "Is this where you pick the pieces for your projects?"

"Yeah. I'll go through them, find one with the right grain or character, then mill it down to what I need."

She stopped in front of a piece of walnut, its edge dark and organic.

Jake crossed to stand beside her. The slab was three inches thick and roughly six feet long, with a natural curve that would work perfectly for floating shelves. The grain ran in tight swirls near the edge, opening into broader strokes toward the center.

"This is walnut; it ages beautifully and gets darker over time," he said.

"How many shelves could you get from this?"

"Three, maybe four. Depends on the dimensions."

Renee reached out and touched the wood, her hand small against its surface.

Jake watched her, the way she studied the grain, like she was reading a story written in the lines. She moved to another slab—this one maple, lighter and softer—and ran her fingers along its edge.

"What would you use this for?"

"Anything that needs a lighter touch. Tables, maybe. Or shelves where you want to keep the space feeling open."

She glanced at him; her smile was warm. "You should teach classes. Share your talent with people."

"I'm not a teacher."

"You're a natural. You explain things so people can understand them."

He didn't know what to say to that, so he stayed quiet, watching her move through his workshop like she belonged there.

Renee paused near the drafting table in the corner, where his sketchbook lay open to a half-finished design for a dining table. She glanced at him, asking permission with her eyes.

"Go ahead," he said.

She turned the pages carefully, studying each drawing. Plans for a chair. A cabinet. A headboard with carved details. His handwriting filled the margins—measurements, notes, and ideas for joinery.

"You design everything before you build it."

"Measure twice, cut once."

She looked up at him, and the expression on her face was something he couldn't quite name. Admiration, maybe. Or something deeper.

"I love this," she said. "All of it. Your house, your workshop, and the way you see the world through what you create."

Jake's throat felt tight. "It's just wood."

"It's not." She closed the sketchbook and set it down gently. "It's you."

Renee walked to the worktable in the center of the room, running her hand over its scarred surface. "How long have you had this?"

"Ten years, maybe more. Built it from an old oak beam Dawson and I salvaged."

She traced one of the deeper cuts with her fingertip. "Every mark tells a story."

"Every mark is a mistake," Jake said. "Or a lesson."

"Same thing, isn't it?"

He watched her standing there in his workshop, surrounded by the tools and wood and unfinished projects that made up so much of his life. She looked right. Natural. Like she'd walked into his world and fit without even trying.

"Let's pick out your wood," he said, needing to move, to focus on something practical.

They spent the next several minutes going through the slabs. Jake pulled out three pieces of walnut, laying them across sawhorses so Renee could see the grain patterns side by side. He explained the differences—the tightness of the grain, the way knots would affect strength, and the character each piece would bring to her kitchen.

Renee listened and asked questions. In the end, she chose two slabs.

"These are perfect," she said.

"I'll start working on them next week. Get them milled and sanded, and figure out the brackets."

"How long will it take?"

"Couple of weeks, maybe. I want to do it right and add multiple layers of sealer."

She smiled. "I trust you."

The words landed harder than they should have. Trust. She trusted him with her inn, with her vision, and with the home she was building. And now she stood in his workshop, surrounded by the pieces of his life he didn't usually share, looking at him like he'd given her something precious.

Jake turned back to the slabs, needing a moment to steady himself. He ran his hand over the walnut, feeling the grain beneath his palm.

When he looked up again, Renee had moved to the window. She stood with her back to him, watching the snow fall beyond the glass. Her reflection showed in the pane—faint and ghostlike—and the lights from above caught in her hair.

She looked as if she belonged here.

She was changing his world without even trying. Making his carefully ordered life feel less like safety and more like waiting.

Renee turned from the window, catching him watching her.

"What?" she asked, her smile curious.

"Nothing," he said.

But it wasn't nothing. It was everything—the way she moved through his space with wonder instead of judgment, the way she saw beauty in sawdust and scarred wood, and the way she made him want to build something more than shelves.

She walked toward him, stopping a few feet away. Close enough that he could see the flecks of darker blue in her eyes. Close enough that the air between them felt charged with something unspoken.

"Thank you for showing me this," she said. "Your home, your workshop. All of it."

"You wanted to see the shelves."

"I wanted to see you. This is who you are. This space. These tools. The things you create."

Jake's hands tightened on the edge of the worktable behind him. "Yeah. I guess it is."

"It's remarkable."

"It's ordinary."

"No." She shook her head, her gaze steady on his. "It's not."

Renee turned back to the walnut slabs, running her hand over the wood again, and Jake watched her.

Maybe this wasn't ordinary.

Maybe she wasn't either.

Chapter 18

Renee stepped back, admiring the soft sage green that transformed her office space from a dated floral disaster to a peaceful sanctuary. Her shoulders ached from three days of painting the walls in her home, but the satisfaction of seeing each room completed made every minute worth it.

She dipped the brush again and continued touching up the wall near the trim. Afternoon light slanted through the glass, warming the freshly painted walls and making the color glow exactly the way she'd imagined. Tomorrow her desk and bookcases would arrive, and this room would finally become the office she'd been planning.

A place to work on the inn's branding. A space to build her marketing consultancy. Somewhere that was completely, undeniably hers.

The sound of heavy footsteps on the stairs pulled her attention from the wall. Multiple sets of boots hit each step in rhythm. Voices carrying up from below—Jake's steady baritone mixed with Billy's laugh and Sam's good-natured ribbing about something.

Renee set the paintbrush across the top of the can and wiped her hands on the old towel she'd been using as a rag. Her pulse quickened, the way it had been doing lately whenever Jake arrived. She'd stopped pretending she didn't notice.

"Renee? You up here?"

"In the office," she called back.

He appeared in the doorway. Tool belt slung low on his hips, flannel shirt rolled to his elbows, dark hair slightly mussed like he'd been running his hands through it. Behind him, Billy, Sam, and Levi filled the hallway, each carrying cabinet pieces wrapped in protective padding.

"We brought your kitchen," Jake said.

Renee smiled. "All of it?"

"The lower cabinets. Picked them up from Dad's store this morning." He glanced past her at the walls. "You finished painting."

"Almost. I'm just touching up a few spots."

Jake walked into the room, his gaze moving across the sage green walls with the same careful attention he gave everything. "I like the color. Calm. Professional. Exactly what an office should be."

"That's what I was going for. Do you need my help to bring everything up?"

"No, we'll get them all up here."

The next fifteen minutes turned into carefully choreographed chaos. The crew moved up and down the stairs, carrying cabinets wrapped in thick padding to protect the finish.

The cabinets accumulated near the kitchenette area—natural oak, unfinished and beautiful, waiting to be installed and sealed. The wood grain swirled in unique patterns on each piece, and the craftsmanship showed in every joint and corner.

"These are gorgeous," Renee said, running her hand over the smooth surface of one cabinet door.

"They're solid," Jake said. "Good construction."

Billy set down the last cabinet and straightened, rolling his shoulders. "That's everything. You need us for the install, or are you good?"

Jake glanced at Renee, then back at his crew. "I've got it. You guys get back to work on the first floor."

"You sure?" Sam asked. "It'll go faster with more hands."

"I'm sure. Renee's going to help me."

Levi's mouth twitched like he was holding back a smile, but he just nodded. "All right. If you need us, just holler."

The three men headed for the stairs, their footsteps echoing through the old Victorian.

Renee looked at the pile of cabinets, then at Jake. "So. Where do we start?"

"Layout first." He pulled a folded paper from his back pocket and spread it on the small dining table. The paper showed a detailed drawing of the kitchenette with measurements and cabinet placements marked in his neat handwriting.

She leaned over the table beside him. "You drew this?"

"Yesterday. Wanted to make sure everything would fit right with the extension." He pointed to the drawing. "The sink base goes here, against the existing plumbing. These two base cabinets flank it on either side. Then we've got a corner cabinet here and two more standard bases completing the run."

"And the upper shelves?"

"I'll install those next week once I finish them." He glanced at her. "I started milling them down yesterday evening."

"I can't wait to see them installed."

"They're going to look good." He refolded the drawing and tucked it away. "All right. Let's get started. The first cabinet is the corner unit. It's the trickiest because of the angle."

They unwrapped the corner cabinet together, peeling away the protective padding to reveal the natural oak underneath. The cabinet was larger than Renee remembered; L-shaped to fit flush against both walls.

Jake crouched beside it, checking the internal mechanisms. "This one has a lazy Susan inside. Makes corner storage actually useful instead of just a black hole where things disappear. You made a good choice in picking this. Wanna help me position it?"

"Sure."

They lifted the cabinet together—Renee taking one side, Jake taking the other. The weight pulled at her arms, but she kept her grip steady as they maneuvered it into the corner. Jake directed her movements with quiet instructions, adjusting the angle until the cabinet sat exactly where he wanted it.

He set the level on top, watching the bubble settle. "It's off by about a quarter inch. The floor's not quite level here."

"Is that a problem?"

"Not if we shim it." He pulled small wooden wedges from his tool belt and slid one under the front corner of the cabinet. The bubble in the level shifted and then centered. "Perfect."

Renee watched him work, the way his hands moved with practiced certainty, testing the level again from different angles to make sure everything was true. He caught her watching and raised an eyebrow.

"What?"

"Nothing. You're just very precise."

"Measure twice, cut once. The same principle applies to cabinets. If they're not level, the doors won't close right, and everything will look off."

He marked where the cabinet sat, then moved it aside to drill pilot holes into the wall studs. The drill whirred, loud in the quiet apartment.

"Hand me that cabinet screw from the box," he said without looking up.

Renee found the box of hardware on the floor and selected a long screw. She placed it in his outstretched hand, and his fingers closed around it.

He drove the screw partway in, then repeated the process for three more mounting points. "All right. Let's get it back in position."

They lifted the cabinet again, and this time Jake guided it into place with more confidence. The screw heads aligned with the pilot holes.

"Hold it steady while I get it secured," he said.

Renee pressed her hands against the top of the cabinet, keeping it from shifting. Jake worked below her, his shoulder brushing against her hip as he maneuvered the drill. The contact was brief and entirely practical, but it sent awareness skating across her skin.

The final screw went in, and he straightened. "You can let go."

She stepped back, and the cabinet stayed exactly where it was, solid and level and permanent.

"One down," Jake said. "Five to go."

The sink base went in next, centered under the window where natural light would fall across the farmhouse sink Jake would install later. Two standard cabinets flanked it, their doors aligned perfectly when Jake adjusted the hinges.

"How are your arms holding up?" He asked as he checked the level again and made a minor adjustment.

"I'm fine."

"You've been painting for three days, and now you're lifting and holding cabinets." He drove another screw in, then glanced at her. "Take a break if you need one."

"I don't need a break. I like helping."

"Why?"

The question caught her off guard. She steadied the cabinet while he secured it, thinking about how to explain. "Because it's my space. I want to be part of building it, not just watching someone else do all the work."

"Most clients would rather watch."

"I'm not most clients."

"No." His voice had gone quieter. "You're not."

The fifth cabinet slid into place with satisfying precision, completing the run along the wall. Only one cabinet remained—a narrow piece designed to fill the gap between the last standard cabinet and the wall.

Jake measured the space twice, then nodded. "This should fit perfectly."

"I still can't believe how beautiful these are. Just the wood itself, without any stain."

"Natural oak has character. Once we seal it, the grain will really pop." He positioned the cabinet, checked for level, and started marking holes. "What made you choose natural over painted cabinets?"

"Honestly? I just really like the natural look." She watched him drill the pilot holes. Jake secured the final cabinet, tested the door swing, and stepped back to survey the complete installation.

"Well?" he asked.

Renee moved to stand beside him, taking in the row of natural oak cabinets that now lined her kitchenette wall.

"Love it. It's perfect," she said.

"You haven't seen it with the countertop and sink yet. Or the live-edge shelves."

"I don't need to. I can already tell it's going to be spectacular."

"I'm glad you're happy with it so far."

"I am. More than happy." She touched his arm, her hand resting on his forearm just above his wrist. "Thank you for all the hard work you've done for me."

He looked down at her hand on his arm. "You're welcome."

"When are you going to ask me out?"

Jake went completely still. His eyes widened slightly, and for three full seconds he just stared at her like she'd spoken in a foreign language.

"What?"

"You heard me."

"I—" He blinked. Swallowed. "You want me to ask you out?"

"I wouldn't have asked if I didn't."

The level slipped from his hand, clattering to the floor.

"I've been trying to figure out the right time to ask," he said finally, his voice rougher than usual.

"Why?"

"I didn't want to mess it up." His gaze held hers, steady and honest.

"You won't mess it up."

"You sound pretty confident about that."

"I am."

He exhaled slowly, and his shoulders relaxed like he'd been holding tension she hadn't even noticed. "Friday night. Dinner. Let me take you somewhere."

"Okay," she said.

"Okay?"

"Yes, I'd like that."

A smile spread across his face—not his usual small curve of amusement, but something wider and more genuine that transformed his whole expression. "Good."

"How should I dress?"

The question made him pause, his head tilting slightly as he considered it. "Casual. Just be yourself. That's who I want to take to dinner."

The sincerity in his voice made warmth bloom in her chest and spread outward until her fingers tingled where they still touched his arm. "That might be the best answer you could have given me."

"It's the truth."

"I know. That's what makes it good."

They stood there in her half-finished kitchen, surrounded by new cabinets and the smell of fresh paint, not quite touching except for her hand on his arm. The space between them felt charged with possibility and promise and all the things they'd been carefully not saying for weeks.

Jake's gaze dropped to where her hand rested against his flannel sleeve, then back to her face. "I should probably finish here. Get the cabinet doors adjusted so they're all aligned right."

"Okay."

But neither of them moved.

"Renee."

"Yeah?"

"I'm glad you asked that question."

"Me too."

Chapter 19

Renee sat cross-legged on the floor of her office, surrounded by stacks of papers that had seemed so organized when they were packed in Manhattan. Now spread across the hardwood in overlapping piles, they looked like chaos with ambition.

Marketing portfolios. Client case studies. Branding examples. Strategy documents from campaigns she'd led three years ago that felt like they belonged to someone else's life.

Her new desk sat in the middle of the room. Solid cherry wood with clean lines and brass hardware—simple but substantial. The two bookcases flanked the window, their empty shelves waiting to be filled. A wooden filing cabinet stood near the door, its drawers empty and smelling faintly of cedar.

She picked up a folder labeled "Luxury Hotel Rebranding—SoHo" and flipped it open. Glossy photos showed sleek lobbies and rooftop bars, sophisticated marketing copy that promised exclusivity and urban elegance. Good work. Professional work.

Work that had nothing to do with a Victorian inn in the Tennessee mountains.

Renee set the folder aside and reached for another stack. Below her, the sound of power tools cut through the old house—a drill whirring, then stopping. Sam's voice was calling out something about measurements. Billy's laugh. The steady rhythm of construction work had become the soundtrack of her days.

"Renee? You up here?"

"In the office," Renee called back.

Her sister appeared in the doorway holding a vase filled with flowers—burgundy dahlias, golden sunflowers, and rust-colored mums arranged with the artistic eye that made Heather's shop the best in town. She wore jeans and a cream cardigan, her honey-blonde hair pulled back with a floral clip.

Heather's gaze swept the room, taking in Renee on the floor, the wrapped desk, the empty bookcases, and the sea of papers. "Wow. This looks like organized chaos had a fight with regular chaos, and nobody won."

"I'm creating a system."

"Uh-huh. What kind of system involves sitting on the floor looking overwhelmed?"

"The kind where I'm trying to decide what's actually useful for my life here versus what's just evidence of my old one." Renee gestured at the portfolio she'd just set down. "Do I really need a case study about luxury hotel marketing when I'm running a six-room inn?"

"Maybe not that specific one." Heather stepped carefully around the papers and set the vase on her desk. "But you worked hard on all of this. It shows what you can do."

"It shows what I used to do."

"Is there a difference?"

Renee looked up at her sister, who stood with one hand on her hip, head tilted.

"I don't know yet," Renee admitted.

Heather crouched down and started gathering papers into neater stacks. "What's the organization system you're going for?"

"I was thinking chronologically, but maybe it should be by industry? Or by type of service?" Renee picked up a folder labeled "Social Media Strategy—Restaurant Group." "See, this one's about restaurants, but it's really about social media. So where does it go?"

"Make two piles. One for examples you'd show clients and one for reference materials you'd use for your own projects. Forget chronological. You're not writing your memoir."

"That's actually smart."

"I have my moments." Heather sat down on the floor across from Renee, tucking her legs beneath her. She reached for a stack of papers and started sorting through them. "Okay, so this one about organic skincare branding—client example or reference?"

"Client example. That campaign won an award."

Heather set it to the right. "This one about email marketing metrics?"

"Reference. That's more about strategy than finished work."

They fell into a rhythm, Heather asking questions while Renee made decisions. The piles grew more organized, and Renee felt the knot in her chest loosen slightly. This was manageable. This was just papers and folders and files that needed homes.

"So," Heather said after several minutes. "How's everything going with the renovation?"

"Good. The first floor's really coming together. They've got drywall up in the kitchen now, and the bathroom's almost ready for tile."

"And Jake's crew? They're working out okay?"

"They're great. Professional, respectful, and know what they're doing." Renee set another folder on the reference pile. "Why?"

"Just asking." Heather picked up a glossy portfolio and studied the cover. "How are things going with Jake?"

"Good."

Heather looked up. "Just good? Come on, give me details. You're glowing."

Heat crept up Renee's neck. "I'm not glowing. I'm sitting on the floor sorting papers."

"Nope. Definitely glowing." Heather set down the portfolio and leaned forward, grinning.

Renee picked up another folder, opened it, closed it, and set it down. Her hands felt restless. "Jake asked me out."

The squeal that came out of Heather was loud enough to be heard on the first floor. She clapped her hands together, bouncing slightly where she sat. "Tell me everything. When did he ask? What did he say? Where's he taking you?"

"Yesterday afternoon. After he installed my kitchen cabinets." Renee said with a grin. "Actually, I asked him."

Heather's eyes went wide. "You asked him?"

"More or less. I asked him when he was going to ask me out."

"Renee Bentley." Heather pressed both hands to her chest like she was having heart palpitations. "That is pretty bold; good for you."

"It just came out. We were standing there in my kitchen, and he'd just finished the install, and I was thinking about how much I enjoy his company; I enjoy being around him. I want to get to know him better. I was tired of waiting for him to make the first move. So I just asked."

"What did he say?"

"He dropped his level." Renee laughed at the memory. "Just completely froze and dropped it on the floor. Then he said He'd been trying to figure out the right time to ask."

"The right time." Heather's voice went soft.

"He said he didn't want to mess it up."

"And then?"

"And then he asked me to dinner."

Heather grabbed Renee's hands and squeezed them. "Where's he taking you?"

"He won't say. Just said to dress casually."

"Casual." Heather released Renee's hands and sat back, her expression turning analytical in that way she got when arranging flowers or solving problems. "Casual means probably not the steakhouse. Maybe Rosa's? Or the new bistro on Oak Street?"

"I have no idea. He said, to just be myself."

"Well, that's perfect. Because yourself is exactly who he's been spending time with for the past few weeks." Heather reached for more papers, resuming the sorting even as she talked. "Client example or reference?"

Renee glanced at the folder. "Reference. And what do you mean, that's who he's been spending time with?"

"I mean, he's seen you covered in paint. He's watched you learn how to strip wallpaper and remove bathroom fixtures." Heather set the folder on the left pile. "He's not asking out Manhattan Marketing Executive Renee. He's asking out the real you."

Renee looked down at her current outfit—old jeans with paint stains on the knees, a faded University of Tennessee t-shirt, and hair pulled back in a messy ponytail.

This was what Jake saw every day.

"I'm nervous," Renee admitted.

"About Friday?"

"About all of it." She picked up a paper and then set it back down without reading it. "My last date in Manhattan was over a year ago. A guy Patricia set me up with. Investment banker. We had dinner at this trendy place in TriBeCa, talked about market trends and quarterly projections, and I spent the whole evening wishing I was home in my pajamas."

"Sounds romantic."

"It was exactly like every other Manhattan date I went on. Professional networking disguised as getting to know each other. Everyone performing their best selves instead of actually being themselves." Renee met her sister's eyes. "This feels different."

"Because it is different."

"That's what scares me."

Heather was quiet for a moment, her hands stilling on the papers she'd been sorting.

"It's one date, Renee. Dinner. Conversation. Getting to know each other outside of cabinet installations and renovation updates. Just let yourself have fun."

"When did you get so wise?"

"I've always been wise. You were just too busy being the responsible older sister to notice."

"Fair point."

They returned to sorting; the piles grew more organized with each decision. Client examples were on the right, and reference materials on the left. Evidence of old work that might inform new projects. The past serving the future without dictating it.

"What if it's awkward?" Renee asked. "After Friday, I mean. What if we go out and realize there's nothing there, and then we still have weeks of renovation left and it's weird between us?"

"What if you go out and realize there's everything there?"

"That might be worse."

"How could that possibly be worse?"

"Because then it's real. Then it's something I could lose."

Heather squeezed her hand tighter. "Renee. Listen to me. You can't protect yourself from hurt by refusing to take chances. That's not living. That's just existing cautiously."

"When did you become a philosopher?"

"When my big sister came home after ten years, I realized she'd forgotten how to let herself be happy." Heather released Renee's hand and straightened. "I should get going. I have three arrangements to finish before this evening."

"Thank you for the flowers. And the help. And the pep talk."

"That's what little sisters are for." Heather headed for the door, then paused at the threshold. "Oh, and Renee? Text me Friday night. Or Saturday morning at the latest. I want details."

"What kind of details?"

"All of them." Heather grinned.

"It's just dinner."

"It's never just dinner." Heather waggled her fingers in a wave. "Trust me on this."

Chapter 20

Jake held the heavy wooden door of the Mistletoe Lodge open, and Renee stepped past him into the warmth of the lobby.

"Thank you," she said, glancing back at him with a smile.

He followed her inside, letting the door swing shut behind them. The century-old lodge stretched out before them in all its rustic elegance—gleaming wood floors, a massive stone fireplace already crackling with a fire, and leather chairs arranged in conversation groups. Vintage photographs of Mistletoe Falls lined the walls, and through an archway ahead, Jake could see the soft glow of the Timberline Dining Room.

His pulse was doing something strange. Not quite racing, but not steady either. Which was ridiculous because he'd been here dozens of times. His parents celebrated their anniversary in this dining room every year. He'd eaten Sunday dinner at those tables more times than he could count.

But this wasn't Sunday dinner with his family. This was a date. His first actual date with Renee, and he wanted it to be right.

The drive from the inn had been easy enough—twenty minutes of comfortable conversation. Nothing heavy. Nothing that required much thought. She'd been waiting for him when he pulled up, stepping out the door before he could even make it up the porch steps. The sapphire blue-colored sweater she wore made her eyes seem impossibly blue, and her dark jeans and boots were simple but somehow perfect.

She looked beautiful. That was the word that kept cycling through his mind, even though it felt inadequate.

"Good evening, Jake." The hostess, a woman named Clara who'd worked here since before Jake was born, smiled at them both. Her silver hair was swept up in an elegant twist, and her burgundy dress matched the lodge's color scheme perfectly. "Your table's ready."

"Thanks, Clara."

"Right this way." She gathered two leather-bound menus and led them through the lobby toward the Timberline Dining Room.

The restaurant opened before them like something from another era. Exposed timber beams crossed the high ceiling, dark with age and character. The massive stone fireplace dominated one wall, its flames casting dancing shadows across the honey-colored log walls. Large windows offered views of the town below, where lights were beginning to twinkle in the gathering dusk. White linen covered generously spaced tables, each with a small oil lamp providing intimate pools of golden light.

In the far corner, a man with graying hair sat on a stool with an acoustic guitar, playing something soft and melodic that blended with the quiet conversation of other diners. The entire space hummed with warmth and life without being loud or overwhelming.

Clara led them to a table near one of the windows but close enough to the fireplace that Jake could feel its warmth. The table was set with simple elegance—white linens, burgundy napkins, and quality silverware that had weight and substance.

"Your server will be right with you," Clara said, placing menus before them. "Enjoy your evening."

Jake held Renee's chair as she sat, then took his own seat across from her. Through the window beside their table, the lights of Mistletoe Falls spread out below them like scattered stars, and beyond that, the dark silhouette of mountains cut against the sky.

"This place is beautiful," Renee said, her gaze moving around the room before settling back on him. "I haven't been here since I was a teenager."

"It hasn't changed much. They update things here and there, but mostly it's the same as it's always been."

"That's what makes it special." She ran her fingers along the edge of the linen tablecloth. "Everything here feels intentional. Like someone cared about every detail."

"Old Man Harrison built this place with his sons back in 1889. Used timber from their own land and stone from the creek bed. According to what my granddad once told me, they worked on it for six years straight." Jake gestured toward the beams overhead. "Those are all hand-hewn. You can still see the ax marks if you look close."

Renee tilted her head back, studying the ceiling. "I love that. That kind of craftsmanship."

"Me too."

Their server appeared, took their drink orders—sweet tea for both—and left them with a promise to return shortly.

Jake opened his menu but found himself watching Renee instead. The firelight caught in her hair, turning it gold at the edges. She was studying her menu with the same focus she brought to everything, her bottom lip caught between her teeth as she read.

She looked up and caught him staring. "What?"

"Nothing. Just thinking."

"About?"

"How glad I am you asked when I was going to ask you out."

A smile curved her lips. "You were taking too long."

"I was being careful."

"Why?"

Jake set down his menu. "Because this matters to me."

Renee's expression softened as she smiled.

"It matters to me too," she said.

The server returned with their drinks, and they ordered—mountain trout for him, herb-crusted chicken for her, and an artisan bread basket to share.

Renee picked up her glass, took a sip, then set it down and looked at him with that direct gaze he'd come to recognize.

"If you could only eat one meal for the rest of your life, what would it be?"

There it was. Classic Renee, jumping straight into personal territory without preamble or small talk.

"That's quite an opening question."

"I don't believe in small talk. We've already covered numerous generic topics on the drive over."

"Fair enough." He leaned back in his chair, considering. "My mom's pot roast. With mashed potatoes and carrots and dinner rolls she makes from scratch."

"Seriously? That's your answer?"

"You asked what I'd want to eat forever. That's it."

"Why?"

"Because it tastes like home. Like being taken care of. Mom makes it the same way every time—the same recipe she learned from her mom.

And whenever I eat it, I'm eight years old again with scraped knees, and my mom's putting food on the table and making everything okay." He met her eyes. "What about you?"

"My grandmother's biscuits with honey butter." Renee's voice went soft with memory. "She used to make them every Sunday morning when we all gathered for breakfast. Heather and I would sit at her kitchen counter and watch her work. She never measured anything, just knew exactly how much flour and buttermilk to use. They were perfect every time."

"Does she still make them?"

"She passed away when I was in college. But my mom has her recipe now. She makes them on special occasions."

"That's what you'd want to eat forever? Your grandmother's biscuits?"

"They taste like being loved. I guess we both picked comfort over complexity."

"Nothing wrong with that."

Their bread basket arrived, and the server set it between them with small dishes of herb butter and local honey. Steam rose from the warm bread, and the scent made Jake's stomach growl quietly.

Renee reached for a piece, tore it in half, and slathered it with honey. "Okay, my turn to ask a real question."

"The first wasn't a real question?"

"That was a warm-up." She took a bite of bread and chewed thoughtfully before asking, "What's something you were afraid of as a kid that you're not afraid of anymore?"

Jake selected a piece of bread, buying time while he thought. "Letting people down."

"You were afraid of that as a kid?"

"Terrified of it. My parents, my teachers, my coaches. I wanted everyone to think I was doing okay. That I had it together." He buttered his bread slowly, deliberately. "Spent a lot of energy making sure nobody saw me struggle."

"And you're not afraid of that anymore?"

"I wouldn't say I'm not afraid. But I've learned that disappointing people is survivable. That people who actually care about you don't disappear when you mess up." He looked at her steadily. "What about you?"

Renee set down her bread and stared at the table for a moment. "I was afraid of not being the best. Of being ordinary."

"That doesn't surprise me."

"Why not?"

"Because you're someone who gives everything one hundred percent. You don't do things halfway."

"I'm learning to be okay with good enough. With being imperfect." She picked up her bread again, tearing off a small piece. "Turns out ordinary can be pretty wonderful if you let it."

"You're not ordinary."

"Neither are you."

They ate their bread in companionable silence, the acoustic guitarist shifting to a new song—something slow and sweet that Jake didn't recognize but liked immediately. Around them, other diners talked quietly, silverware clinked against plates, and the fire crackled and popped.

"What's the best gift you've ever received? Not the most expensive. The most meaningful."

Jake didn't have to think about this one. "The crooked birdhouse I made when I was eight."

Renee's eyebrows rose. "You made it yourself? How is that a gift?"

"I made it in my grandfather's workshop. He helped me measure and cut the wood and showed me how to drive the nails without smashing my thumb. It came out all crooked—one side higher than the other, the roof at a weird angle. I was so disappointed because it didn't look like his birdhouses."

"What did he say?"

"He said it was perfect because I made it with my own hands. That it would get better with practice, but this first one would always be special because it was the beginning." Jake smiled at the memory. "My mom still has it. It's on a shelf in their living room."

"That's really sweet."

"What's yours?"

"A cookbook. My grandmother's recipes, all handwritten. My mom gave it to me after she passed. Every page has notes in the margins—little tips or variations or memories about who liked which dish." She looked up at him. "I rarely cooked from it when I lived in Manhattan. I didn't have time. But now I'm thinking I want to use some of those recipes for the inn."

"You should."

"Will you eat my terrible first attempts?"

"Absolutely."

Their entrees arrived, and for a few minutes they focused on the food. Jake's trout was perfectly cooked, flaky, and seasoned with herbs he couldn't name but enjoyed. Renee had let him try a bite of her chicken, and he'd traded her a piece of fish. It felt natural, easy, like they'd been doing this for years.

The guitarist transitioned to something upbeat, and Jake noticed a few couples swaying near the small stage area. The entire room felt alive with warmth and connection, and he was aware that he was part of it—sitting across from a beautiful woman who made him want to share things he normally kept to himself.

"My turn," Jake said, setting down his fork. "What's something you're surprisingly good at that most people wouldn't guess?"

Renee grinned. "Parallel parking."

"That's your secret skill?"

"Don't underestimate it. I can parallel park in spaces most people wouldn't even attempt. Manhattan teaches you that or you never go anywhere."

"I'm not sure that counts as surprising."

"Okay, fine. I'm really good at estimating time. Like, I can tell you almost exactly how long something will take without looking at a clock. It drove my coworkers crazy because I was always right."

"That's actually useful."

"What about you? What's your hidden talent?"

Jake considered. "I can whistle really well. Like complicated songs. My crew makes fun of me for it."

"Prove it."

"Right here?"

"Nobody's paying attention."

He whistled a few bars of the song the guitarist was playing, matching the melody perfectly. Renee laughed, the sound bright and genuine, and Jake felt something warm settle in his chest.

"Okay, you win," she said. "That's impressive and completely unexpected."

They ate in comfortable silence for a few minutes, and Jake relaxed into the evening. The nervousness from earlier had evaporated, replaced by something easier and more natural.

"Can I ask you something?" Renee said, pushing her vegetables around her plate.

"No need to ask permission. Let's hear your next random question."

She set down her fork and looked at him directly. "If you could have dinner with anyone, living or passed on, who would it be?"

"Besides you?"

She rolled her eyes but smiled. "Yes, besides me."

"My grandfather." The answer came immediately from somewhere deep and honest. "He passed when I was fifteen. And I'd want to ask him about his life before I knew him. About building his workshop, about what he dreamed about when he was young, and about what he wished he'd done differently."

"Why?"

"Because I only knew him as an old man with weathered hands and endless patience. But he was young once. He had hopes and fears and probably made mistakes. I'd like to know that version of him." Jake paused. "What about you?"

"Aunt Holly." Renee's voice was soft. "I'd ask her if she were happy. If running the inn was everything she hoped it would be, or if there were things she wished she'd done differently. If she had regrets."

"Why does that matter to you?"

"Because I'm following in her footsteps. And I want to know if this path leads where I hope it does."

"I think she was happy. Everyone who knew her said she loved that inn more than just about anything. That she poured her heart into it."

"That's what I'm afraid of."

"What do you mean?"

"What if I pour my heart into it and it's not enough? What if I fail?"

"Then you'll figure it out. Just like you've figured out everything else." Jake leaned forward slightly. "You're brave, Renee. Braver than you give yourself credit for."

She looked at him for a long moment, something unreadable in her expression. Then she smiled, small but genuine. "Thank you for saying that."

The server cleared their plates and offered dessert menus, but Jake was already full. Still, when Renee suggested they share a slice of bourbon pecan pie, he agreed immediately.

While they waited for dessert, Jake asked his next question. "What does a perfect Saturday look like for you? Not what you think it should be—what actually makes you happy."

Renee tilted her head, considering. "Slow morning. A pot of fantastic coffee. Relaxing and doing nothing special. Afternoon with family or friends. Simple dinner. A long, steaming hot bubble bath. Reading before bed." She paused. "That probably sounds boring."

"Not at all."

"What about you?"

"Cell phone turned off. Fishing as the sun comes up. Coffee on my porch a little later. Working in my shop on something personal, not a job. Simple lunch. Maybe a hike if the weather's good. Nothing complicated."

"We have very similar definitions of perfect."

"I noticed that."

Their dessert arrived, and the server set it between them with two forks. The pie was still warm, topped with a scoop of vanilla ice cream that was already starting to melt into the bourbon-spiked filling. Jake took a bite and nearly groaned at how good it was—sweet and rich with just enough salt to balance it out.

Renee took her own bite and closed her eyes. "This is dangerous."

"Why's that?"

"Because now I know it exists. I'll be thinking about it constantly."

The conversation continued to flow easily between them. Jake found himself watching her more than eating—the way she smiled when she got a particularly good bite, the way she gestured with her fork when she was making a point, and the way her eyes lit up when she laughed at something he said.

"Okay, serious question," Renee said, scraping up the last bit of ice cream. "What's something you believed about yourself that turned out to be wrong?"

Jake set down his fork. "I thought I was only good at one thing. That without football, I didn't have much to offer."

"And?"

"And losing it showed me I was capable of more. That my worth wasn't tied to how far I could throw a ball or how many touchdowns I scored. Turned out I'm pretty good with my hands. That I can build things that matter. That I can run a business and take care of my crew and create something I'm proud of."

"That's a good thing to learn."

"What about you?"

Renee was quiet for a moment, her finger tracing patterns on the tablecloth. "I thought success meant climbing higher. Earning more. Achieving constantly. Always in motion, hurrying here, running there to achieve the next big thing. That's what I was good at, so that must be what I was meant to do."

"But?"

"But that was someone else's definition. Maybe society's definition, or my industry's definition, but not mine." She looked up at him. "I'm happiest here. I'm enjoying being alive with the freedom to choose who I want to be. I'm enjoying the quieter moments in life. Turns out success doesn't have to be loud to be real."

The guitarist had shifted to something slower, more intimate. A few couples had moved to the small space near the stage, swaying together in the dim light. Jake watched them for a moment.

"Dance with me?" He asked as he stood and held his hand out to her. For a moment he thought she might say no, that he'd pushed too far too fast. But then she smiled and placed her hand in his.

He led her to the small space where other couples were dancing.

They swayed to the music, and Jake tried not to think about how right this felt and how natural it was to hold her like this.

"I didn't expect this," Renee said quietly, her voice almost lost in the music.

"Didn't expect what?"

"To feel this comfortable. I thought first dates were supposed to be awkward."

"Maybe it's not really a first date."

"What is it then?"

Jake pulled back slightly so he could see her face. "Feels more like coming home."

He cupped her face with one hand, his thumb brushing across her cheekbone, and leaned down slowly. Gave her time to pull away if she wanted to. But she didn't. Instead, she rose slightly on her toes, closing the distance between them.

The kiss was soft, and brief—a gentle press of lips that lasted only a heartbeat. Nothing demanding or complicated. Just honest and real and exactly right.

When he pulled back, Renee's eyes were still closed. She opened them slowly, and the smile that spread across her face made Jake's chest tighten.

She leaned into him, and they swayed to the music, not quite dancing anymore but not ready to let go either. Jake's hand stayed on her back, and hers remained on his shoulder, and the moment stretched out peacefully and perfectly.

And he didn't mind at all.

Chapter 21

Renee's phone buzzed on the desk in her office, where she'd been sitting for the past hour, staring at paint samples trying to decide on colors for each of the themed rooms on the second floor of the inn. Her mind kept drifting back to last night—the restaurant, the conversation, the dancing. The kiss.

She picked up the phone.

Jake: *Morning. You busy right now?*

Her pulse jumped.

Renee: *Not really. Why?*

The three dots appeared immediately, disappeared, and appeared again.

Jake: *The Winter Market is happening at the community center today. Thought you might want to check it out. Local artisans, Christmas stuff, and food samples. Figured you could find decorations for the inn.*

Renee: *That sounds perfect. When?*

Jake: *I'm in town running errands. Could pick you up in about 30 minutes if you'll be ready?*

She glanced at the clock. Thirty minutes. She needed to shower, fix her hair, and attempt to look like an actual human being.

Renee: *I can be ready in an hour?*

Jake: *Sounds good. See you soon.*

The shower was quick, the hair situation handled in 20 minutes, and the wardrobe choice surprisingly easy. Dark jeans, boots with good tread for walking, a soft burgundy sweater that was warm but not bulky, and her wool coat. Simple. Comfortable. Herself.

She was pulling on her second boot when she heard his truck pull up outside.

Renee grabbed her purse and phone and hurried down both flights of stairs. Through the front window, she could see Jake climbing the steps on her porch. He wore jeans and work boots and a charcoal henley under his winter coat, and when he looked up at the inn and saw her through the glass pane on the door, he smiled.

That smile did something to her chest that shouldn't be legal.

She opened the door before he could knock.

"Hi," she said.

"Hi." His gaze moved over her, warm and unhurried. "You look nice."

"Thanks. So do you."

Jake extended his hand toward her.

She slipped her hand into his, his fingers warm despite the cold.

The chilly air bit at her cheeks as they walked to the truck, and she was grateful when he opened her door and she could climb into the warmth. He'd left the engine running, and country music played softly from the radio.

Jake climbed into the driver's seat and put the truck in reverse, backing out carefully. "How was your morning?"

"Productive. I unpacked more boxes and found a few things I'd forgotten I owned."

"That's the best kind of unpacking. Finding treasures."

"What about you? What errands brought you to town?"

"Hardware store. My drill battery died yesterday, and I needed a replacement before Monday." He turned onto Mistletoe Lane, heading toward downtown. "Figured while I was out, I'd see if you wanted to come to the market."

"I'm glad you did."

He glanced at her, and the corner of his mouth lifted. "Yeah?"

"Yeah."

They drove through downtown, past The Ginger Jar and Pinecone & Ivy, past the Fireside Diner and Morrison's Hardware Store. The streets were busy for a Saturday—people bundled in coats and scarves, carrying shopping bags, stopping to talk with neighbors.

"The market's been going for about four years now," Jake said. "Started as a way to support local artisans during the holidays. Give them a place to sell directly instead of having to go through online stores or shops in Gatlinburg."

"Sounds like it was a good idea."

"It's been popular. Gets bigger every year. You'll see a lot of the same vendors every week through Christmas, but some rotate in and out."

He turned left onto Pinecone Pass. "I thought you might find things for the inn. Decorations, maybe some art for the walls. And there's always food samples."

"You had me at food samples."

He laughed. "Yeah, the food samples get me every time."

The community center came into view—a large building with a peaked roof and wide front steps. Cars filled the parking lot, and people moved in and out of the main entrance, their breath making clouds in the cold air.

Jake found a spot near the back. "Fair warning, it can be overwhelming at first. Lots of booths and plenty of people. If you need a break, just say so."

"I think I can handle it."

"I know you can. I'm just saying the offer stands."

They climbed out into the cold, and Renee pulled her coat tighter around herself. Jake came around the truck and fell into step beside her. When they reached the entrance, he pulled the door open and gestured her to go through first.

Warmth hit her immediately, along with sound and light and scent all at once. The community center had been transformed into something magical.

Renee stopped just inside the doorway, taking it in.

Rows of vendor booths stretched across the main floor, each draped in lights and garland and decorated with the vendor's personal style. Overhead, strings of Edison bulbs crisscrossed the ceiling, casting a warm golden light over everything. Christmas music played from speakers somewhere—not loud, but present, weaving through the hum of conversation and laughter.

The smell was almost overwhelming in its richness. Cinnamon and pine, fresh-baked goods and something savory, scented candles, and the sweetness of honey and apple cider. It smelled like Christmas distilled into one space.

"Wow," Renee said.

Jake stood beside her, watching her reaction. "Pretty great, right?"

"It's amazing."

In the far corner, a small stage had been set up where a man with a guitar sat on a stool, playing something soft and melodic. Near the entrance, a table offered hot cider in paper cups, steam rising in delicate spirals. Everywhere she looked, people browsed and talked and laughed, their voices blending into a comfortable murmur.

"Where do you want to start?" Jake asked.

"I have no idea. There's so much."

"How about we just wander? See what catches your eye."

"That works."

They moved into the main aisle, and immediately Renee felt the energy of the place wrap around her. It wasn't frantic or rushed like the holiday markets in Manhattan had been. This felt warmer, slower, and more intentional. People stopped to actually talk with vendors, asking about the work, sharing stories, and laughing together.

The first booth they approached displayed hand-carved wooden items—cutting boards, bowls, serving trays, and small decorative pieces. Everything gleamed with an oil finish, the grain of the wood rich and beautiful.

Jake slowed, his attention caught by a large cutting board with a live edge. His fingers traced the natural curve of the wood, and Renee saw something shift in his expression. Not just appreciation—recognition. The look of someone who understood the work that went into creating something like this.

"Jake Morrison." The vendor, a man probably in his sixties with silver hair and weathered hands, grinned. "Wondered if I might see you here today."

"Hey, Carl. How's business?"

"Can't complain. Sold three cutting boards already this morning." Carl gestured to the board Jake had been examining. "That one's cherry. Took me two weeks to get the finish right."

"It's beautiful work."

"Coming from you, that means something." Carl's gaze shifted to Renee, and his smile widened. "Who's this?"

"This is Renee Bentley. She bought the Jingle Bell Inn and recently moved back here. Renee, this is Carl Weber. Best woodworker in Mistletoe Falls."

"Now you're just flattering an old man." But Carl looked pleased as he extended his hand to Renee. "Nice to meet you, Renee. I heard her niece bought it. Good to see it staying in the family."

"Thank you. It's good to be back."

"Jake here built my workshop five years ago. Finest building I've ever worked in."

"He's exaggerating," Jake said.

"I'm not. That workshop stays warm in winter and cool in summer, and the light is perfect for detail work." Carl picked up a small wooden ornament carved to look like a snowflake, intricate and delicate. "Tell you what, this is on the house. Welcome home present."

Renee started to protest, but Carl pressed it into her hand. "No arguments. Hang it on your first Christmas tree at the inn."

The wood was smooth and warm against her palm, the carving so detailed she could see individual branches in the snowflake design. "Thank you. That's very kind of you."

"It's good to know the inn will be open again someday." Carl's attention shifted back to Jake. "You taking care of this one?"

"Trying to."

"Good man."

They moved on, and Renee held the ornament carefully, studying it as they walked. "That was sweet of him."

"Carl's one of the good ones. Been carving since he was twelve. Learned from his father."

"He said you built his workshop."

"A few years back. Nothing fancy, just a solid building with good light and ventilation."

"He seemed pretty grateful."

Jake shrugged. "He needed a space to work. I built it."

She looked at him—the way he brushed off the compliment, the way he talked about his work as though it were simple instead of meaningful. Like building someone a space to create wasn't a gift in itself.

"What?" he asked, catching her watching him.

"Nothing. Just thinking."

"About?"

"About how you don't take compliments very well."

His mouth quirked. "Maybe I just don't need them."

"Everyone needs them."

They reached the next booth—Christmas ornaments. Hundreds of them. Glass baubles painted with winter scenes, wooden ornaments carved into stars and angels, and fabric ornaments stitched with snowflakes and trees. They hung on display racks in layers, catching the light and spinning slowly.

Renee stopped, her hands reaching out almost instinctively to touch a delicate glass ball painted with a snow-covered Victorian home that looked startlingly like the Jingle Bell Inn.

"That's nice," Jake said, stepping close beside her.

"It looks like the inn."

"It does."

The vendor, a woman in her forties with kind eyes, smiled at them. "That's one of my custom pieces. I paint local landmarks. The inn's been on my list for years."

"You painted this?"

"All by hand. I do about two hundred ornaments every season. Takes me from June through November to finish them all."

Renee lifted the ornament carefully, turning it to see the detail. The windows of the painted inn glowed with golden light, and tiny evergreen trees flanked the front porch. It was perfect.

"I'll take this one," Renee said.

"Wonderful choice. Would you like me to wrap it?"

"Please."

While the vendor wrapped the ornament in tissue paper and placed it in a small box, Jake browsed the other displays. He picked up an ornament shaped like a snowflake—not carved like Carl's, but made of delicate wire twisted into an intricate pattern.

"This one too," he said to the vendor, handing it over.

The vendor wrapped both ornaments and placed them in a small bag. Jake paid before Renee could argue, and when they walked away from the booth, he handed her the bag.

"Thank you," she said.

They wandered deeper into the market, pausing at a pottery booth where a woman demonstrated throwing clay on a wheel. Her hands moved with practiced precision, shaping the spinning clay into a bowl that seemed to grow out of nothing. Jake and Renee stood watching for several minutes, neither speaking, just observing the process.

"I could never do that," Renee said.

"Why not?"

"I'd want it perfect immediately. I don't have the patience."

"You stripped all the wallpaper in your apartment."

"That's different."

"How?"

"That was just removal. This is creation."

"Still, it takes patience."

The potter looked up and smiled. "It takes quite a few bad bowls before you make a good one. Patience and a tolerance for failure."

"See?" Renee said to Jake. "I'd quit after the first few flops."

"I don't believe that."

They moved on to a booth displaying handmade soaps and candles. The vendor had arranged them by scent—floral, woodsy, seasonal, and fresh. Renee picked up a candle labeled "Winter Woods" and lifted it to her nose. Pine and cedar, with something slightly sweet underneath. It smelled like the mountains, snow, and evergreens.

"That's one of my bestsellers," the vendor said. "I make it with essential oils from local trees. No artificial scent."

Renee set it down and picked up another—this one labeled "Christmas Morning." Cinnamon, orange, and a hint of clove. Warm and inviting.

Jake leaned in, his shoulder against hers, and sniffed. "That smells like a kitchen during Christmas."

"It does."

She set that one down too and reached for a third. "Frosted Cranberry." This one was sharp and sweet at once, tart and fresh.

"That one's nice," Jake said.

"They're all nice. How am I supposed to choose?"

"Get all three."

"I can't buy three candles."

"Why not?"

"Because that's excessive."

"You're decorating an entire inn. Three candles is barely a start."

The vendor, a young woman with curly hair and an enthusiastic smile, nodded. "He's right. And I'll give you ten percent off if you buy three or more."

Renee looked at the candles, then at Jake, then back at the candles. "Fine. All three."

"Excellent choice. These are soy wax, so they burn clean. About forty hours each."

While the vendor wrapped the candles in paper and placed them in a bag, Jake pulled out his wallet.

"Jake Morrison, I can pay for my own candles."

"I know you can." He handed cash to the vendor before Renee could stop him.

"You're impossible."

"Thank you," he said to the vendor, taking the bag. Then to Renee: "You can get the next one."

"There's going to be a next one?"

"Probably several."

"You're going to spoil me if you keep buying me things."

"That's sort of the idea."

She bumped his shoulder with hers. "You're trouble."

"You're just figuring that out?"

They walked on, and Renee found herself smiling despite her protest. There was something sweet in his wanting to buy things for her. Not because she needed him to, but because he wanted to. Because it made him happy to do it.

The next booth sold jams and preserves—rows of mason jars with handwritten labels. Strawberry, blackberry, peach, apple butter, pepper jelly. The vendor, an older woman with white hair pulled back in a bun, offered samples on small crackers.

"Try the apple butter," she urged. "Made it with apples from my own trees."

Renee took a cracker and bit into it. The apple butter was smooth and rich, sweet with just a hint of cinnamon. "Oh, that's good."

Jake tried one next. "Really good."

"I've been making preserves for fifty years," the woman said with obvious pride. "Same recipes my mother used."

"Do you sell these year-round?" Renee asked.

"Just seasonally. I make about two hundred jars every fall, and when they're gone, they're gone."

"I'll take two jars of the apple butter." Renee pulled out her wallet before Jake could. "And one of the strawberry."

The woman wrapped the jars carefully and placed them in a bag. Renee paid, feeling victorious, and when they walked away, she said, "See? I can buy things too."

"Never doubted it."

They passed a booth selling hand-knit items—scarves, hats, blankets, and mittens. Everything looked soft and warm, the colors rich jewel tones that would stand out beautifully against winter snow. Renee ran her hand over a deep sapphire blue scarf, feeling the texture.

"That color would look good on you," Jake said.

"You think?"

"Brings out your eyes."

She looked up at him, and he was watching her with that steady gaze that made her feel like she was the only person in the room. Her pulse skipped.

"You're good at this," she said.

"At what?"

"Noticing things. Saying things that make me feel—" She stopped, not sure how to finish that sentence.

"Make you feel what?"

"Special."

His expression softened, and he reached out to tuck a strand of hair behind her ear. His fingers lingered for just a moment against her cheek before he pulled back. "Good."

They moved toward a food vendor offering samples of various dishes—small paper cups with bites of pulled pork, chicken salad on crackers, and a white queso dip with tortilla chips. The vendor explained each one enthusiastically, and Jake and Renee sampled them all, comparing favorites.

"The queso is dangerous," Renee said.

"You want a full order?"

"I shouldn't."

"That's not what I asked."

"Yes. I want a full order."

Jake ordered one for them to share, and they found a high table near the wall where they could stand and eat. The queso came with a basket of warm chips.

"This is really good," Renee said.

"Better than Manhattan food?"

"Different. Not better or worse. Just different."

"What do you miss about Manhattan?" Jake asked. "Besides the coffee."

She thought about it while chewing. "The museums. The variety of restaurants. Being able to walk everywhere." She took another chip. "But I don't miss the noise. Or the crowds. Or the feeling that I was always rushing somewhere."

"You seem calmer now than when you first moved back."

"I feel calmer here. Like I can breathe."

"Good."

They finished the queso and threw away the container. Jake picked up the bags they'd accumulated and carried them without being asked.

Near the back of the market, Renee spotted a booth that made her professional instincts activate immediately. A woman sat behind a table displaying beautiful handmade soaps arranged in a wooden crate. The soaps themselves were gorgeous—swirled colors, natural ingredients, lovely scents. But the display was minimal, almost apologetic. No signage explaining the process, no pricing clearly visible, and no samples set out for people to touch and smell.

"Hold on," Renee said to Jake.

She approached the booth, and the woman looked up with a hesitant smile. She was probably in her early thirties, with dark hair and uncertain eyes.

"These are beautiful," Renee said, picking up a lavender-colored bar. "Do you make them yourself?"

"I do. Everything's handmade with natural ingredients. No chemicals, no artificial colors or scents."

"How long have you been doing this?"

"About three years. I started making soap for myself because my daughter has sensitive skin. Friends kept asking me to make them some, and eventually I just started selling."

Renee looked at the display again—at the potential being hidden by a lack of marketing knowledge. "Can I give you some advice?"

The woman's eyebrows rose. "Sure."

"You need signage. Something that tells your story—why you started, what makes your soap special, and what ingredients you use. People connect with stories." Renee gestured to the soaps. "And samples. Let people touch them and smell them. Once someone holds your product, they're more likely to buy it."

"I never thought about that."

"Also, your pricing isn't visible. Make it clear and easy to see. Remove barriers between people and purchase."

The woman nodded slowly, taking it in. "That makes sense. Are you in marketing?"

"I was. I'm starting a consultancy to help small businesses in Mistletoe Falls." Renee pulled a business card from her purse—one she'd had printed last week with her name, number, and email. "If you'd like to talk more about how to grow your business, give me a call. The first consultation is free."

The woman took the card; her face brightened. "Really? That would be wonderful. I've been struggling to figure out how to reach more customers."

"That's exactly what I do. Call me whenever you're ready."

"Thank you so much."

Renee bought three bars of soap—lavender, lemongrass, and something called "Mountain Morning"—and when she walked back to where Jake waited, he was smiling.

"What?" she asked.

"Nothing. Just watching you work."

"I wasn't working. I was shopping."

"You were networking. And you were good at it."

"She makes beautiful soap. She just needs help to get it in front of people."

"And now she has your business card."

"Maybe she'll call."

"She'll call." Jake shifted the bags to one hand and reached for hers with the other. His fingers threaded through hers, warm and solid. "Come on. There's more to see."

They wandered through more booths—a jewelry maker displaying pieces made with local stones, a quilter showing intricate designs, and a leather worker demonstrating how he tooled patterns into belts and bags. At each one, Jake knew someone or had a story. He'd worked at the jewelry maker's house last spring. He'd built custom shelves for the leatherworker's shop. He'd helped the quilter move her studio to a bigger space.

Everywhere they went, people greeted him warmly, teased him gently, and looked at Renee with open curiosity and approval.

"You know everyone," she said as they walked away from the quilter's booth.

"Small town. Can't avoid it."

"They like you."

"I like them too."

"It must be nice. Having that kind of community."

"It is." He squeezed her hand. "You'll have it too; just give it time."

"You think so?"

"I know so. You're a Bentley. Your family's been here forever. People already know you—they're just waiting for you to settle in."

She wanted to believe that. Wanted to feel like she belonged here the way Jake so clearly did.

They reached a booth selling fresh evergreen wreaths and garland, and Renee stopped. The scent of pine was strong here, real and sharp and exactly what she needed for the inn.

Wreaths of all sizes hung from display racks—some plain, some decorated with pine cones and berries, and some with ribbons and bells. One in particular caught her eye. It was full and lush, made with Fraser fir and white pine, and decorated with natural pine cones and clusters of red berries. Simple but elegant.

"That one," Jake said, following her gaze.

"You like it?"

"It's perfect for the inn. Classic but not fussy. Like you."

She looked at him, caught off guard by the compliment wrapped in such casual words. "Like me?"

"Yeah. Elegant and timeless."

"That might be the nicest thing anyone's ever said to me."

"Then people haven't been paying attention."

The vendor, a man in his fifties with weathered hands and a ready smile, lifted the wreath down. "Good choice. This is one of my best. I can add a ribbon if you'd like."

"No ribbon," Renee said. "Just like it is."

"You want garland too? I've got some that match."

She looked at Jake. "What do you think?"

"You need something for the mantel in the sitting room. Garland would look good there."

"Okay. Twenty feet of garland, please."

The man measured and cut the garland, wrapped both it and the wreath in brown paper to protect them, and Jake paid before Renee could reach for her wallet.

"I was going to get that one," she protested.

"Next time."

"You said that three booths ago."

"And I'll keep saying it."

She shook her head but couldn't stop smiling. "You're ridiculous."

"Probably."

They carried the wreath and garland toward the front of the market. The market was quieter now, winding down as afternoon shifted toward evening. Some vendors had started packing up, and the crowd had thinned to just a handful of people still browsing.

The guitarist on stage played something slower, more intimate, and Renee found herself drawn toward the music. Jake followed, still holding her hand, and they stood near the edge of the small stage, listening.

The song was pretty—something about snow and coming home and finding love in unexpected places. The guitarist's voice was rough but sincere, and Renee felt the words settle somewhere deep in her chest.

Jake's arm came around her shoulders, and she leaned into him without thinking. His warmth seeped through her coat, solid and steady, and she realized this was becoming normal. This easy physical closeness. The way they fit together.

"You okay?" he asked.

"Yeah. Just listening."

"Good song."

"Really good song."

They stood there through the rest of it, not talking, just being. When the song ended and another began—something upbeat and cheerful—Jake squeezed her shoulder gently.

"Should we load up the truck?" he asked.

"Probably. Before I see something else, I think I need."

They collected all the bags and the wreath and garland, Jake carrying most of it, Renee insisting on taking at least a few things. The cold air outside felt sharp after the warmth of the community center.

At the truck, Jake arranged everything carefully in the back, making sure the wreath wouldn't get crushed and the jars of preserves wouldn't roll around. He worked with the same attention to detail he brought to everything, making sure each item was secure.

"You're very methodical," Renee said, watching him.

"Can't have your stuff getting broken."

When everything was loaded, Jake closed the tailgate and turned to face her. They stood there in the parking lot as daylight faded to dusk, the temperature dropping, breath visible between them.

"Thank you for today," Renee said. "For thinking of me. For bringing me here."

"Thank you for coming."

"I had fun."

"Me too."

She looked at the truck bed full of Christmas decorations, thought about hanging the wreath on the inn's front door, arranging the candles around the sitting room, and displaying the ornaments. All the pieces of making the inn feel like home.

But it wasn't the decorations that made her chest feel full. It was this. Standing in a parking lot with Jake as the sun set behind the mountains, with cold air biting at her cheeks, and his eyes steady on hers.

It was the ease of spending a whole afternoon together and never once feeling like she had to hurry or be anyone other than exactly who she was. It was his carrying her bags without being asked, buying her small gifts just because he wanted to, and introducing her to people in his world like she already belonged there.

It was realizing that when she'd imagined coming back to Mistletoe Falls, she'd pictured the inn and her family and building a business.

She hadn't pictured him.

"Renee?"

"Yeah?"

"I'm really glad you came back to Mistletoe Falls."

"Me too."

Chapter 22

Renee stared at the spreadsheet on her laptop screen, trying to make sense of the numbers she'd been calculating for the past twenty minutes. Room rates. Seasonal pricing. Occupancy projections. The cursor blinked at her from the cell where she'd stopped typing, waiting for her to decide whether seventy-five dollars per night was too low for a weeknight in January or exactly right for attracting guests during the slower season.

Outside her office window, snow fell thick and steady. The radio on her bookshelf played a country song low and easy.

Papers covered her desk—printed templates for social media calendars, notes about local wedding venues she wanted to partner with, and a hand-drawn sketch of what the inn's website homepage might look like. She'd been working since seven o'clock, and her coffee mug sat empty beside her laptop.

The marketing plan was taking shape slowly. She had ideas. Good ones. A blog featuring local businesses and Mistletoe Falls attractions. A partnership program with the Christmas tree farm and other seasonal destinations. An email newsletter highlighting upcoming events and special packages. But turning ideas into an actionable strategy required focus she was struggling to maintain.

Renee rubbed her eyes and reached for her coffee mug, then remembered it was empty.

"Renee? You up here?"

Jake's voice carried up the stairwell from the second floor.

"In my office," she called back.

His footsteps sounded on the stairs, steady and unhurried. Then Dawson's voice, lower and muffled by distance.

"Careful, don't bang it on the railing."

Renee stood and walked to her doorway, curiosity pulling her from the spreadsheet she'd been staring at too long.

Jake appeared at the top of the stairs, moving backward, hands gripping one end of a long wooden plank. No—not a plank. A shelf. The live-edge shelf he'd been working on for weeks.

Her breath caught.

The wood glowed in the light from the stairwell window, warm honey tones streaked with deeper amber and gold. The natural edge curved along one side, following the tree's original shape, rough bark stripped away to reveal the organic line beneath. The grain ran in waves across the surface, tight and beautiful, the kind of pattern that only came from slow growth in good soil.

Dawson came into view behind Jake, carrying the other end. He glanced up, saw Renee standing in her doorway, and grinned.

"Special delivery."

Renee opened her mouth to say something—anything—but no words came out.

Jake glanced over his shoulder at her, then back at the shelf in his hands. "Careful. Pivot left."

They maneuvered the shelf onto the landing, and Jake set his end down gently against the wall. Dawson did the same, and both men straightened.

"Where's the second one?" Renee managed to ask, her voice coming out smaller than she intended.

"Coming right up," Dawson said as he and Jake disappeared back down the stairs and returned a moment later carrying another shelf, just as beautiful as the first. They leaned it beside its mate.

Renee moved toward the shelves. The surfaces were smooth as glass. Not cold like stone or metal, but warm, alive, holding some memory of the tree it had been. Her fingers traced the live edge on one of the shelves, following the curve, feeling the subtle texture where Jake had left the natural line intact.

"I finished the sealer early yesterday morning," Jake said. "They're ready to install."

She couldn't stop touching the wood. Couldn't stop seeing the hours of work in every inch—the milling, the sanding, and the multiple layers of finish that made the grain shine like it was lit from within.

Her throat went tight.

"Renee?"

She pressed her lips together, trying to hold it back, but her eyes were already burning and she knew what was coming.

"Hey." Jake's voice shifted, concern creeping in. "What's wrong?"

"Nothing." The word came out thickly. She blinked hard, but it didn't help. The first tear slipped free and tracked down her cheek before she could stop it.

Jake's shoulders went rigid. His weight shifted back half a step, and his eyes widened just slightly, the kind of look a man got when he'd just realized he'd walked into something he didn't understand and had no idea how to fix.

"I'm sorry," Renee said, swiping at her face with the back of her hand. "I don't—I'm not—"

Another tear fell. Then another.

"Okay." Jake looked at Dawson, then back at Renee, then at Dawson again. He made a gesture with his hand—quick and subtle, just a small movement that said, go.

Dawson caught it immediately. "I'll, uh, go check on that delivery. We're supposed to get those electrical panels this afternoon."

"Yeah. Thanks."

Dawson headed for the stairs, moving fast, and his footsteps faded down toward the first floor.

Jake stood there looking at Renee as if she might break if he said the wrong thing.

"I'm sorry," she said again. "This is so stupid. I don't know why I'm crying over shelves."

"They're just shelves," he said, but his voice was careful.

"They're not." Renee pressed her palms to her face, trying to pull herself together and failing. "They're beautiful. You made them. For me. And I've been sitting in that office all morning trying to figure out pricing structures and build a website and write marketing copy, and I'm stressed about getting everything done before the opening, and then you walk up here with these, and they're so—"

Her voice broke.

Jake closed the distance between them in two steps. His arms came around her, solid and sure, pulling her against his chest before she could say anything else.

She let him. Let her forehead rest against his shoulder, let the tears come because trying to stop them wasn't working, anyway. His flannel shirt was soft under her cheek, and he smelled like sawdust and the outdoors, like cold air and pine.

He didn't say anything. Didn't tell her it was okay, or that she didn't need to cry, or any of the useless things people said when they wanted crying to stop. He just held her, one hand flat between her shoulder blades, the other resting at the small of her back, steady and patient.

The tightness in her chest began to ease. Her breathing slowed. The tears stopped as quickly as they'd started, leaving her feeling wrung out and slightly embarrassed but also lighter than she had in days.

She stepped back, and Jake's arms dropped away immediately, giving her space.

"Sorry," she said, fanning her face with both hands. "I'm fine. Really."

"You don't have to apologize."

"I just—sometimes everything gets to be too much, and this is how I deal with it. I hold it all in until something pushes me over the edge, and then I cry for a few minutes, and I'm fine." She laughed, but it came out shaky. "You probably think I'm losing it."

"I don't think that."

"You looked terrified when I started crying."

His mouth twitched. "I don't handle women crying well."

"I noticed."

"Most guys don't."

"That's true." She wiped under her eyes with her fingertips, checking for smudged mascara. "But you didn't run away."

"Didn't seem right to leave you standing here crying by yourself."

The simplicity of it—the quiet decency in that single sentence—made her chest go warm.

"Thank you," she said.

Jake glanced at the shelves leaning against the wall, then back at her. "I was hoping you'd like them. Didn't expect tears."

"Happy tears. Overwhelmed tears. Good tears." She moved to the shelves again, running her hand along the edge of the top one. "These are the most beautiful shelves I've ever seen."

"They'll look better once they're installed."

"I can't imagine them looking better than this."

"Trust me." He picked up the first shelf, testing its weight. "I'd like to get them up today if that's okay with you. Finish your kitchen."

"Yes. Please. I've been waiting for this."

"Let me grab my tools from the truck."

He headed downstairs, and Renee walked back into her office. She closed her laptop and stacked the papers into a neater pile, then picked up her empty coffee mug and carried it to the kitchenette.

The cabinets she and Jake had installed looked perfect—natural oak with clean lines and black hardware. The butcher-block countertops gleamed with an oil finish. The small farmhouse sink sat deep and white below the window. Everything was ready. Waiting for the final piece.

She rinsed her mug and filled it with fresh coffee from the pot she'd made earlier, adding cream until the color turned pale caramel. The first sip was hot enough to warm her all the way down.

Jake's footsteps sounded on the stairs again, and he appeared carrying a toolbox in one hand and a drill case in the other. He set both on the counter, then went back for the shelf.

Renee pulled out one of the two chairs at her small table and sat down, cradling her coffee mug between her hands.

Jake brought the first shelf into the kitchenette and held it up against the wall above the cabinets, eyeing the placement. He set it down, pulled a tape measure from his toolbox, and started marking measurements on the wall with a pencil.

The radio in her office was still playing, the music drifting through the open door. Another country song, this one about autumn fields and mountain roads.

"How's Thanksgiving looking for you?" Renee asked.

Jake glanced at her, then back at his measurements. "Pretty standard. Mom's doing turkey, Dad's in charge of mashed potatoes. Dawson's bringing pies from the bakery because nobody trusts him to actually bake anything."

"Smart."

"He tried making a pie once. It was like eating sweet concrete." Jake marked another measurement. "After we eat, Dad and Dawson and I usually head out to the river for a couple of hours. Try to catch some trout."

"In November?"

"They're still biting. Water's cold, but they're there." He pulled a level from his toolbox and held it against the wall, checking the line he'd drawn. "It's more about getting outside than catching anything. Dad likes the tradition."

"That sounds nice."

"What about you?"

"First Thanksgiving at home since I was twenty-two." Renee took another sip of coffee. "Mom's going all out. Turkey, ham, three kinds of potatoes, her special cornbread dressing, green bean casserole, rolls, cranberry sauce—both kinds, jellied and whole berry—and four pies."

Jake looked over his shoulder at her, eyebrows raised. "Four pies?"

"Pumpkin, pecan, apple, and chocolate cream."

"That's a lot of pie."

"She's excited I'm home."

"I can tell." He turned back to the wall and picked up his drill, fitting a bit into the chuck. "Your sister coming?"

"Heather and her boyfriend. And probably half the neighbors will stop by at some point because that's what happens at my parents' house during holidays."

"Sounds about right for Mistletoe Falls."

The drill whirred as Jake made the first hole, and the sharp scent of fresh-cut drywall dust joined the smell of coffee and wood. He worked methodically, measuring twice before drilling, checking his level after each hole.

Renee watched him over the rim of her mug. His movements were efficient and precise—no wasted motion, every action purposeful. He'd pushed his sleeves up to his elbows, and she could see the flex of muscle in his forearms as he worked.

"I was on the town website this morning," she said after a few minutes.

"Yeah?" Jake set down the drill and picked up the first shelf, lifting it carefully.

"The Christmas tree lighting is this Friday night."

"That's right. Day after Thanksgiving." He positioned the shelf against the wall, lining up the brackets with the holes he'd drilled. "I forgot about that."

"I haven't gone since I was twenty-two."

Jake paused, the shelf still in his hands, and turned his head to look at her. "You want to go?"

"I do."

He set the shelf down and crossed to where she sat. The kitchenette was small enough that it took him only three steps. He stopped in front of her chair, and she had to tilt her head back to meet his eyes.

"You asking me to take you?" he said.

"I'm asking if you'd like to go with me."

"There's a difference?"

"Not really."

His mouth curved into a smile—the real one, the one that made his whole face change and reached all the way to his eyes. "Yeah. I'd like that."

"Good."

"I haven't been in a few years either." He reached out and tucked a strand of hair behind her ear, his fingers gentle. "Seems like a good year to start going again."

Jake went back to the shelf and lifted it again, positioning it against the wall. He worked the first screw into the bracket, then the second, checking the level again before tightening everything down.

The shelf held firm against the wall, suspended on hidden brackets so it looked like it was floating. The live edge faced outward, that beautiful natural curve drawing the eye.

"Can you hand me the other one?" Jake asked.

Renee set down her coffee and went to get the second shelf from where it leaned against the wall on the landing. It was heavier than she expected, solid wood through and through, and she carried it carefully into the kitchenette.

Jake took it from her and repeated the process—measuring, checking the level, drilling, positioning, screwing the brackets tight. When he stepped back, both shelves were installed, perfectly level, their grain patterns catching the afternoon light from the window.

Renee stared at them.

They transformed the entire kitchenette. What had been functional and nice now felt custom and intentional, like someone had designed this space specifically for her and no one else. The natural edge added organic warmth that complemented the oak cabinets. The honeyed tones of the wood made everything feel richer.

"Well?" Jake was watching her face.

"I love it."

"You sure? Not too high? Too low?"

"They're exactly right." She moved closer, running her hand along the bottom shelf. "I don't even know what I'm going to put on them."

"You'll figure it out. Cookbooks. Coffee mugs. Whatever you want."

"I want to leave them empty so I can just look at them for now."

"That defeats the purpose of shelves."

"I don't care. They're too pretty to cover up."

Jake started packing his tools back into the toolbox, fitting the drill back into its case. The radio shifted to a new song, something slower with a steel guitar winding through the melody.

Snow still fell outside the window, heavier now, piling on the sill and blurring the view. The afternoon light had a diffused quality it got during snowfall, soft and gray and peaceful.

Renee returned to her chair and picked up her coffee. It had cooled enough to drink easily now, and she took a long sip, watching Jake clean up his workspace. He wiped down the counter where drywall dust had scattered, then swept it into his palm and threw it away.

"You didn't have to finish these before Thanksgiving," she said.

"Wanted to." He closed his toolbox. "Figured you'd like having a finished kitchen before the holiday."

"I do."

"Good." He leaned against the counter, arms crossed, and looked at her. "You feeling better?"

"Much."

"No more tears?"

"Not over shelves, anyway."

"What about other things?"

"Depends on the day." She smiled. "But I'm okay. Really. Today was just one of those days where everything hit at once."

"The marketing plan?"

"And the website. And trying to figure out room rates. And wondering if anyone's actually going to want to stay here once I'm open." She turned the mug in her hands. "Normal business anxiety, I guess."

"People are going to want to stay here."

"You sound sure."

"I am sure."

The confidence in his voice steadied something in her chest that had been wobbling all morning.

"Thank you," she said quietly.

"For what?"

"For showing up with beautiful shelves. For not running away when I cried. For installing them the week of Thanksgiving so I'd have something to be grateful for." She met his eyes. "For being exactly who you are."

Jake's expression shifted—his jaw tightened just slightly, and he looked away, out the window at the falling snow. When he looked back at her, the intensity in his gaze made her breath catch.

"Friday night," he said. "Tree lighting. I'll pick you up at seven."

"I'll be ready."

He grabbed his toolbox and drill case, moved toward the door, then stopped at the threshold and turned back.

"Renee?"

"Yeah?"

"You're going to be fine. The inn. The marketing. All of it. You know how I know?"

She shook her head.

"Because you care enough to cry over shelves." He smiled. "That's the kind of person who makes things work."

Then he was gone, his footsteps descending the stairs, and she was alone in her kitchenette with its beautiful new shelves and her cooling coffee and the snow falling outside.

Renee stood and walked to the shelves, running her hand along the smooth wood one more time. The grain pattern swirled under her fingertips, dark and light flowing in waves that told the story of seasons and years, of a tree that grew slowly and strong in good soil.

Jake had made these. For her kitchen. With his own hands.

And in three days, he'd pick her up at seven o'clock to take her to see the Christmas tree lighting in the town square.

She smiled, picked up her coffee, and stood at her window watching the snow fall and feeling grateful for shelves that were more than shelves, and for a man who held her when she cried.

Her laptop waited in the office, with the marketing plan half-finished and demanding attention. But for just this moment, Renee let herself stand here in her completed kitchen with its floating shelves and falling snow and the knowledge that downstairs Jake Morrison was possibly thinking about Friday night.

Just like she was.

Chapter 23

Jake and Renee walked hand in hand down Icicle Lane toward the town square, snow falling steadily and softly, catching in her hair and melting on the shoulders of her deep green coat. She'd wrapped a cream-colored scarf around her neck, and every few steps she'd look up at him and smile like they were the only two people in the world instead of part of a crowd heading toward the biggest event of the season.

The street glowed with lights. Every business they passed had decorated for Christmas—garland wrapped around lampposts, wreaths hung on doors, window displays filled with holiday scenes that drew people close to look. Music drifted from somewhere ahead, faint but present, mixing with voices and laughter and the crunch of boots on snow-covered sidewalks.

They passed the North Pole Café with its red-and-green striped awnings and twinkling lights outlining the roofline. Through the windows, Jake could see families gathered around tables, mugs of cocoa steaming in front of children whose faces were flushed from the cold.

"I love this town during Christmas. I always looked forward to coming home when I lived in Manhattan," Renee said.

"It's something."

"Did you go to the tree lighting every year growing up?"

"Every year. My mom organized the volunteers who decorated the entire square back then, so we didn't have much choice." Jake squeezed her hand gently. "What about you?"

"Every year until I graduated from college. Then after that, I was always too busy with work or plans with friends in the city." She glanced at the shops they were passing. "I forgot how magical it feels."

They reached the corner where Icicle Lane met Mistletoe Lane, and Jake paused. The view opened up ahead—the town square spread out before them, transformed into something from a Christmas card.

The enormous Fraser fir stood in front of the Victorian gazebo, twenty-two feet of evergreen waiting to be lit for the first time this season. Even without lights, the tree dominated the square, its branches heavy with fresh snow and its top reaching toward the sky like a promise.

Thousands of people had already gathered. Mistletoe Lane had been closed to traffic, and the crowd filled the street and sidewalk on all sides of the square. Families bundled in winter coats stood close together, and children balanced on parents' shoulders to get a better view.

The buildings surrounding the square glowed with holiday displays. The Fireside Diner had strung lights across its entire front, and through the windows Jake could see every booth filled with people warming up before the ceremony. The Once Upon a Time Bookshop had created a window display featuring a village scene made entirely of stacked books. Even the Sugarplum Bakery had gone all out with a display of gingerbread houses and a Christmas tree full of vintage ornaments that drew people to press their faces against the glass.

"It's beautiful," Renee breathed.

"Come on. Let's get closer." Jake guided her forward, weaving through the crowd with the ease of someone who knew this town and its rhythms. People called out greetings as they passed. Mrs. Filmore from the library waved. Carl Weber, the woodworker from the craft market, nodded and smiled. Everyone knew everyone here, and Jake had forgotten how comforting that could feel.

They made their way toward the square's center, where three white tents had been set up at different locations around the square. The smell of freshly baked goods and coffee drifted on the cold air, and Jake recognized the setup immediately.

"Sugarplum Bakery," he said, nodding toward the tents.

Claire Whitfield stood at the center of one of the tents, directing her staff as they handed out steaming cups of coffee and hot chocolate to anyone who approached. Plates of decorated sugar cookies—snowflakes and Christmas trees and candy canes—sat arranged on tables inside the tent, free for the taking.

"That's generous," Renee said.

"Sugarplum Bakery does it every year. Claire recently took over the bakery after her grandmother passed away, and she's carrying on the tradition."

They approached the tent, and Claire looked up from the coffee urn she was filling. Her face lit up when she saw Jake.

"Jake Morrison. Good to see you."

"Hey Claire."

Claire's attention shifted to Renee, curiosity bright in her eyes. "And who's this?"

"Claire Whitfield, this is Renee Bentley. She bought the Jingle Bell Inn."

"Holly's Inn." Claire's expression warmed immediately. "Oh, honey, I'm so glad someone's bringing that place back to life. Holly was a dear friend to my grandma."

"Thank you," Renee said. "Holly was my aunt. I have wonderful memories of spending time with her there when I was young."

"Then you're exactly the right person to own it." Claire reached for two cups and began filling them with hot chocolate. "Enjoy and grab some cookies too."

Jake accepted both cups, handing one to Renee, then picked up two snowflake cookies from the nearest plate. The chocolate was rich and warm, and the cookie melted on his tongue, sweet and buttery.

"Thank you," Renee told Claire.

"You're welcome, honey. Come by the bakery sometime. I'd love to hear about your plans for the inn."

They moved away from the tent, sipping their hot chocolate and watching the crowd continue to grow. Vendors had set up carts along the edges of the square, selling roasted nuts and caramel apples.

"Jake!"

He turned at the sound of his brother's voice. Dawson pushed through the crowd, Laura beside him. She had her arm looped through Dawson's, bundled in a thick burgundy coat with a white knit hat pulled low over her dark hair.

"Thought you might be here," Dawson said when they reached him.

"Hey Dawson," Jake said and then nodded at Laura. "Good to see you."

"You too." Laura's attention moved to Renee, interest clear on her face. "You must be Renee. Dawson's told me so much about you."

"All good things, I hope," Renee said, smiling.

"Mostly." Laura's eyes sparkled with humor. "I'm Laura Morrison. It's nice to finally meet you."

"You too. Jake mentioned You and Dawson are renovating a house?"

"Attempting to renovate, yes. It's a work in progress." Laura laughed. "Last weekend we spent six hours stripping wallpaper from the upstairs bedrooms. I'm still finding bits of it in my hair."

"I know the feeling." Renee touched Jake's arm. "Jake's been teaching me how to do renovation work at the inn. I've become intimately familiar with wallpaper removal."

"Then we're kindred spirits." Laura said as she glanced at the tree. "Have they started yet?"

"Not yet. Should be any minute now."

They stood together in a loose group, finishing their hot chocolate and watching the square fill. The crowd had grown massive—easily a couple thousand people, maybe more. Kids darted between adults, their laughter rising above the general murmur of conversation. Someone near the gazebo was handing out small battery-operated candles, and people lit them one by one until the square glowed with hundreds of tiny flames.

A microphone crackled to life near the gazebo, and the crowd quieted.

A group of elementary school children climbed the gazebo steps, arranged in neat rows by their teacher. They wore matching red scarves and held sheet music in their gloved hands. The pianist from the school positioned herself at a keyboard someone had wheeled onto the gazebo, and she played the opening notes of "Jingle Bells."

The children sang, their voices high and clear, carrying across the square. Some of them were on key. Others were enthusiastically off, but it didn't matter. The crowd loved it, smiling and swaying along with the music.

They sang three songs—"Jingle Bells," "Frosty the Snowman," and "We Wish You a Merry Christmas"—before their teacher thanked everyone and led them off the gazebo to applause that echoed across the square.

Mayor Roger Hayes stepped up to the microphone next, his silver hair catching the light from the surrounding buildings. He waited for the applause to die down, then smiled out at the crowd.

"Good evening, Mistletoe Falls."

The crowd responded with cheers and whistles.

"Welcome, welcome everyone!" His greeting echoed across the square. "What a beautiful evening to celebrate the official start of our Christmas season here in Mistletoe Falls!"

The crowd cheered, the sound rising like a wave before settling back into attentive silence.

"I want to take a moment to thank all the volunteers who came together this past week to decorate this magnificent tree and transform our town square into the winter wonderland you see before you." Mayor Hayes gestured broadly. "Their hard work and dedication make events like this possible."

More applause rippled through the crowd.

"I also want to extend my gratitude to Gabe Mills, owner of the Mistletoe Christmas Tree Farm, for once again donating this stunning Fraser fir. Gabe, wherever you are out there, thank you for your generosity!"

"Tonight represents more than just turning on some lights," the mayor continued, his tone shifting to something more reflective. "It represents our community coming together, year after year, to celebrate what makes Mistletoe Falls special. We're not just a town—we're a family. And like any good family, we show up for each other, we support one another, and we find reasons to celebrate together."

Renee had gone still beside Jake, her attention focused entirely on the mayor's words.

"So as we light this tree tonight, let's remember what this season is truly about—connection, generosity, and the joy that comes from being part of something bigger than ourselves." Mayor Hayes raised his hand, his voice lifting with renewed energy. "Now, who's ready to see this tree light up?"

The crowd roared in approval, children bouncing with excitement and adults calling out affirmations.

"And now," Mayor Hayes announced with a theatrical flourish, "the moment we've all been waiting for. In ten seconds, our magnificent community Christmas tree will officially welcome the holiday season to Mistletoe Falls!"

"Let's count it down. Ten!"

"Nine!" the crowd shouted back.

Jake turned toward Renee. She was already looking at him, her eyes bright with excitement.

"Eight! Seven! Six!"

He pulled her closer, his arm sliding around her waist. She came willingly, leaning into him, her shoulder fitting perfectly beneath his.

"Five! Four! Three!"

Her hand rested against his chest, fingers curled into the fabric of his coat.

"Two! One!"

The tree exploded with light.

Thousands of tiny white bulbs blazed to life, transforming the Christmas tree into something magical. The branches sparkled, the lights reflecting off the snow and creating halos of gold and silver that seemed to shimmer in the falling flakes. The star at the top glowed brilliantly white, and the crowd erupted in cheers and applause.

Jake looked down at Renee.

She was already looking up at him.

Her eyes held his for a heartbeat, then she rose onto her toes and kissed him.

Her lips were cold from the winter air but soft, and Jake's hand moved to the small of her back, holding her steady as the surrounding crowd faded into background noise. The kiss was brief—sweet and unhurried—and when she pulled back; she was smiling.

"That was perfect," she said quietly, her breath visible in the cold.

"Yeah," Jake agreed. "It was."

The crowd began to disperse slowly, people drifting toward the refreshment tents or heading home, but many stayed to admire the tree from different angles or take photographs with family. The lights cast everything in a warm glow, and the snow kept falling, adding to the magic of the moment.

"That tree is gorgeous." Laura said. "But I'd love to walk around the square and see all the window displays up close. Jake, Renee... want to join us?"

"I'm in," Renee said immediately.

"Sounds good," Jake added.

They moved as a group toward the edge of the square, where the businesses stood in neat rows around Mistletoe Lane. The sidewalks were wide, cleared of most of the snow, and people moved at a leisurely pace, pausing at each window to admire the displays.

The Fireside Diner had created a scene featuring vintage Christmas decorations and an old sled propped against artificial snow. Once Upon a Time Bookshop's display featured the book village Jake had noticed earlier, complete with tiny lights and miniature people ice skating on a mirror that represented a frozen pond.

Laura and Renee moved ahead, stopping at each window to point and comment. Jake could hear Renee's laughter carrying back to where he and Dawson walked behind them, and the sound made him smile.

"She's good for you," Dawson said quietly.

Jake glanced at his brother. "Yeah?"

"Yeah. You're happy." Dawson's hands were shoved in his coat pockets, and he walked with that easy confidence he'd always had. "How's it going? With her, I mean."

"Good. Really good."

"You care about her."

It wasn't a question, but Jake answered anyway. "I do."

Jake watched Renee pause at the window of Stitches Quilt Shop, her hand pressed to the glass as she pointed out something to Laura. The lights from the display caught in her hair, and when she turned her head to say something, her entire face lit up with delight.

"She's the one," Jake said.

Dawson stopped walking. Jake stopped too, meeting his brother's eyes.

"Yeah?"

"Yeah." The words came out steady and certain.

"Does she know?"

"Nope. But she will."

Dawson studied him for a long moment, then nodded slowly. A smile spread across his face—the genuine kind that made his eyes crinkle at the corners. "Good. I'm glad, Jake. You deserve this."

"Thanks."

"Laura's going to be thrilled. She's been asking about you two since the first time I mentioned Renee's name."

"I figured."

They resumed walking, catching up to where Laura and Renee stood at the window of Holly Belle Boutique. The display featured mannequins dressed in cozy sweaters and sparkly accessories, all arranged around a Christmas tree made of vintage hat boxes.

"This is adorable," Laura said. "I need to come back here during regular hours."

"Same," Renee agreed.

They continued around the square, pausing at each business. Mountain Brew Coffee Shop had stacked its window display with bags of coffee arranged to look like wrapped presents. The Ginger Jar featured a gingerbread village that must have taken Cindy days to create. Pinecone & Ivy Florist—Heather's shop—had decorated with fresh evergreen arrangements and red berries that looked almost too perfect to be real.

By the time they'd made it all the way around the square, the crowd had thinned considerably. The snow was falling harder now, and the temperature had dropped enough that Jake could see his breath even when he wasn't speaking.

They ended up back at the corner of Icicle Lane and Mistletoe Lane.

Laura pulled her coat tighter and tucked herself closer to Dawson's side. "I hate to be the one to say it, but I'm tired. I'm ready to go home."

"I'm with you," Dawson said. He looked at Jake. "You two heading back to the inn?"

"Yeah."

"Good seeing you both." Dawson shook Jake's hand, then gave Renee a warm smile. "Nice spending time with you, Renee."

"You too. Both of you."

Laura hugged Renee quickly. "Let's do this again soon. Maybe coffee or lunch and then shopping?"

"I'd love that."

They said their goodbyes, and Dawson and Laura headed toward where they'd parked their truck several blocks away. Jake watched them disappear into the crowd, then turned to Renee.

"Ready?"

"Ready."

They walked north on Icicle Lane, retracing their earlier path. The street was quieter now, most people having dispersed after the ceremony. Most of the businesses they passed were closed.

Renee walked close beside him, her arm looped through his, and they didn't talk much. They didn't need to. The silence between them was easy, comfortable, the kind that came from being with someone who didn't require constant conversation to feel connected.

The Jingle Bell Inn appeared ahead, its white Victorian structure glowing under the porch lights Renee had left on before they'd left. The burgundy trim looked almost black in the darkness, and snow had piled on the porch railings and gathered in the corners of the steps.

They stopped at the bottom of the porch stairs, and Jake turned to face her.

Renee looked up at him, snowflakes catching in her eyelashes. Her cheeks were pink from the cold, and her scarf had come slightly loose, revealing the collar of her coat.

"I had a wonderful time tonight," she said.

"Me too."

She smiled, but she didn't move toward the stairs. Neither did he. They stood there in the falling snow, and Jake knew he should say goodnight, should let her go inside where it was warm, but he wasn't quite ready for the evening to end.

Renee solved the problem by stepping closer and kissing him again.

This kiss was unhurried. Her hands came up to rest against his chest, and Jake's arms wrapped around her waist, pulling her close. She tasted like hot chocolate, and when she finally pulled back, her eyes held his for several long seconds.

"Goodnight, Jake."

"Night."

She turned and climbed the porch steps, her boots leaving prints in the fresh snow. At the door, she paused to look back at him, gave a small wave, then disappeared inside.

Jake stayed where he was, listening for the sound of the lock clicking into place. When he heard it, he finally moved, walking down the sidewalk toward where he'd parked his truck in the lot beside the inn.

The engine started with its usual rough rumble, and Jake let it idle for a minute while he brushed snow off the windshield. His breath came out in clouds, and his hands were cold despite his gloves, but he didn't care.

He climbed into the cab and sat there with the heater running, staring at the inn.

The words he'd said to Dawson earlier came back to him, clear and undeniable.

She's the one.

Jake put the truck in reverse and backed out of the parking spot. As he drove down Icicle Lane toward home, snow falling steadily in his headlights, those three words repeated in his mind with the rhythm of certainty.

She's the one.

Chapter 24

The scraping sound came again, steady and rhythmic, metal against concrete.

Renee looked up from her laptop screen, her fingers pausing mid-type over the website mockup she'd been tweaking for the past hour. The sound was coming from outside, from the front of the inn.

She pushed back from her desk and crossed to her office window, peering down through the glass.

Jake stood on the sidewalk below, pushing a snow shovel in long, even strokes. He'd cleared about half the walkway already, piling snow in neat mounds along the edges.

Six inches of snow had fallen overnight, blanketing everything in fresh white. She'd woken to it covering her windowsills and transforming the backyard into something from a winter postcard. Beautiful, but she'd been dreading the thought of clearing the walks.

And here was Jake. Sunday morning, ten o'clock, shoveling her sidewalk.

She turned from the window and hurried out of her office, grabbing her thick, fluffy bathrobe from the hook behind her bedroom door. The fabric was soft, cream-colored fleece, warm and oversized, and she wrapped it around her pajamas as she rushed down the stairs.

By the time she reached the first floor, her messy bun had come half loose and her fuzzy socks were sliding on the hardwood.

She unlocked the front door and pulled it open. Cold air hit her immediately, sharp enough to make her catch her breath.

"Good morning!" she called out.

Jake looked up from the shovel, and his entire face changed. His mouth curved into the grin she'd come to love.

"Mornin'." He walked toward the porch, still holding the shovel. "You better get back inside and stay warm."

"What are you doing here?"

"Shoveling snow." He climbed the porch steps, his boots leaving prints in the thin layer of white that had accumulated on the wood.

"I can see that. I meant, why are you here shoveling my snow?"

"Because it needed to be done."

"Jake." Her voice came out softer than she had intended. "You drove all the way from your house to shovel my sidewalk?"

"It's not that far."

"It's Sunday morning."

"I was up anyway." He leaned the shovel against the porch railing.

The warmth in her chest spread outward, filling her whole body despite the cold air coming through the open door.

"Thank you," she said. "That's really thoughtful."

He shrugged, and his eyes moved over her bathrobe, pajamas, and fuzzy socks. The corner of his mouth twitched. "Nice outfit."

"I was working."

"In your pajamas?"

"It's Sunday morning." She pulled the robe tighter. "Not all of us are out doing manual labor before noon."

"Some of us have ambition."

"Some of us have warmth and coffee."

"Fair point." He shifted his weight, and snow fell from his boots onto the porch. "What are your plans for the day?"

"Nothing much. Just working on the website. Why?"

"Want to go cut down a Christmas tree?"

The question took her completely by surprise. Her brain needed a full three seconds to process what he'd just asked.

"A Christmas tree?"

"For your living room. You want one, right?"

"I—yes. I do. I hadn't even thought about it yet."

"I figured." His grin widened. "So what do you say? Want to go to Mistletoe Christmas Tree Farm and pick one out?"

Joy burst through her chest like fireworks as she launched herself forward, rising onto her toes and throwing her arms around his neck.

Jake caught her easily, his hands coming to her waist to steady her.

"I take that as a yes," he said, and she could hear the smile in his voice.

She pulled back just enough to look at him, her arms still around his neck. "It most certainly is. Give me thirty minutes, and I'll be ready."

"Take your time."

Renee kissed his cheek, then stepped back and hurried inside, closing the door behind her.

She ran up both flights of stairs, her fuzzy socks sliding on every other step, and burst into her bedroom with her heart racing.

A Christmas tree. With Jake. At the Christmas tree farm.

She threw open her closet and started pulling out clothes. She'd need warm layers. Long underwear, thick socks, jeans, a thermal shirt, and a sweater. Her puffer coat. Gloves. That cute winter hat Heather had given her last year—cream-colored with a red pompom on top.

As she dressed, pulling on layer after layer, her mind kept circling back to the image of Jake standing on her sidewalk with that shovel. He'd driven over here. On a Sunday morning. Just because he knew the snow needed clearing and wanted to make sure she didn't have to do it herself.

That kind of thoughtfulness meant something. It meant he was thinking about her when they weren't together. It meant he cared about making her life easier. It meant—

Renee yanked the thermal shirt over her head and reached for her sweater.

It meant he was a good man. The kind of man who showed up and did the work without needing credit or praise or thanks. The kind of man who thought about small practical kindnesses that made a real difference.

The kind of man she was falling for.

The thought should have scared her. Instead, it just made her move faster.

She pulled on her jeans, then her thick wool socks, then grabbed her boots from the closet. Her hair was still a disaster from sleeping on it, so she pulled out the messy bun and ran a brush through it quickly before twisting it back up into something more presentable. A touch of lip balm. That was enough.

She grabbed her puffer coat, gloves, and hat, then headed back downstairs.

When she stepped outside, Jake was leaning against his truck, parked in the lot beside the inn. He'd finished the sidewalk while she was getting ready, and the cleared path stretched from the porch steps all the way to the parking lot.

He looked up when she appeared, and his eyes tracked over her winter gear.

She locked the door behind her and walked down the cleared sidewalk toward him. "Thanks again for shoveling. You didn't have to do that."

"I know."

She reached the truck, and he opened the passenger door for her. The interior was warm, and country music played softly from the speakers.

Renee climbed in and buckled her seatbelt while Jake walked around to the driver's side. He slid behind the wheel and put the truck in reverse, backing out of the parking spot with easy confidence.

"Do you go to the tree farm every year?" Renee asked as they turned onto Icicle Lane.

"Yeah. Mom picks out a tree, and Dad and I cut it down."

"I haven't been out there since I was a teenager."

"It's probably a lot bigger now than what you remember. Gabe's expanded the whole operation."

"Gabe?"

"Gabe Mills. Owns the place. Fifth generation."

"Wow. The name sounds familiar."

"His family's been growing Christmas trees there since 1924." Jake turned left onto a side road that wound north out of town. "It's become a pretty big deal. People come from all over during the holidays."

The road climbed higher into the mountains, following curves that offered glimpses of the valley below. Snow-covered everything—trees, fields, and the peaks in the distance. The sky was gray but bright, the kind of overcast that made the white landscape almost glow.

"Did you bring a saw?" Renee asked.

Jake's mouth curved. "In the truck bed."

"Of course you did. I haven't cut down a real tree in years."

"Manhattan didn't have Christmas tree farms?"

"Manhattan had tree lots on street corners where they'd already cut them down and tied them up. Very efficient. Zero charm. I bought a fake tree my second year there. Easier to store." Renee shook her head. "Looking back, that feels sad."

"You're here now."

"I am."

"About to cut down a real tree."

"With you."

Jake's hand reached across the center console and found hers. His fingers laced through hers, warm and solid.

They drove in comfortable silence for a few minutes, just the sound of the engine and the soft country music filling the space. The heater hummed, keeping the cab warm while snow-covered trees passed by.

A sign appeared ahead: Mistletoe Christmas Tree Farm—2 Miles.

"Almost there," Jake said.

Another sign: Christmas Magic Ahead—1 Mile.

Then: Welcome to Mistletoe Christmas Tree Farm—Est. 1924.

The entrance appeared around a curve—two stone pillars topped with enormous evergreen arrangements, and between them a hand-carved wooden sign that read "Mistletoe Christmas Tree Farm—Est. 1924—Mills Family" in elegant lettering. Smaller signs below announced "Choose & Cut," "Wagon Rides," "Gift Shop," and "Hot Chocolate."

Jake turned onto the paved drive, and the farm opened up before them.

Renee's breath caught.

A sweeping drive curved between towering Fraser firs that created a tunnel of evergreen beauty. Ahead, the drive split at a charming traffic circle where a vintage red truck—a 1952 Ford loaded with wreaths, garland, and twinkling lights—sat permanently displayed like a piece of art.

"Oh wow," Renee breathed.

"Wait until you see the rest."

They followed the drive past the red truck and into the main area. The farm stretched across rolling hills and flat meadowlands, with neat rows of Christmas trees marching across the landscape in perfect formation. Different sections were clearly marked—some for taller trees, others for smaller ones, areas for different varieties.

A restored red barn with white trim stood near the center, and beside it was a newer building with large windows and a sign that read "North Pole Trading Post." People moved between the buildings and through the tree fields—families with children, couples holding hands, and staff members in red vests over their coats helping customers.

Jake parked in the gravel lot near the barn, and they both climbed out. The cold hit Renee immediately, sharp and clean, making her grateful for all the layers she'd put on.

"This is amazing," she said, turning in a slow circle to take it all in.

"It's something." Jake moved to the back of his truck and lowered the tailgate. A handsaw lay in the bed, along with a coil of rope and a tarp. He grabbed the saw. "Ready to find your tree?"

"Absolutely."

They walked toward the main path that led into the tree fields. A staff member in a red vest smiled at them from near the barn, and Jake nodded in acknowledgment.

"Do you know what kind you want?" Jake asked.

"What are my options?"

"Fraser firs have good needle retention, classic shape. Noble fir if you want something that can hold heavier ornaments. Virginia pine if you're on a budget."

"Fraser fir sounds good."

"That's the 40-acre section." He pointed to the path marked with a wooden sign. "This way."

They walked side by side down the path, snow crunching under their boots. On either side, Christmas trees grew in perfect rows, their branches heavy with fresh snow. The trees ranged from waist-high to twelve feet tall, all carefully tended and shaped.

Other families moved through the surrounding fields—a young couple with a toddler balanced on the father's shoulders, an older couple debating the merits of two nearly identical trees, and a group of teenagers laughing as they tramped through the snow.

"How tall do you want to go?" Jake asked.

"My living room ceiling is about eight feet. So maybe six feet? Leave some room for a tree topper?"

"Six feet. That's manageable." He scanned the rows ahead. "Let's walk through and see what catches your eye."

They moved deeper into the Fraser fir section. The trees here were gorgeous—full and symmetrical, with that perfect Christmas tree shape that appeared in every holiday movie. The branches were dense with blue-green needles, and the fresh scent was almost overwhelming in its richness.

Renee stopped at one tree, walking around it slowly to examine it from all sides. "This one's pretty."

Jake came over and studied it. "It's nice. A little sparse on that side, though. See how the branches aren't as full?"

She looked where he pointed and saw what he meant. "You're right."

They kept walking.

Renee paused at another tree—this one slightly taller, fuller on all sides. "What about this one?"

"Better," Jake said as he walked around it. "Good shape. Dense needles. No major gaps." He looked at her. "You like it?"

"Yep. I like it."

"Let me show you how to check if it's healthy." He moved closer to the tree and gripped one of the branches gently. "See how the needles stay on when I pull? That means it's good and healthy. If they were coming off easily, it means they're showing signs of disease or weakness."

Renee reached out and tested a branch herself. The needles stayed firmly attached.

Jake stepped back and surveyed the tree one more time. "You wanna keep looking, or is this the one?"

She studied the tree—really looked at it. It was about six feet tall, full and symmetrical, with that rich blue-green color that screamed Christmas. And it was perfect. Not too big, not too small. Just right for her living room.

"This is the one."

"You sure? We can keep looking."

"I'm sure."

Jake's smile was warm and genuine. "All right then. Let's cut it down."

He knelt in the snow at the base of the tree, examining the trunk. Renee crouched beside him, watching as he positioned the saw.

"The trick is to cut straight through," he said. "You want to go slow and steady. Let the saw do the work."

"Can I help?"

He glanced at her. "You want to help cut it?"

"Yes."

"Okay. Let me start it. Get the cut going." He positioned the saw against the trunk about two inches from the ground. "Ready?"

"Ready."

Jake began sawing in long, even strokes. The blade bit into the wood, and the sound of it—that rhythmic back-and-forth—filled the cold air. His breath came faster as he worked, visible in white clouds.

After a minute, he stopped and sat back. "Your turn. Just keep the same rhythm. Don't force it."

Renee moved into position and gripped the saw handle. The wood was warm where Jake's hands had been. She started sawing, trying to match the steady rhythm he'd set.

The blade caught and stuck.

"Ease up on the pressure," Jake said. "Let the blade do the work."

She adjusted, pulling lighter, and the saw moved more smoothly. Back and forth. Back and forth. Her arms started to burn after thirty seconds.

"This is harder than it looks," she said.

"Keep going. You're doing good."

She kept sawing, falling into the rhythm of it. Her breath came faster, and she could feel sweat starting under all her layers despite the cold.

"Okay, my turn again." Jake took the saw from her and resumed cutting. His strokes were confident and measured, and within two minutes the trunk gave a sharp crack.

"It's going," he said. "Stand back."

Renee stepped away, and Jake made three more cuts before the tree tilted slowly to the side. He caught it with one hand, guiding it down gently so it landed in the snow rather than falling hard.

"There we go." He stood and brushed snow from his knees. "Got yourself a Christmas tree."

Renee looked at the tree lying in the snow, its branches still perfect, its needles still densely packed. They'd cut it down. Together.

Pride swelled in her chest, warm and unexpected.

"We did it."

"We did." Jake grabbed the rope from his pocket and began tying it around the trunk. "Now we just have to get it back to the truck."

He handed her the saw, and Renee took it, feeling the weight of it in her hand. Jake grabbed the rope with his right hand and reached for her left hand with his.

His fingers laced through hers, warm despite the cold.

They started walking back toward the parking area, Jake dragging the tree behind him with his other hand. The branches made a soft shushing sound as they moved through the snow, leaving a wide trail behind them.

Renee's hand felt small in Jake's, safe and secure. She looked up at him. His jaw was set with concentration as he pulled the tree, and his breath came out in white clouds. Snow had caught in his dark hair, and the cold had brought color to his cheeks.

He looked over and caught her staring. "What?"

"Nothing. Just thinking."

"About?"

"About how I'm going to make you help me decorate this tree when we get it into my living room."

Jake's laugh was genuine and warm. "Is that right?"

"That's right. You helped me pick it out and cut it down. That means you're invested now. You have to see it through to the end."

"Do I?"

"You do."

They walked a few more steps; the tree making that soft shushing sound behind them.

"Whatever you want, that's fine with me," Jake said, his voice casual but his hand tightening slightly on hers.

Chapter 25

"Watch the railing."

Jake angled the top of the tree away from the carved wooden banister as they maneuvered up the main staircase from the first floor. The trunk end was heavier, which meant he was walking backward, trusting Renee to guide him and warn him before he backed into anything.

"You're good," Renee called from behind him. "Keep going."

His boot found the next step. Then the next. The tree was unwieldy—six feet of Fraser fir with branches that wanted to catch on everything.

They reached the second-floor landing, and Jake paused to catch his breath. "One more flight."

Renee's face appeared around the side of the tree, flushed and grinning. "This is harder than I thought it'd be."

He adjusted his grip on the trunk and grinned. "Ready?"

"Ready."

They climbed the second set of stairs.

"Left," she said. "No, your other left."

"There's only one left."

"Then go that way."

They reached the third-floor landing, and Jake backed through the doorway into Renee's living room.

"Where do you want it?" Jake asked.

"By the window in the living room. Right there in that corner."

He backed up until his heel hit the wall, then they both set the tree down and stepped back.

The tree looked massive in the space.

"It's bigger than I thought," Renee said.

"It'll look good in this space."

"You sure?"

"Positive." Jake pulled off his coat and draped it over the back of her couch. "You've got the stand?"

"Yes, hold on." She disappeared into her bedroom and returned a moment later with her arms full of shopping bags. She set them on the floor near the tree, then went back for more.

Jake counted five bags in total by the time she finished. Department store logos, craft store names, all stuffed with boxes and tissue paper.

"You've been busy," he said.

"I had to start from scratch." She knelt beside the bags and started pulling things out. "I gave all my Christmas stuff to charity before I left Manhattan."

She pulled out a box and held it up. "Tree stand. Assembly required, apparently."

Jake took it from her and examined the picture on the box. Standard four-legged design, nothing complicated. "I can handle it. Where do you keep your tools?"

"Kitchen drawer. Second from the left."

He found a screwdriver and returned to the living room. Renee had cleared space near the window, pushing her small side table out of the way. Jake opened the box and spread the pieces across the floor.

The stand came together quickly—four legs screwed into the base, the center post tightened down, and the water reservoir checked for cracks. He positioned it in the corner where Renee had indicated, then looked up at her.

"I'm going to need your help to get it in."

"What do I do?"

"Hold it steady while I get the trunk positioned in the center. Then I'll tighten the screws while you make sure it's straight."

They lifted the tree together, and Jake guided the trunk into the stand's opening. The fit was snug, which was good. He knelt and started tightening the first screw, then the second, working his way around while Renee held the trunk vertical.

"Is it straight?" he asked.

"Tilt it a little to the left. Your left."

He adjusted.

"More."

He shifted again.

"Perfect."

Jake tightened the remaining screws until the tree stood solid and secure. He stood and stepped back to check his work. The tree rose straight and tall, its branches spreading in balanced layers, the top nearly brushing the ceiling.

"It looks good," Renee said.

"It does."

She pulled another bag toward her and started removing boxes. Christmas lights—five boxes of them, still in their packaging.

White lights, the kind that gave off warm color rather than the harsh blue-white of LEDs.

"I wasn't sure how many strands I'd need," she said. "So I bought extra."

"Better to have too many than not enough."

They opened the boxes and untangled the first strand. Jake plugged it into the wall outlet to test it, and the lights blazed to life. He unplugged them and started at the top of the tree, weaving the strand in and out through the branches while Renee fed him more length from the spool.

"Do you wrap them around the branches or just drape them?" she asked.

"Depends on the look you want. Wrapped looks fuller but takes longer. Draped is faster, but you see more cord."

"Which do you prefer?"

"Whatever makes you happy."

She smiled at that, and Jake realized he'd give the same answer to just about any question she asked recently. Whatever made her happy. That's what mattered.

They settled on a compromise—wrapped on the front of the tree where it would show most, draped toward the back. Jake worked methodically, checking each section before moving to the next, while Renee opened the remaining boxes and handed him fresh strands as he needed them.

"What was Christmas like when you were a kid?" she asked as he wove lights through a particularly dense section of branches.

"Pretty traditional. Big dinner at my parents' house, usually turkey and all the sides. Mom would bake for days beforehand—cookies, pies, and bread. The house would smell of food for a week straight."

"That sounds wonderful."

"It was. Still is, actually. She hasn't slowed down any." He secured the end of one strand and reached for the next. "What about you?"

"Similar. My mom's the same way with the baking. And my dad always insisted on reading 'The Night Before Christmas' on Christmas Eve, but he'd do different voices every year. One year all the characters were pirates. Another year they were all cowboys."

Jake laughed. "I'd like to see that."

"It was ridiculous. Heather and I would be trying not to laugh, and he'd just commit fully to whatever accent he'd chosen."

"Your dad seems like a good man."

"He is. Both my parents are." She handed him another strand of lights. "I'm lucky."

Jake had reached the lower branches now, where the work went faster.

"Dawson and I tried to catch Santa once when we were little," Jake said.

"What?"

"We were probably eight and ten. Old enough to have doubts but young enough to still want to believe." He grinned at the memory. "We rigged this elaborate trap system with string and bells, stretched across the living room from the fireplace to the Christmas tree."

"Did it work?"

"It worked too well. Dad came down in the middle of the night to adjust the thermostat and walked right into it. The bells went off, Dawson and I came running down the stairs, and there was Dad tangled up in string with bells hanging off him."

Renee's laugh was bright and unguarded. "What did he do?"

"Claimed he'd scared Santa off. He said he heard sleigh bells on the roof right before he tripped. We went back to bed believing him too." Jake secured the last strand and stepped back to check his work.

"That's sweet."

"We were gullible."

"You were children. That's what children are supposed to be."

Jake plugged in all the lights, and the tree came alive with a warm white glow. Even in the afternoon light, the effect was striking. The branches looked fuller, the green deeper, and the whole tree transformed into something magical.

"It's so magical, I love Christmas," Renee said as she grabbed another bag and pulled out boxes of ornaments. Glass balls in red and gold, some plain and some glittered. A box of silver icicles. Another box with ornaments shaped like snowflakes. She'd chosen classic colors, traditional shapes, and nothing trendy or modern.

They established a rhythm—Jake holding the box, Renee selecting ornaments, and hanging them on the tree. She worked thoughtfully, turning each ornament to catch the light, testing different branches before committing to a placement.

"Heather and I used to make gingerbread houses every year," she said as she hung a gold snowflake near the middle of the tree. "We'd get these kits from the craft store with the pre-baked walls and the icing in bags, and we'd spend an entire afternoon decorating them."

"Did they turn out good?"

"They were disasters. The walls never wanted to stay together, and we'd use so much icing trying to cement them that the whole thing would start sliding. One year, the roof collapsed while we were eating dinner. Just caved in on itself while we were in the other room."

"But you kept doing it."

"Every year until I left for college. It was our thing." She hung another ornament, this one a plain red ball that caught the light and reflected it in miniature points. "I should do that with her again this year."

"You should."

They continued working, the ornament boxes slowly emptying as the tree filled with color and light. Renee hummed along to Christmas music playing from her phone—Bing Crosby singing about white Christmases and chestnuts roasting on open fires.

She pulled something from one of the bags and held it up. A small wooden ornament carved to look like a snowflake, intricate and delicate.

"From the market," Jake said.

"Yep, the one Carl gave to me." She found a spot near the front and hung it carefully. Then she pulled out the other ornaments he'd bought her that day and hung them on the tree.

They finished the ornaments in comfortable quiet; the tree becoming more complete with each addition. Renee stepped back periodically to check the balance, sometimes moving ornaments from one branch to another, adjusting until everything was exactly how she wanted it.

Finally, only one bag remained. She opened it and pulled out a box containing a gold star tree topper. The star was classic in design, about eight inches across, with a clip on the back to secure it to the top branch.

"I need to be taller," she said, looking up at the tree.

"I can lift you."

"You sure?"

"Positive. Come here."

Renee brought the star over, and Jake positioned himself behind her. "Ready?"

"Ready."

He placed his hands on her waist, his grip firm and steady, and lifted. She rose smoothly, her weight no challenge for him, and he held her there while she reached up toward the top of the tree.

"A little higher," she said.

He adjusted, lifting her another few inches.

She worked the star onto the top branch, adjusting it until it sat straight and secure.

"Got it," she said finally.

He lowered her slowly, and when her feet touched the floor, she turned in his arms. They were close enough that he could see the gold flecks in her brown eyes and count the freckles across her nose.

"Thanks," she said.

"Welcome."

She stepped away and walked to the wall outlet where all the light strands converged into a power strip. She looked back at him; her face bright with anticipation.

"Ready to see it?"

"Ready."

She plugged it in.

The tree exploded with light. Warm white bulbs illuminated every branch, making the ornaments sparkle and the gold star at the top glow as if it held its own sun. The whole tree seemed to radiate warmth, and the corner of the living room that had been empty and dark was now the brightest, most welcoming spot in the entire space.

Renee pressed both hands to her mouth, her eyes wide.

Then she spun toward him, grinning.

"I love it!"

She crossed the small space between them, grabbed his shirt with both hands, and pulled him down to kiss her.

The kiss was sweet and unhurried, her lips soft against his. Jake's hands found her waist again, holding her close, and for a moment the world narrowed to just this—the warmth of her mouth, the pine scent from the tree, and the glow of Christmas lights reflecting off the walls.

When she pulled back, she didn't go far. Her hands stayed fisted in his shirt, and her eyes held his with an intensity that made his breath catch.

"How did I ever get so lucky to find someone like you?" she said.

Jake's throat went tight. He'd been asking himself the same question in reverse for weeks now. How had he, a contractor who lost his football scholarship, ended up here with this brilliant, accomplished woman who looked at him like he was something rare and precious?

"I'm the lucky one," he managed.

"No. I am." She shook her head, and her grip on his shirt tightened. "You showed up this morning to shovel my snow. You took me to cut down a tree. You spent your whole Sunday hauling a six-foot Fraser fir up three flights of stairs and stringing lights and hanging ornaments because I asked you to. You make me laugh. You make me feel special and cherished." Her voice dropped to barely above a whisper. "You make me feel like I'm home."

Jake cupped her face with both hands, his thumbs brushing her cheeks. The tree lights cast gold and white patterns across her skin, and her eyes shimmered with unshed tears that she was trying hard to blink away.

"You are home," he said. "This is where you belong."

"With you?"

"With me."

She rose onto her toes and kissed him again, and this time when she pulled back, she was smiling through the tears that had finally spilled over.

Chapter 26

"Yes, I understand. Thursday delivery works perfectly." Renee's voice carried through the open doorway of her office as Jake reached the third-floor landing. "Thank you so much. I sincerely appreciate it."

He waited at the threshold, not wanting to interrupt. Through the doorway, he could see her sitting at her desk, laptop open, papers spread across the surface in organized stacks. Her hair was pulled back in a ponytail, and she wore jeans and a sweater that looked soft and comfortable.

She glanced up and saw him. Her whole face brightened, and she held up one finger—just a minute.

"Perfect. Yes, please send the confirmation to that email address. Thank you again." She hung up and set her phone on the desk. "Sorry. That was the linen company. They're delivering tablecloths and napkins next week."

"You're making progress."

"Slowly but surely." She stood and stretched, rolling her shoulders. "What's up?"

"I wanted to see if you're ready."

"Ready for what?"

"To see the kitchen. And the bathroom." He leaned against the doorframe. "They're done."

Renee went completely still. Her eyes widened, and she pressed both hands flat on the desk like she needed to steady herself.

"Done? As in finished? Everything's installed?"

"Everything. Appliances, fixtures, countertops, backsplash. All of it."

"When did you finish?"

"A few minutes ago. Sam just installed the last sconce in the bathroom."

She walked around the desk so fast she nearly knocked over her coffee mug. "Let's go. Right now. I want to see."

Jake grinned and stepped aside to let her pass. She practically ran to the stairs, and he followed at a more reasonable pace.

They descended from the third floor to the second-floor landing, where Danny was installing a new outlet in the hallway. He looked up when they passed and nodded a greeting.

"Looking good up here," Renee said.

"Getting there. Should have all the electrical done soon."

They continued down the main staircase to the first floor, where she reached for his hand, and they walked toward the kitchen

Her free hand came up to cover her mouth when she first saw it. She stood there without moving, taking it all in.

The kitchen looked exactly like the elevation drawings Jake had shown her weeks ago, but better. Real. Finished. Ready to be used.

Soft white Shaker-style cabinets lined the walls in perfect formation, their clean lines complementing the inn's Victorian character without competing with it. The Calacatta Mist quartz countertops caught the light from the window above the farmhouse sink, their soft gray surface veined with delicate white that looked like marble but would hold up to daily use for decades.

The island dominated the center of the space—six feet by three feet of functional beauty with storage drawers on one side and space for bar stools on the other. The same quartz topped it, and the cabinet doors matched the wall units.

The residential-commercial range stood against the far wall, its six burners and double ovens ready for serious cooking. The counter-depth refrigerator sat beside it, its custom white panels making it blend seamlessly with the surrounding cabinetry.

Behind the sink, the backsplash of soft white subway tile with gray grout created subtle color that kept the space from feeling too stark.

Light poured through the windows and reflected off every surface—the white cabinets, the polished countertops, and the traditional bridge-style faucet over the farmhouse sink.

Dawson stood near the island, arms crossed, watching Renee's face. Billy leaned against the counter by the range. Sam waited near the doorway to the bathroom, and Levi stood by the pantry, his hands in his pockets.

They'd all been waiting for this moment.

Renee's hand slowly dropped from her mouth. Her eyes moved across the space, taking in every detail. She released Jake's hand and walked toward the island. She ran her hand over the countertop, her fingers trailing across the smooth quartz.

"It's beautiful," she said quietly.

"Wait till you see the rest." Dawson gestured toward the island. "Open one of the drawers."

She moved to the island and pulled on one of the drawer handles. The drawer glided out smoothly on soft-close hinges, revealing deep storage space lined with protective felt.

She pushed it closed and opened another. Then another. Each operated with the same smooth precision, and her smile grew wider with each test.

"This is amazing."

"Good quality hardware," Billy said. "Those'll last you twenty years easy."

Renee walked to the range and opened the oven doors, checked the burners, and examined the controls. She moved to the refrigerator and pulled it open, revealing stainless-steel shelving and LED lighting.

"It's huge."

"You can fit food for a week's worth of full-house breakfasts in there," Jake said.

She closed the refrigerator and walked to the sink. The white porcelain gleamed against the gray countertop, deep enough to wash large pots and pans. She turned the bridge-style faucet on and watched water flow into the basin, then turned it off and examined the fixtures.

"This is exactly what I imagined." She looked at the backsplash, stepping closer to see the tile work. "The grout lines are perfect."

"Levi did those," Sam said. "Took him two full days."

"It was worth it." Renee touched the tile gently. "It's gorgeous."

She turned in a slow circle, taking in the whole kitchen from this new angle. The afternoon sun slanted through the windows and made the white cabinets glow. The quartz countertops looked almost translucent where the light hit them directly.

Jake watched her face. She looked happy. No—more than happy. She looked like she was seeing a dream become real.

"Can I see the bathroom?" she asked.

"Through here." Sam said as he slid open the pocket door beside the pantry.

The bathroom had been transformed from the cramped, outdated space it was before into something functional and beautiful. The expansion had been worth the compromise of shrinking the office nook—this space felt twice as large now.

Gray quartz topped the vanity, matching the kitchen counters to create visual flow between the spaces. The white porcelain sink sat in a vessel style, and the mirror above it reflected the sconce lighting on either side that cast warm, even light.

Subway tile covered the walls from floor to ceiling, creating a clean backdrop for the clawfoot tub that dominated one corner. A curved shower curtain rod arched above it, fitted with a rainfall showerhead.

The floor featured hexagon tiles in soft gray that complemented the vanity top, and the pattern created visual interest without overwhelming the small space.

Renee walked to the tub and turned on the rainfall shower. Water cascaded down, and she looked up at it with delight.

"This will be so nice as a spare bathroom for guests. I'm glad I ordered the same showerheads for the second-floor bathrooms."

"The water pressure's good," Sam said. "Upgraded the line when we did the rough plumbing."

She turned off the shower and tested the tub faucet, checked the sconces, and opened the vanity drawers. Everything operated smoothly, and Jake could see her satisfaction in every movement.

"I love it. All of it." She turned to face the crew. "Thank you. Really. You've done such beautiful work, and I know you've been working ahead of schedule to get these spaces done. I can't tell you how much I appreciate it."

Billy straightened slightly, his chest puffing up just a bit. "It's been a good project. One of the better ones we've worked on."

"Well-built house," Levi added. "Nice to work on something with good bones."

"Your aunt knew what she was doing when she ran this place," Sam said. "We're just helping bring it back to life."

Renee's eyes got bright, and she blinked a few times. "She would have loved this. All of it."

Dawson cleared his throat and moved toward the kitchen door. "We're going to head into the sitting room. Need to install some new outlets and light fixtures before we call it a day."

"And tomorrow we'll start sanding the floors," Billy said. "Should have them ready to stain by early next week."

"That's wonderful." Renee followed them back into the kitchen. "Thank you again. All of you."

Jake and Renee walked back into the finished kitchen.

She walked to the island and leaned against it, both hands flat on the quartz surface. She stared at the range, the refrigerator, the beautiful backsplash—all of it.

"It's really happening," she said quietly.

"It is."

"The kitchen's done. The bathroom's done. The second-floor rooms are being worked on. The floors are next." She turned to look at him, and her expression had changed. The joy was still there, but something else had crept in around the edges. "This is real now. It's actually going to open."

"That's the goal."

"But I have so much to do." Her voice rose slightly. "I need to stock this entire kitchen. Pots, pans, dishes for twelve guests, glasses, coffee mugs, serving dishes, utensils—" She counted on her fingers. "Pantry items, cleaning supplies, a commercial coffee maker, probably two coffee makers because people drink coffee all day—"

"Renee—"

"And that's just the kitchen. I still need to order new mattresses for the guest rooms, order linens for all six beds plus the bathrooms, stock toiletries, get towels and washcloths, bath mats, shower curtains—" She pressed both hands to her forehead. "I need to set up a booking system. And double-check I've got enough insurance. And pass health inspections. And I haven't even started marketing properly—"

Jake crossed to where she stood and took both her hands in his. She looked up at him, her eyes wide and her breathing quick.

"Just breathe," he said.

"I'm breathing."

"Slower."

She took a deliberate breath in, then let it out. Then another.

"Better?"

"A little." But her hands gripped his tight. "This is a lot, Jake. More than I thought it would be. Looking at spreadsheets and making lists is one thing. Standing in this finished kitchen and realizing I have to actually run an inn is something completely different."

He tugged her hands gently until she stepped closer. "You know what I've watched you do over the past several weeks?"

"What?"

"I watched you help gut a kitchen. Learn how to strip wallpaper. Install cabinet hardware. Paint your entire living space on your own. Make a hundred decisions about tile and fixtures and countertops." He squeezed her hands. "You left your job in Manhattan. I watched you come back here to Mistletoe Falls and tackle your aunt's inn with determination."

"That's different."

"How?"

"That was just—" She stopped. Frowned. "Okay, when you say it like that, it sounds impressive."

"It is impressive. You're impressive." He lifted one of her hands and kissed her knuckles, his lips warm against her skin. "You've got this, Renee. I know you do."

"What if I don't?"

"Then you'll figure it out. That's what you do. You figure things out."

She was quiet for a moment, her gaze fixed on where his hand held hers. Then she looked up at him, and her eyes had cleared. The panic had receded, leaving something steadier behind.

"You really believe that."

"I do."

"Why?"

"Because I believe in you." He released one of her hands but kept hold of the other. "You've got this. And you're not doing this alone. You've got your parents. Your sister. Me."

"You?"

"Yeah, me." He pulled her closer. "I'm not going anywhere."

Her free hand came up to rest against his chest, over his heart. "Promise?"

"Promise."

She rose onto her toes and kissed him, quick and sweet, then pulled back with a small smile.

"Okay," she said. "I can do this."

"I know you can."

"But I'm still going to panic occasionally."

"That's allowed."

"And you're going to talk me down?"

"Every time."

She laughed, and the sound filled the empty kitchen, bouncing off the new cabinets and echoing against the tile backsplash. "You're going to regret volunteering for that job."

"I don't think I will."

Chapter 27

Jake's wrench slipped on the coupling, and his knuckles scraped against the copper pipe. He pulled his hand back and shook it, then reached for the rag tucked into his back pocket to wipe away the thin line of blood.

The bathroom in the Silver Bells Room on the second floor of the inn was small. Sam had roughed in the new water lines yesterday afternoon, and now Jake was finishing the connections before they could move on to hang drywall.

The work was straightforward. Methodical. The kind of task that usually cleared his head and let him think.

Except this morning, his thoughts kept circling back to a week and a half ago and the Christmas tree. The decorating. The way Renee had pulled him down to kiss her, her hands fisted in his shirt like she never wanted to let go.

The way she'd told him he made her feel at home.

Jake tightened the coupling another quarter turn, then tested the connection with his hand. Solid. He stood and backed out of the cramped space, rolling his shoulders to work out the stiffness.

"Jake."

He turned to find Dawson standing in the doorway, paint samples in one hand and his phone in the other.

"Yeah?"

"Renee pick out paint colors for the rooms yet? Billy's asking. The Evergreen Room and the Mistletoe Room are ready for paint once we finish the electrical."

Jake wiped his hands on the rag. "I think so. She mentioned something about it earlier this week."

"You think so, or you know?"

"I'm not sure."

Dawson raised an eyebrow. "Can you go ask her?"

"Right now?"

"Billy needs to know before we break for lunch so he can run and get the paint."

Jake tossed the rag onto his toolbox. "All right. I'll go check."

He moved past Dawson into the hallway. The second-floor hallway stretched in both directions, doors open to the other guest rooms where various crew members worked. Billy's radio played classic rock from the Star of Wonder Room at the far end. The smell of fresh joint compound hung in the air, mixing with sawdust.

Jake walked up the main staircase and started climbing. His boots made soft thuds with each step. The third-floor landing came into view, and he could see light spilling from Renee's office doorway.

He was about to call out when he heard her voice.

"No, I understand what you're saying."

Jake slowed. She was on the phone.

He should announce himself. Walk back down and come up louder next time. Give her privacy.

But her tone stopped him. Something in her voice he couldn't quite identify. Not upset exactly, but serious. Focused.

"Chicago?"

Jake froze halfway up the last few steps.

"That's... that's a significant opportunity."

His hand gripped the banister.

"The salary you're offering is very generous."

The air left his lungs in one slow breath.

She was talking to someone about a job. In Chicago.

Jake stood there on the stairs, his pulse loud in his ears. He should move. Walk up or walk down. Do something besides stand here listening to a conversation that wasn't meant for him.

But his feet wouldn't cooperate.

"I see." Pause. "Mm-hmm." Another pause. "I understand."

Her voice drifted through the open doorway, clear and steady, and every word landed like a stone in his chest.

Chicago. A job offer. Generous salary.

The phrases looped through his mind, each repetition tightening something behind his ribs.

He backed down one step. Then another. His hand slid along the banister, the polished wood smooth under his palm. When his boots hit the second-floor landing, he turned and walked back down the hallway toward the Silver Bells Room.

His mind moved fast now, sorting through options and plans the way it did on job sites when something unexpected came up and required immediate adjustment.

Renee was considering leaving.

Or maybe she'd already decided.

Maybe she'd been thinking about it for days, weighing her options, and just hadn't told him yet because she didn't know how.

His jaw tightened.

He reached the doorway where Dawson stood examining paint samples, and he looked up when Jake approached.

"Did she pick colors?"

"You and me," Jake said. "Let's go."

Dawson blinked. "What?"

"Now. We're leaving."

"Leaving? Jake, what are you—"

Jake turned toward the Star of Wonder Room, where Billy stood on a ladder installing a new light fixture. "Billy."

Billy looked down, screwdriver in hand. "Yeah, boss?"

"You're in charge. We'll be back later."

Billy's eyebrows went up. "In charge? Where are you going?"

But Jake was already moving past Dawson toward the main staircase. His brother's footsteps followed a second later, quick and confused.

"Jake, what's going on?"

Jake took the stairs two at a time, his hand sliding down the banister. He hit the first-floor landing and kept walking.

He opened the front door and stepped onto the porch. The December air hit his face, cold and sharp. He walked down the steps and across the cleared sidewalk to where his truck sat in the parking lot.

"Jake!" Dawson's voice came from behind him, footsteps crunching on the salted concrete. "Would you stop and talk to me?"

Jake reached his truck and unlocked it. The beep echoed across the quiet lot. He climbed into the driver's seat, inserted the key, and turned the engine over. It caught immediately, rumbling to life.

Through the windshield, he saw Dawson standing beside the passenger door, arms spread in a gesture of complete bafflement. Jake reached across and unlocked the door manually.

Dawson pulled it open but didn't get in. "What is going on?"

"Get in."

"Not until you tell me what's going on."

Jake's hands gripped the steering wheel. "Dawson. Get in the truck."

Something in his tone must have cut through because Dawson climbed into the passenger seat and pulled the door shut, the sound sharp in the quiet cab.

He turned to face Jake. "What in the world, Jake?"

Jake shifted into reverse. The truck rolled backward. He didn't look at his brother. Didn't explain. Just backed out of the parking space, turned the wheel, and pointed the truck toward downtown Mistletoe Falls.

Chapter 28

Jake turned left onto Sugarberry Lane, the truck's tires crunching over the brick-paved street that curved along the west side of town. The gas lampposts were wrapped in evergreen garland, and shop windows displayed Christmas scenes that drew clusters of pedestrians to pause and look.

Dawson sat in the passenger seat, silent. His hands rested on his thighs, and he stared straight ahead through the windshield. He hadn't said a word since they'd left the inn.

Jake scanned the storefronts as he drove slowly down the block.

Sterling & Stone Fine Jewelers occupied a corner building with large display windows that gleamed under strategically placed spotlights. The exterior was painted a soft cream with hunter green trim, and a hand-carved wooden sign hung above the door.

He pulled into an open parking space directly in front of the store and shifted into park. The engine idled for three seconds before he turned the key and the rumble died.

Jake pulled the keys from the ignition and opened his door. He climbed out and closed the door behind him with a solid thunk.

He walked around the front of the truck and stopped on the sidewalk, waiting. Through the windows, he could see glass cases arranged in neat rows, each one lit from within so the jewelry sparkled against dark velvet displays.

The passenger door opened. Dawson stepped out and shut it.

"Jake, what is going on?"

Jake met his brother's eyes. "I need your help. I've never done this before."

Dawson's gaze shifted past Jake to the jewelry store. His mouth opened, then closed. He looked back at Jake.

"I think I know where this is heading, but can you give me a few more details?"

"Follow me."

Jake turned and walked toward the entrance. The door was heavy oak with beveled glass panels and a brass handle that felt cold against his palm. He pulled it open, and a soft chime sounded overhead.

Warmth enveloped him immediately. The interior was quieter than he'd expected; the sound muffled by thick carpet beneath his boots. Classical music played softly from hidden speakers—something instrumental with piano and strings.

The space was larger than it appeared from outside. Glass display cases formed neat aisles throughout the showroom, each one filled with rings, necklaces, bracelets, and watches arranged on dark velvet. Track lighting highlighted every piece, making the diamonds catch and throw light in small, brilliant sparks.

Several customers browsed the displays. A young couple stood near the back, bent over a case while a salesperson showed them something.

An older woman examined watches near the front window. A man in a business suit spoke quietly with another employee near the register.

Jake stood just inside the doorway, his hands at his sides. The store felt too clean, too polished. He glanced down at his flannel shirt and work jeans, both dusty from the job site. A streak of joint compound marked his left sleeve, and his boots had tracked in a bit of dirt despite the mat at the entrance.

A woman approached from the left, her heels clicking softly on the hardwood border that framed the carpeted center. She wore a black dress and pearls, her dark hair pulled back in a neat bun. Her smile was professional and warm.

"Good afternoon. Welcome to Sterling & Stone. How can I help you today?"

Jake looked at her. "Engagement rings."

Her smile widened. "Wonderful. Right this way."

She turned and walked toward the back of the store, her posture perfect. Jake followed, aware of Dawson's footsteps behind him. They passed display cases filled with earrings and pendants, bracelets with tiny diamonds set in intricate patterns, and watches with faces that probably cost more than his truck payment.

The salesperson stopped at a large L-shaped display case that dominated the back corner of the showroom. The case stretched at least twelve feet in one direction and eight feet in the other, every inch filled with rings.

Hundreds of them.

Solitaires with round diamonds. Three-stone settings. Halos. Vintage styles with filigree details. Modern designs with clean lines. Yellow gold, white gold, rose gold, and platinum. Every possible combination of metal and stone, arranged in neat rows that blurred together under the bright lights.

Jake placed both hands on the glass case and leaned forward slightly. His eyes moved across the display, trying to make sense of what he was seeing. Too many options. Too many choices.

The rings were all beautiful. Every single one. But which one was right?

Dawson came up beside him. He didn't say anything. Just stood there, looking down at the same overwhelming display.

Jake's jaw tightened. He scanned the rows again, slower this time. Round diamonds. Princess cuts. Oval stones. Emerald cuts. Each style had its own section, each section containing dozens of variations.

His hands pressed harder against the glass.

"Which one?" he asked.

Dawson took a step back. Jake heard the movement, the soft rustle of his brother's flannel shirt, the shift of his weight.

"Jake." Dawson's voice was quiet. "Buddy, this is your choice. This is all on you."

Jake turned his head to look at him. Dawson stood with both hands raised, palms out, like he was backing away from something dangerous.

"What do you think she'd like?" Dawson asked.

Jake looked back at the display. His eyes moved across the rings, row after row, and nothing stood out. Nothing felt right.

"I have no idea."

The salesperson moved closer, her hands clasped in front of her. "May I ask you a few questions? It might help narrow things down."

Jake straightened but kept his hands on the case.

"Tell me a little about the special lady you're looking to buy a ring for," she said. Her tone was gentle, encouraging. "What's she like?"

"She's beautiful," he said. "Classy. Elegant. I need a ring that says all that."

The salesperson's expression shifted, her smile growing more genuine. She nodded once, then moved to the case and unlocked it from the back. The glass panel slid open with a soft whisper.

She reached inside and carefully removed six rings, placing each one on a black velvet pad she'd set on top of the case. The diamonds caught the light immediately, throwing tiny rainbows across the dark fabric.

Jake's eyes moved across the six options. They were all gorgeous. Each one displayed the kind of quality and craftsmanship that made them worth whatever price tag came with them.

But one caught his attention immediately.

A marquise-cut diamond, at least two carats, set in what looked like platinum. The center stone was surrounded by a delicate halo of smaller round diamonds that followed the marquise's distinctive shape. More diamonds continued down both sides of the band, decreasing gradually in size but maintaining the same brilliant sparkle.

It was stunning. Classic but not old-fashioned. Elegant but not fussy. The marquise cut had a timeless quality that wouldn't look dated in ten years or fifty.

It was perfect.

Jake pointed at it. "That one."

The salesperson's eyebrows lifted slightly. "Would you like to hold it? Look at it closer?"

"No need. Just ring me up."

She picked up the ring carefully, examining it in the light, then looked back at him. Her mouth curved into a grin, and her eyes held genuine approval.

"I like a man who knows what he wants."

She placed the ring back in its slot on the velvet pad and gathered the other five rings, returning them to the display case with the same careful precision. Jake watched her lock the case, then lift the velvet pad with the single ring still resting on it.

"Follow me to the register, and we'll get you all set up."

She walked toward the front of the store, carrying the ring as if it were made of glass. Jake followed, his heart beating steadily and strongly in his chest.

At the register, he pulled his wallet from his back pocket, extracted his debit card, and handed it across the counter. The salesperson began entering information into the computer. Her fingers moved quickly across the keyboard, and the printer beside the register hummed to life.

Jake felt a hand clap down on his shoulder. Solid. Firm.

He turned his head to find Dawson standing beside him.

"You did good, Jake."

The printer stopped. The salesperson pulled a receipt from the tray and set it on the counter along with a pen. Jake picked up the pen and signed without reading the total.

The transaction took less than three minutes.

The salesperson placed the ring in a small navy-blue box with Sterling & Stone embossed in gold on the lid. She closed it with a soft click, then slipped the box into a matching navy bag with rope handles and tissue paper folded neatly inside.

"Congratulations," she said, handing him the bag. "I hope she loves it."

"Thank you."

Jake took the bag and turned and walked toward the door, Dawson beside him. The chime sounded overhead as they stepped back outside into the snowy December afternoon.

The sidewalk was busier now, people moving between shops with bags in their hands and conversations floating on the winter air.

Jake walked to his truck and opened the driver's door. He set the navy bag carefully on the center console, then climbed in behind the wheel.

Dawson got in on the passenger side and pulled his door shut. He looked at Jake, then at the small bag between them, then back at Jake again.

"So," Dawson said. "You going to tell me what brought this on?"

Jake started the engine. He shifted into drive, checked his mirrors, and pulled out of the parking space.

"Later."

He pulled onto Sugarberry Lane and pointed the truck back toward Icicle Lane.

Chapter 29

Jake took the stairs two at a time.

His boots hit each step hard, the sound echoing through the inn. The navy bag swung from his hand, rope handles twisted around his fingers. His other hand gripped the banister, steadying himself as he climbed.

The crew's voices drifted from the guest rooms as he hit the second-floor landing—Billy's radio playing, someone hammering, the murmur of conversation. Jake ignored it all. He hit the third-floor staircase without slowing and kept climbing, his breath coming faster now, not from exertion but from what he was about to do.

The third-floor landing opened before him. Her office door stood open, but she wasn't there. He turned toward the main living space.

Renee stood at the kitchenette counter, her back to him. She wore jeans and a pink sweater, her hair loose around her shoulders. She was pouring coffee into a white mug, steam rising in a thin curl.

She turned, coffee pot still in hand, and smiled when she saw him.

Then her smile faded.

Her eyes moved across his face, reading something there. She set the coffeepot down. "Jake, what's wrong?"

She glanced down at the navy bag in his hand, her eyebrows drawing together.

Jake didn't answer. He walked toward her, his boots loud on the hardwood floor. The bag crinkled as his fingers worked at the rope handles, pulling the tissue paper aside. He reached inside and found the small velvet box, his hand closing around it.

He tossed the bag onto the counter. It landed beside the coffeepot with a soft thump.

Renee's eyes tracked the movement, then came back to his face. "Jake—"

He dropped to one knee and looked up at her, his heart hammering against his ribs.

She went completely still. Her hand came up to cover her mouth, fingers pressed against her lips. Her eyes went wide, shining with something that made his chest pound even harder.

He opened the box.

The ring caught the afternoon light streaming through the dormer windows. The marquise diamond threw tiny rainbows across the room, and the halo of smaller stones sparkled as if they were lit from within.

"Will you marry me?"

Renee's breath hitched. A sound escaped her throat, half laugh and half sob, and tears spilled over onto her cheeks.

"Yes." The word came out choked. "Yes, yes, of course yes."

He stood and pulled the ring from the box. He took her shaking left hand and slid the ring onto her finger. The fit was close to perfect. The marquise diamond sat exactly where it should, elegant and timeless, catching light with every tiny movement of her hand.

She stared at it, her fingers splayed, and more tears tracked down her face.

Then she threw her arms around his neck.

Jake caught her, his arms wrapping around her waist, pulling her close. She was crying into his shoulder, her whole body shaking, and he held her tighter.

"I love you," he said against her hair. "I love you, Renee."

She pulled back just enough to look at him, her hands framing his face. Her eyes were red, tears still streaming, but she was smiling so hard it changed her entire face.

"I love you too." Her voice broke on the words. "I love you so much."

She kissed him.

Her lips were wet from crying, salty, and warm. Jake's hand came up to cup the back of her head, his fingers threading through her hair. The kiss was soft and sweet and carried the weight of everything they'd built together over the past weeks.

When she pulled back, she was still crying. She pressed her forehead against his, her hands sliding down to rest against his chest.

"What brought this on?" Her voice was barely above a whisper. "When you walked in here, you looked like you'd seen a ghost."

Jake's hands rested on her waist, his thumbs moving in small circles against the soft fabric of her sweater. He took a breath.

"I heard you on the phone."

Her eyebrows drew together. "What?"

"Earlier. I was coming upstairs to ask you about paint colors for the second-floor rooms. I heard you talking to someone." He paused. "You said Chicago. Said something about a significant opportunity. A generous salary. I don't want you to leave. I want you here with me."

Understanding dawned on her face. Her mouth opened, then closed. She pulled back slightly, her hands still on his chest.

"Jake." Her voice was gentle. "That was Patricia. My old colleague from New York."

His jaw tightened. He'd been right. A job offer.

"She called to tell me about another position opening up. A friend of hers is starting a consulting firm in Chicago and wanted to know if I'd be interested." Renee's hands moved to his shoulders, her grip firm. "I told her no before she even finished the pitch."

Jake went still. "You told her no?"

"Of course I told her no, Jake; I'm not going anywhere. This is my home. The inn is my future. You—" Her voice caught. "You're my future."

Relief hit him so hard his knees almost buckled. He exhaled a long breath.

"I wasn't considering it for a second," she continued. "I'm not interested in big things anymore." She leaned closer, her eyes locked on his. "I'm interested in this. In building a life here. In you."

Jake's hands tightened on her waist. "I shouldn't have jumped to conclusions."

"You couldn't have known. You only heard part of the conversation." Her thumbs brushed across his collarbone. "But even if you'd heard the whole thing, the answer would've been the same. No, absolutely not."

"I'm sorry for eavesdropping."

"Don't be." She smiled, fresh tears gathering in her eyes. "If you hadn't, I wouldn't have this ring on my finger right now."

Jake looked down at her hand, still resting against his chest. The diamond caught the light again, sending small sparks dancing across the ceiling.

"Do you like it?" he asked.

"Like it?" She pulled her hand back and held it up, examining the ring from different angles. "Jake, it's the most beautiful thing I've ever seen. It's so me... it's perfect. How did you—" She stopped, shaking her head. "You just knew, didn't you?"

"I saw it and thought of you. Beautiful. Classy. Elegant."

More tears spilled over. She wiped at them with her free hand, laughing at herself. "I can't stop crying."

"That's all right."

She stepped back into his arms, her cheek pressed against his chest. They stood there in the quiet of her living room, snow beginning to fall outside the dormer windows.

Jake rested his chin on top of her head, breathing in the scent of her shampoo, feeling her heartbeat steady and strong against him.

She pulled back suddenly, her eyes bright with that particular look he'd come to recognize—the one that meant she was about to say something that would catch him completely off guard.

"When?" she asked.

"When what?"

"When can we have the wedding? How soon?"

Jake grinned. The question was so perfectly Renee—immediate, enthusiastic, already three steps ahead. He'd learned over the past weeks that when she got excited about something, she wanted to make it happen yesterday.

"Whenever you want," he said. "That's fine with me."

Epilogue

Renee stood before the full-length mirror in the Mistletoe Room on the second floor of The Jingle Bell Inn, her reflection staring back at her in a dress that felt like it belonged in a dream.

The gown was ivory silk, fitted through the bodice with delicate lace cap sleeves that sat perfectly on her shoulders. The neckline was modest but elegant, a subtle sweetheart cut that needed no embellishment. The skirt flowed from her waist in soft, clean lines that pooled slightly on the hardwood floor. No train. No excessive beading. Just simple, timeless elegance.

Her hair was swept up in a loose chignon, with a few curled tendrils framing her face. Heather had insisted on the hairstyle, claiming it was both romantic and practical.

"You look beautiful, sweetheart."

Renee turned from the mirror to find her mother standing in the doorway, hands clasped together, eyes already shining with unshed tears.

"Mom, don't cry; you'll get me started."

"I can't help it." Michelle crossed the room and took both of Renee's hands in hers. "You look beautiful."

Renee squeezed her mother's hands.

"Jake's a good man."

"He is."

"Your father and I are so proud of you."

Renee's throat tightened. "Thanks, Mom."

Michelle kissed her cheek, then stepped back and smoothed an imaginary wrinkle from Renee's skirt. "I should go check on your father. He's been pacing downstairs for the past ten minutes."

"Nervous?"

"About walking his daughter down the stairs? Absolutely." Michelle smiled. "I'll send him up in a few minutes."

She left, and Renee turned back to the mirror one last time.

The marquise diamond on her left hand caught the light from the window, throwing tiny rainbows across the ivory silk. Six weeks. That's all it had been since Jake had dropped to one knee in her living room. Six weeks of planning a small, intimate wedding. Six weeks of finalizing the inn's last details. Six weeks of falling more in love with him every single day.

A knock sounded at the door.

"Come in."

Her father entered, and Renee watched his face transform. His expression went soft, his eyes misting immediately.

"Dad—"

"You look just like your mother did on our wedding day." His voice was rough. "Beautiful."

Renee crossed to him and took his hands. "Are you ready for this?"

"To walk you down the stairs? Yes." He cleared his throat. "To give you away? Not even a little bit."

She laughed, the sound shaky. "You're not giving me away. You're just... sharing custody."

Carter pulled her into a hug, careful not to wrinkle her dress. "Jake's going to take good care of you. I know that. But you'll always be my little girl."

"I know, Dad."

He pulled back and offered his arm. "All right. Let's go get you married."

Renee took his arm, and they walked out of the Mistletoe Room into the second-floor hallway. The inn was quiet except for the soft murmur of voices drifting up from the first floor. Twenty people. That's all they'd invited. Close family. The construction crew and their families. Cindy.

They reached the top of the main staircase, and Renee looked down.

The sitting room opened before her, transformed.

All the furniture had been removed. White folding chairs sat in two small sections on either side of a center aisle, burgundy ribbons tied to each one. Candles in tall glass hurricanes lined the aisle, their flames flickering softly. Evergreen garland draped the mantel of the stone fireplace, interspersed with white roses and burgundy dahlias—Heather's work, stunning and perfect.

And at the front, beside the fireplace, stood Jake.

He wore a classic black tuxedo, crisp white shirt, and black bow tie. His hands were clasped in front of him, and his eyes were already locked on her.

Renee's breath caught.

Her father patted her hand. "Ready?"

"Yes."

They descended the stairs together, her hand resting lightly on his arm. One step. Then another. The guests stood as she came into view—her mother dabbing at her eyes, Betty Morrison beaming, and Tom with his hand over his heart. Dawson grinned at his brother. The crew members stood in the back row, all dressed in their Sunday best, Billy already wiping at his eyes.

But Renee saw only Jake.

His jaw tightened as she came down the stairs. His eyes stayed locked on hers.

They reached the bottom of the staircase and crossed into the sitting room. The makeshift aisle stretched before them, lined with candlelight and the faces of people who loved them. Heather stood at the front on the left, wearing a deep burgundy floor-length gown. Dawson stood on the right in his tuxedo, his expression warm and proud.

Carter walked Renee down the aisle, and with each step, her heartbeat steadied.

They reached the front, and Carter turned to face her. He lifted her veil—just a short one that had covered her face—and kissed her cheek.

"I love you, sweetheart."

"I love you too, Dad."

He placed her hand in Jake's, squeezed once, then stepped back to sit beside Michelle in the front row.

Jake's hand was warm and steady. His thumb brushed across her knuckles, and when Renee looked up at him, his eyes held everything she needed to see.

The officiant—a kind-faced man named Reverend Hayes who'd known Jake's family for decades—smiled at them both.

"Dearly beloved, we are gathered here today to witness the union of Jake Morrison and Renee Bentley in holy matrimony." His voice was gentle, carrying easily through the small space. "Marriage is a sacred covenant, built on love, trust, and mutual respect. Jake and Renee have chosen to share their lives with one another, and we're honored to stand witness to their commitment."

He looked at Jake. "Jake, do you take Renee to be your lawfully wedded wife? Do you promise to love her, honor her, support her, and remain faithful to her for all the days of your life?"

Jake's voice was steady and clear. "I do."

Reverend Hayes turned to Renee. "Renee, do you take Jake to be your lawfully wedded husband? Do you promise to love him, honor him, support him, and remain faithful to him for all the days of your life?"

"I do."

"The couple prepared their own vows." Reverend Hayes stepped back slightly.

Jake turned to face Renee fully, both her hands now in his. He took a breath.

"Renee, the day you came into my life, everything changed. I never understood what love was until I met you. I promise to love you every day. To support your dreams. To be your partner in everything and cherish you forever."

Renee's eyes burned. She blinked, trying to keep the tears at bay, but they spilled over anyway.

She squeezed his hands and found her voice.

"Jake, you showed me what home really means. You taught me that success isn't measured in promotions or paychecks, but in the life you build and the people you love. You make me laugh. You challenge me. You make every day better just by being in it." Her voice broke slightly. "I promise to love you with everything I have. To be your partner, your best friend, and your biggest supporter. To build our lives together, one day at a time."

Reverend Hayes stepped forward again. "The rings, please."

Dawson produced two simple gold bands and handed them to the reverend, who held them up.

"These rings are symbolic of unending love. A circle with no beginning and no end. May they remind you both of the commitment you make today."

He handed Jake's ring to Renee first.

She took Jake's left hand and slid the band onto his ring finger. It fit perfectly; the platinum catching the candlelight.

Then Jake took her ring—a simple platinum band that would sit perfectly against her engagement ring—and slid it onto her finger with hands that were completely steady.

"By the power vested in me, I now pronounce you husband and wife." Reverend Hayes beamed at them both. "Jake, you may kiss your bride."

Jake's hands moved to Renee's waist. His eyes held hers for one heartbeat, two, and then he pulled her close.

His arm wrapped around her waist, and he dipped her backward.

Renee gasped, her hands flying up to grip his shoulders, and then his mouth was on hers.

The kiss was sweet and thorough and absolutely perfect. The room erupted in applause and cheers, but Renee barely heard it. All she felt was Jake—solid, warm, steady—holding her like she was the most precious thing in the world.

When he pulled her upright, she was breathless and grinning.

"Show-off," she whispered.

"Had to make it memorable." His voice was low, just for her.

They turned to face their guests, and the applause grew louder. Billy whistled. The Reverend clapped Dawson on the shoulder. Michelle was crying openly, and Carter had his arm around her.

Renee and Jake walked back down the aisle hand in hand, their guests standing and cheering as they passed. Through the sitting room doorway into the foyer, then straight back to the kitchen.

The kitchen gleamed under the pendant lights. The white cabinets, the gray quartz countertops, the subway tile backsplash—all of it looked exactly as it had the day Jake finished the renovation. But tonight, the island was covered with a white tablecloth, and in the center sat a simple two-tier wedding cake with white buttercream frosting and fresh flowers cascading down one side.

Their guests filed in behind them, filling the kitchen with warmth and laughter and conversation. Heather handed Renee and Jake a knife, and they cut the first slice together, his hand over hers on the handle.

They fed each other small bites—no smashing, no mess, just sweetness and laughter—and then stepped back while Heather and Michelle served slices to everyone else.

The kitchen filled with the sounds of forks on plates, quiet conversation, and the occasional burst of laughter. Billy told a story about Jake nearly falling off a ladder during the second-floor renovations. Tom Morrison raised his glass of sparkling cider and toasted to "the hardest-working couple I know." Cindy hugged Renee tight and whispered, "I knew you two would end up together."

Renee stood beside Jake, his arm around her waist, and looked around the kitchen. The crew members, with their wives and children. Her parents were standing near the sink, her father's arm still around her mother. Laura was laughing at something Dawson said. Betty Morrison was cutting another slice of cake for someone.

This was home. This was family. This was everything.

Jake's hand tightened on her waist. When she looked up at him, he was checking his watch.

"You ready?" he asked quietly. "We've got an hour to get to the airport."

Renee's heart jumped. Colorado. A week in the mountains. Just the two of them.

"I'm ready."

Jake turned to Dawson and said something too low for Renee to hear. Dawson nodded, grinned, and set down his plate.

Then Jake bent and scooped Renee into his arms.

She gasped, her arms flying around his neck. "Jake—"

"Can't walk out the door without carrying my bride across the threshold." His eyes held a familiar gleam—the one that always made her pulse skip.

He looked at Dawson. "Open the door."

Everyone stopped talking. Heads turned. Smiles spread.

Dawson walked to the front door and pulled it open.

"Goodbye!" Michelle called out, laughing and crying at the same time.

"Have a wonderful honeymoon!" Betty added.

"Don't forget to send pictures!" Heather shouted.

Jake carried Renee through the kitchen, into the foyer, and straight toward the open front door. Everyone followed, crowding into the doorway, calling out goodbyes and well-wishes.

He stepped through the door onto the front porch.

Snow was falling. Soft, gentle flakes that caught in Renee's hair and on Jake's shoulders. The inn's Christmas lights—still up because, after all, this was a Christmas-themed town—glowed warm against the white Victorian siding.

Jake walked down the porch steps, steady and sure, Renee secure in his arms. His shoes crunched on the salted sidewalk as he carried her toward his truck parked at the curb.

"You know I can walk, right?" Renee said, laughing.

"Where's the fun in that?"

"You're going to throw out your back."

"Worth it."

He reached the truck and somehow managed to open the passenger door without setting her down. Then he lifted her onto the seat, her dress pooling around her legs.

Before she could say anything, he leaned in and kissed her. Slow and sweet.

When he pulled back, snowflakes dusted his dark hair, and his eyes held hers with an intensity that made her chest tighten.

"Ready for Colorado, Mrs. Morrison?"

Mrs. Morrison. The name still felt new, strange, and wonderful.

Renee reached up and brushed snow from his shoulder. "Ready for anywhere, as long as it's with you."

Jake's grin widened. He kissed her once more—quick and light—then closed her door and walked around to the driver's side.

Through the passenger-side window, Renee could see everyone still gathered on the porch, waving. Her parents with their arms around each other. Heather blowing kisses. The crew members with their families, all smiling.

The Jingle Bell Inn stood behind them, lit and beautiful, ready for its grand opening in two weeks.

Home.

Jake climbed into the driver's seat and started the engine. He reached across the console and took her hand.

"You good?" he asked.

Renee looked at their joined hands—his wedding band gleaming beside hers, the engagement ring catching light from the dashboard.

She looked back at the inn, at the people she loved waving goodbye, and at the snow falling soft and steady on the town she'd come home to.

She looked at Jake.

"I'm perfect."

He squeezed her hand, then shifted into drive and pulled away from the curb.

Leave A Review

I f you enjoyed this book, please consider leaving an honest review
on Amazon

Visit Our Website:

www.tarabaisden.com

Visit Our Amazon Author Page HERE

Find Us On Social Media:

Facebook

Facebook Author Page

Instagram

Also by Tara Baisden

<u>Laurel Ridge Series</u>

#1. Season of Hope

#2. Finding Grace

#3. His Perfect Plan

#4. Love Redeemed

#5 Snowbound Blessings

#6 Sheltered Hearts

#7 Restoring Faith

#8 Love Rekindled

#9 Where She Belongs

#10 Shelter in His Arms

#11 Where Love Stands

#12 The Pieces We Mend

#13 Where Love Grows

#14 Where Hearts Heal

#15 Harvest of the Heart

#16 Heart of the Season

#17 Season of Forgiveness

#18 Threads of Grace

<u>Riverbend Valley Series</u>

#1 A Cowboy's Second Chance

#2 Wanderlust & Wild Horses

#3 Heartstrings on the Horizon

#4 Runaway in Riverbend Valley

#5 Mended Hearts

#6 Healing Hearts

#7 Home to Lost Creek

<u>Mistletoe Falls Series</u>

#1 Whisk Me Under the Mistletoe

#2 Once Upon a Christmas

#3 The Mistletoe Express

#4 Candy Canes & Sweet Dreams

#5 Wrapped Up in Christmas

#6 Jingle All the Way Home

About The Author

Tara Baisden writes the kind of sweet, wholesome romances that feel cozy, comforting, and full of heart. She's the author of the beloved *Laurel Ridge* and *Riverbend Valley* inspirational series, as well as the *Mistletoe Falls* series, where Christmas magic and small-town charm are always on the menu.

A proud West Virginian, Tara makes her home on a peaceful stretch of mountain land where deer wander past her windows, the garden never quite weeds itself, and her pets supervise her writing schedule with great dedication. When she's not dreaming up stories of love, faith, and second chances, you'll likely find her quilting, digging in the dirt (sometimes successfully), hiking in the mountains, or curled up with a good book.

Family means everything to Tara, and some of her favorite moments are spent on the porch with loved ones—sharing stories, laughter, and maybe a slice of pie (because every good gathering needs pie). She also loves exploring the rich history of her home state and can't resist stopping at any bookstore she comes across.

Tara's readers often say her characters feel like family and her fictional towns like places they'd love to visit. Through every story, she hopes to inspire faith, celebrate love, and remind readers of the beauty found in life's simple joys.

You can connect with Tara at www.tarabaisden.com or follow her on social media for new releases, behind-the-scenes peeks, and the occasional glimpse of country life.

About Mistletoe Falls

Welcome to the fictional town of Mistletoe Falls, Tennessee!

Where Christmas Magic Lives Year-Round

*H*igh *in the Tennessee mountains, where winter lingers longer and Christmas spirit fills the air year-round, lies a town that feels almost too perfect to be real and looks like it stepped straight out of a holiday postcard.*

The winding mountain road to Mistletoe Falls tells you this isn't just any destination. Scenic Route 265 climbs higher into the Smoky Mountains with each breathtaking curve, past ancient trees heavy with snow that arch over the road like nature's own cathedral. But it's the final approach that steals your breath—crossing the enchanting Snowbell Covered Bridge, draped in evergreen garland and twinkling lights, as it spans the crystal waters of Mistletoe Creek below.

Beyond the bridge, the Welcome Pavilion greets every arrival with a hand-carved wooden sign: *"Welcome to Mistletoe Falls—Home of the Christmas Spirit."* The cheerful red pavilion, complete with candy cane striping and an archway of year-round twinkle lights, promises that something wonderful awaits just around the bend.

Mistletoe Falls (population 6,200) nestles in a perfect valley where the musical sound of cascading waterfalls mingles with church bells and children's laughter. The town spreads gracefully along Mistletoe Creek, whose series of waterfalls create the melodic backdrop to daily life.

This is Tennessee's beloved Christmas Town—because Christmas simply lives here. From the gas lamp streetlights wrapped in evergreen garland to the horse-drawn carriages clip-clopping down brick streets, every detail whispers of simpler times and sweeter moments.

The town square draws everyone like a magnet, centered around a Victorian gazebo where carols drift through the air and community life unfolds. Ancient oak trees frame the square, their branches creating natural shelter for the wooden benches below—each dedicated to a beloved neighbor who helped shape this special place. Thousands of lights transform the square into pure magic.

Mistletoe Lane curves gently around the town square before branching into charming side streets lined with century-old brick buildings. Each storefront tells a story through hand-carved details and cheerful striped awnings in hunter green, burgundy, and cream. Wide brick sidewalks invite leisurely strolls, while cozy benches appear just when you need them most.

The architecture whispers of careful love—original stonework preserved alongside modern conveniences, ensuring comfort while honoring the past. Three-story buildings house everything from the town bakery to the bookshop, with apartments above where business owners live.

From November through February, Mistletoe Falls transforms into a living snow globe. The special mountain microclimate ensures gentle snowfall that blankets everything in pristine white, while temperatures hover between 15 and 45 degrees—perfect for outdoor adventures and cozy indoor moments.

The partially frozen waterfalls become nature's chandeliers, catching winter light like thousands of diamonds. Snow-covered trails wind through frosted forests where the only sounds are your footsteps and the distant laughter from the town below. Long winter evenings mean crackling fireplaces, hot cider, and the kind of conversations that matter.

The Mistletoe Lodge stands as the town's crown jewel—a century-old mountain lodge with wraparound porches and stone fireplaces where love stories begin over morning coffee and evening wine. Its guest rooms blend historic charm with modern comfort, creating the perfect retreat for visitors who never quite want to leave.

The Snowbell Covered Bridge serves as more than transportation; it's where proposals happen and first kisses are shared, sheltered from mountain weather while framing perfect views of the approaching town.

The Mistletoe Christmas Tree Farm spreads across rolling hills on the town's outskirts, where families create memories among rows of Fraser firs and the air smells like pine and possibility.

What makes Mistletoe Falls magical isn't just its picture-perfect setting—it's the people who call it home. Three generations often work side by side in family businesses, while newcomers quickly discover they're not visitors but neighbors-in-waiting.

Local business owners coordinate holiday decorations and community events with the kind of collaboration that creates the seamless magic visitors remember long after they've returned home. This isn't performed charm—it's the real thing, preserved and protected by people who understand what they have.

In Mistletoe Falls, Christmas isn't a season—it's a way of life. The town square's gazebo hosts summer concerts alongside winter caroling. Local shops maintain touches of holiday magic through every season, because visitors quickly learn that any time is the right time to discover this special place.

The waterfalls provide cooling mists in summer and ice sculptures in winter. Mountain trails offer wildflower walks in spring and dramatic vistas in fall. But somehow, every season here feels like it's building toward December's grand celebration.

www.ingramcontent.com/pod-product-compliance
Lightning Source LLC
Chambersburg PA
CBHW011849300726

48970CB00009B/2711